Praise for Corinne Holt Sawyer's previous mysteries!

MURDER BY OWL LIGHT

"Angela Benbow and Caledonia Wingate solve three murders in this enjoyable tale.... Diverting."
—*Publishers Weekly*

MURDER IN GRAY AND WHITE

"Sawyer has written this novel with wit and a sharp eye for whimsical detail.... The energetic and humorous plot has enough twists and red herrings to make it puzzling and fun."
—*Tallahassee Democrat*

THE J. ALFRED PRUFROCK MURDERS

"What's most enjoyable about this murder mystery is the characterization of its elderly protagonists, formidable women in their 70s who haven't surrendered their roles as mistresses of all they survey."
—*St. Louis Post-Dispatch*

Also by Corinne Holt Sawyer
Published by Fawcett Books:

THE J. ALFRED PRUFROCK MURDERS
MURDER IN GRAY AND WHITE
MURDER BY OWL LIGHT

THE PEANUT BUTTER MURDERS

Corinne Holt Sawyer

FAWCETT CREST • NEW YORK

A Fawcett Crest Book
Published by Ballantine Books
Copyright © 1993 by Corinne Holt Sawyer

Library of Congress Catalog Card Number: 92-54456

ISBN 0-449-22172-5

This edition published by arrangement with Donald I. Fine, Inc.

Manufactured in the United States of America

First Ballantine Books Edition: February 1995

10 9 8 7 6 5 4 3 2 1

To Jake—with all my thanks.
It's been a great couple of years.

And to my sister, Madeline Holt Campillo.

Prologue

"THE SHORTEST distance between two points is a straight line."

Carmella Riego de Dios might not have finished high school, but she knew that much. And though she might have been wearing comfortable, loose-fitting, flat-heeled sandals, she still wanted to walk as short a distance as possible. Therefore, Carmella was marching along the railway line, because although the respectable route to work ran through Camden's city streets, that way was perhaps a fifth of a mile farther than following the railroad right-of-way to Daffodil Street and then cutting north one block to the back door of the office.

Carmella was overweight. She stood 5'4" in her huarached feet and weighed something near to 170 soft, rounded pounds. Food was her only sin of the flesh—and the sin was as large as the flesh subsequently became. She dieted constantly, she cheated on her diet continually, she exercised as little as possible, and she bored all her friends talking about weight-losing programs she could not or would not follow past the first week.

Carmella was the secretary for a local lumberyard in that tiny town not too far up the coast from San Diego, and she was the only employee of whom it could be said that she was literally indispensable. She not only brought order to their chaos and dealt with their daily emergencies with constant good humor and unfailing good sense, she also was

1

the only person—even including her two bosses—who had mastered the Macintosh computer which posted their books, wrote letters to their customers, kept their tax records, juggled their employees' vacation schedules, composed ads for the newspaper, and reminded Mr. Contreras of his wedding anniversaries. (Mr. Contreras was the married partner, Mr. Dunlop having lost his wife some years earlier to the sales rep for a plywood firm.) Without Carmella, the business would have had to file under Chapter 11, and one or both of the partners would long since have been committed to a mental institution.

Carmella was underpaid—a common problem with women returning to the work force whose formal education stopped in high school to accommodate an early marriage (thanks, in Carmella's case, to an early and wholly unexpected pregnancy). But Carmella managed to support herself and her two children, now that the once-handsome former quarterback who was responsible for her shortened education had deserted her and the kids.

She wept when he left—and then suddenly realized that she should be celebrating instead. He would not beat her anymore when he came home tired and frustrated from his job with a highway repair crew—she would no longer risk a third pregnancy from his insultingly matter-of-fact sexual assaults—the children would not have to pretend Daddy was sick when the priest stopped by to check on the family and Daddy lay in a stupor after a binge. Carmella dried her eyes as she thought that perhaps now she really had a chance at last, however small, to make something of herself. So she did not try very hard to locate the missing Victor Riego de Dios, and as soon as she could, she filed for divorce on the grounds of desertion, despite the disapproval of the young priest, who could think of no practical arguments to dissuade her.

Carmella moved herself and her kids in with her parents, at least temporarily. She got a job as a waitress during the day, and at night she set about relearning her typing by practicing on her mother's antiquated portable machine set up on the kitchen table, far enough away from the living room that the kids, asleep with one on each end of the sofa, couldn't hear the tapping.

As soon as she dared, she applied for a secretarial job—the job with the lumberyard. She was surprised to be hired at that first, tentative attempt, with her limited background and her lack of experience. The partners, Contreras and Dunlop, were surprised anyone would take the job at all, at the tiny wages they could offer and considering the dismal confusion of their books, their inventory, their billing system . . .

Carmella had changed shambles to order in a month, had saved them enough money to get the Macintosh, and had learned to use the computer in the same way she'd learned typing—by reading a manual and by practicing. In short order she made herself the absolute pride and joy of Camden Lumber and Building Supply Company, Contreras & Dunlop, Owners (Closed Sundays).

"Leave and I slash my wrists," Mr. Contreras assured her, slipping her a bonus—larger than he had agreed with his partner—on her first Christmas with them.

"Marry me," Mr. Dunlop urged. "I love you," he insisted. "You're the only woman I ever met with any brains," he pursued. Carmella knew he was joking, of course. He was balding and potbellied—older than her own father, and soured on marriage in general. But she dimpled at his teasing, and he regularly furnished flowers for her desk and sent her candy to feed her twenty-dollar-a-week habit—chocoholism.

The partners gave her as many raises as they could. The business was still small, though it flourished with Carmella's help and the new inventory procedures she and the Macintosh had introduced. But she was still underpaid and scrimping, since, over the protests of her parents, she had taken a place of her own shortly after she stopped being a waitress and started being a secretary. Between the rent and food and clothes for the kids and the cost of a day-care center, Carmella was always broke.

Because she made such a small salary, Carmella's car was elderly, battered, and afflicted with a permanent case of the hiccups. Today, for a change, instead of choking and coughing and spluttering when she pressed the starter, the little Ford merely sighed and went back to sleep, a sleep from which she could not rouse it. Joe from the garage down the street towed the rust-spotted Falcon into intensive care before 8:00 A.M., a special favor to Carmella, whom he adored.

Ordinarily Carmella drove to and from work. Not today. She was frowning as she trudged along, thinking of the probable size of the garage bill. Joe said he'd have the car out tomorrow or the next day, but he'd also shaken his head over the starter and muttered things like ". . . replace" and ". . . rebuild" and that all sounded like money.

Walking in the loose gravel beside the tracks was too much like walking in loose sand—you kicked up a lot of stone, your feet slid sideways, and you worked extra hard to make progress. Carmella was already puffing and out of breath, although she had gone only half the distance. So Carmella was walking up on the tracks, taking extra-long steps to avoid the gravel, hippety-hopping as she bounced from wooden tie to wooden tie.

Walking along a railroad can be foolhardy, but she was in no great danger. The morning train from San Diego up to Los Angeles was already past. It sailed through Camden at about 6:00 A.M., no longer stopping at the ornate little one-story wooden railway station. (The station had been turned into a club for senior citizens and the former station parking lot into a grassy park where the elderly played checkers and shuffleboard during the slow California after-noons.)

Early in the morning, an express left San Diego bringing a large group of commuters to their work in the Los An-geles area—and just after the close of work at night, an express roared back to San Diego, returning the same commuters home. (Amtrak was wonderfully efficient, even though it wasn't as much fun as trains had been in the old days, when they groaned and puffed and chuffed along, stopping dutifully at Laguna Beach, Capistrano Beach, San Clemente, Oceanside . . . every station along the coast.) These canny commuters had the pleasure of living in a smog-free town that possessed many of the better features that Los Angeles boasts, but without the splendid tackiness, the gaudy bad taste, and the ever-present squalor that have become the visible badges of the City of the Angels.

These people didn't drive to and from town, ruining their digestions and shortening their life spans as they fought the parking and the traffic. They smiled cheerfully from Amtrak's streaked and grubby windows as they sailed past struggling motorists, lane-cutting and cursing and stalling on their way in to work. And each night, they exulted as they left Los Angeles behind to return to breathable air and a gentler pace. Amtrak's express service between San Diego and Los Angeles did a good business.

This morning, the express had already gone by, and Carmella knew there was not another train until mid-morning. So, using the tracks as a sidewalk was perfectly safe—although she would have warned her children otherwise.

Hitching along and half jumping from tie to tie required Carmella to look down at her feet with close attention. If the track had passed through spectacular scenery, it still would have been lost on Carmella, busily concentrating on her footing. As it was, all she was ignoring were the backs of business establishments, a scrap iron yard, tall board fences shielding a few dust-streaked residential gardens, the pale blue morning glory vine growing wild in the right-of-way, and the body beside the tracks.

At least, Carmella did not really see the body—not at first. She noted with the corner of her vision and one corner of her mind what seemed to be a pile of dark-colored cloth heaped on the gravel beside the track—a little off to one side and crushing a tangle of the morning glory. If she thought about it at all as she passed the dark shape, she thought how careless people were with their trash—even people on trains. Of course motorists were the worst. America was turning into a series of linear junk heaps arranged horizontally along the interstate system . . .

She stopped abruptly and turned back. Something about that mound of cloth had reached her conscious level of thought. Something odd . . .

There was a red-brown stain soaked into the chalky gray gravel—splashed on the leaves of the vine—gluing together the folds in that mound of cloth. There was a human hand protruding from one corner of the tangle.

Carmella took a deep breath, closed her eyes and said a quick prayer, then took a reluctant step back toward the mound lying beyond and below her by perhaps three or four feet, down the small embankment. She did not reach out to touch, but she assured herself by peering closer that it was a real hand, not the hand of a wax dummy or a large doll, and that the hand appeared to be attached to an arm. The limp pile appeared to be a crumpled human shape, huddled below and beside the track, and there was dried blood everywhere in the immediate vicinity.

Carmella cut down the shallow embankment on the other side of the track, puffing with exertion, and jiggled as fast as she could move up Catalpa Street to the drugstore, already open even at this early hour. She whisked straight through the aisle to the back, where the manager, Mr. Hazledon, was arranging some new inventory on a shelf, and she whispered in his ear. (No use upsetting the red-headed teenager, working near him in sulky indolence, a girl with a wad of gum the size of a baby's fist apparently embedded in her cheek.)

Mr. Hazledon listened a moment, looked startled, nodded, and then went with Carmella to the office in the back, where together they phoned the police.

Then Carmella called Mr. Dunlop, who always came to work early, to tell him that she thought that today she might be coming in a little late.

Chapter 1

CALEDONIA WINGATE threw her tremendous head back and laughed a laugh that Jack of beanstalk fame would have found ominously familiar. "I cannot imagine myself," she rumbled to Angela Benbow, her tiny friend and fellow resident in the retirement home of Camden-sur-Mer, "cutting up lettuce and poking it through the bars of a cage to feed some canary. Even if it's a *blue* canary—or whatever that ratty-looking thing is!"

"It's a budgerigar . . . a parakeet . . ." Angela protested, slightly annoyed. "And they're not only very lovely, they're very intelligent birds!"

"Sure," Caledonia barked skeptically. "Intelligent. Uh-huh. Well, you may not believe it, but I kept a canary once myself . . ."

"No! Oh, Caledonia, I didn't know that," little Mary Moffet breathed. "How absolutely marvelous. I would never have guessed you were a bird-fancier, too!"

Mary was not the brightest resident at the beautiful retirement center named after both the town of Camden, in which it stood, and after its location at the ocean's edge, "Camden-sur-Mer." Nor was Mary the most sophisticated of the group now gathered in the shadowy lobby of the converted Spanish-style hotel, waiting for the dining room doors to open for the residents' noon meal. In fact, Mary had a tendency to literal-mindedness, and that led to a great deal of good-natured teasing by her friends—exactly what

Mrs. Wingate, Adm. Herman Wingate's titanic widow, had in mind now.

"Yes," she sighed hugely, "I kept the little fellow near the window, in a cage that hung by a macramé holder." Right then, Mary should have realized she was being told a fib. Caledonia had some very peculiar tastes, it's true; for instance, she kept by her bed a plastic Garfield figurine that concealed a telephone—the only jarring note among exquisite antiques and furnishings that were designer originals. But it was the "macramé" that gave the game away; macramé was not likely to be among Caledonia's possessions. She had often enough remarked that she considered most handcrafts to be inventions of the devil, and folksy, rustic crafts to be the bottom rung of the ladder! She made no secret of her distaste for quilts hung as tapestries, rocking chairs made from unpeeled branches, all varieties of lumpy-faced, soft-sculpture dolls that might or might not have been born in a cabbage patch, and anything crocheted.

"Anything that looks as though it had been made in a commune by leftover flower children," Caledonia remarked to Angela at a showing of local artists' work in San Diego, "should be bundled up and shipped to Yoko Ono for her living room. Collect." She waved a hand at a stand full of dung-colored pottery on one side of the aisle—at a stand beyond that was showing leather hats and vests.

"Look! Just look!—" She pointed again, this time at a stand featuring macramé plant hangers, owls and frogs made with macramé and beads, and a huge abstract "painting," which on closer inspection proved to be made entirely out of rope in several thicknesses and colors, tortuously twisted and knotted and hung from a broomstick fixed horizontally to the wall behind the stand. "That," she had said, "is simply beyond forgiving!"

So Angela, at least, was sure that Caledonia was teasing now, even if Mary was completely unaware of the joke.

"It was really very sad," Caledonia continued her story, sighing deeply. "Very sad. That poor little bird got out one day. Someone left the cage open when we delivered his weekly ration of cuttlebone, and he escaped. Got tangled up in all that knotted twine of the macramé around the cage and broke his little neck. But there were so many lumps of rope and wooden beads laced into the macramé that he hung there quite a while before anybody noticed. By the time we found him . . ."

"You never noticed he was gone?" Mary squeaked. "You didn't miss him?"

"What's to miss?" Caledonia shrugged. "Nobody even commented on it, because nobody really liked him. He was a grumpy bird—never sang—didn't do any tricks . . . just ate and fouled the paper in the cage. We kept right on putting seed into that little china cup and changing the newspaper. Oh, I grant you it smelled a little peculiar in that corner of the room, after a while. But you know bird cages—so we never suspected a thing! And it was—oh, I don't know, maybe two weeks, before . . ."

"You are kidding me, aren't you?" Mary gasped, in an accusing tone. "You have to be joking!"

"Of course she is, Mary," Angela snapped. "Good glory!—" Herself an admiral's widow, and a woman who moved, thought, and talked quickly, Angela did not suffer fools gladly—or silently. "You bring it on yourself, you know. Naturally Caledonia's never owned a bird! Have you, Cal?"

"Nope," Caledonia admitted cheerfully. "I never kept a pet at all. I'm not really fond of birds. And I lived in one city or another most of my life, so a dog or cat would have had to be kept inside. But the only thing I could ever stand to see confined is a goldfish, and they're not very satisfactory pets. You can't cuddle 'em on your lap, they don't welcome you home at night, and they never seem to listen when you talk to 'em. But at least," she went on with an enormous sigh, "they don't jump on you with muddy fins, they don't shed scales all over the house, and they never have fleas."

She glared across the lobby, now full of little groups of residents, scattered about like the discards in a draw-poker game . . . here a pair, there a group of four, here another group of only three, there a single person gazing dreamily out at the sunlit garden. They were waiting for the West-minster Chimes that summoned them to lunch. Twice daily, the management played a recording of the familiar tune through the lobby loudspeaker, the signal for residents to approach the double doors of the dining room. (Breakfast was an "open seating." One could arrive any time between 7:00 and 9:00, and there were therefore no reminder-bells for breakfast.)

Actually, only the most forgetful among the residents needed a reminder; there aren't too many time-dependent events in the average retiree's day, and for ten or fifteen minutes just before lunch and supper, residents drifted into the lobby to chat with each other and to gaze wistfully at the dining room doors, which, despite the constant, hopeful pressure, never opened early.

Now the object of Caledonia's baleful stare was a new addition to the lobby. When the old hotel had been bought and refurbished as an apartment building for the aging, the lobby had been restored as it was in the days when Camden-sur-Mer had been a favorite stop-off between Hol-lywood, a Tijuana divorce, and back to Hollywood—or Hollywood, the racetrack at Del Mar, and Hollywood again. Al Jolson had chased starlets between the potted palms. Errol Flynn had spent a noisy weekend entertaining a mys-tery woman everyone swore was Greta Garbo. Russ Co-lumbo had sung to Mary Astor at the grand piano across from the giant hooded fireplace.

The advent of the freeway had allowed traffic to bypass Camden. The town's residents had been grateful—but the town's biggest attraction, the old hotel, died of neglect.

It took an investment firm from the East to bring it back to life as one of the best-run retirement centers in all of California . . . and 225 happy residents paid a premium

price for one- and two-room apartments that featured infra-
red heat lamps in the bathroom ceilings, chromium "crash
bars" in showers and tubs, extra-wide doors to accommodate walkers and wheeled chairs, water taps that turned
themselves off if a forgetful resident did not, built-in
remote-control switches for ceiling lights and TV sets, extra
phone jacks placed strategically in every wall, extra closet
and storage space for the memorabilia the old cannot bear
to part with, and built-in rolling steps with which to reach
the top closet shelves.

A wide variety of services were available—here a nurs-
ing staff was on duty twenty-four hours a day; a recreation
director planned and supervised activities and hobby work,
including weekly bingo games and daily exercise classes;
three superior meals a day were provided by a gourmet
cook, who knew the small helpings and strong flavorings
that would coax the elderly to take in their daily nutritional
requirements; and there were movies, a chapel, a hair-
dresser/barber, and a chiropodist operating—each on their
own appropriate schedule—right in the building. Someone
manned the switchboard twenty-four hours a day, someone
drove the retirement center van (because many of the elderly gave up their own cars) for shopping and banking errands and for visits to doctors and dentists, and there was
a maintenance staff to repair leaks, hang new curtains,
move the furniture around if one redecorated, and repaint
when the walls got too shabby. And residents got free
weekly maid service and linen laundry.

Camden-sur-Mer was not just a home for the elderly, it
was everybody's ideal living situation; residents were cared
for, fed, waited on, guarded—and yet retained their independence. It cost—but it was worth every penny! Residents, who hadn't shopped for their food, toilet paper,
cleaning supplies, or movie tickets for years, complained
constantly about the rising rental fees—but their payments
were still a bargain. And for the elderly living alone, away
from close family, such a center offered the one indispens-

able gift for the lonely—built-in companions. And what is more, companions who were roughly contemporaries. There's something cozy and comforting about knowing that people will understand you if you talk about "Fletcherizing" your food, if you refer to roadhouses and marathon dancers, or if you compare something to the pointed grill on a Packard. It's nice not to have to explain a reference to Grover Whalen, Marie of Rumania, Douglas Corrigan, Helen Twelvetrees, or Pudge Hefflefinger. It's nice to have friends who don't say, "What do you mean?" when you refer to "... eyebrows like Senator Borah ..." or "... as many wives as Tommy Manville!"

Camden had, in addition, a perfect location—by the sea and within "The Golden Crescent," that blessed little strip of California from San Diego northward to, approximately, Laguna Beach, where the temperature never varies much from an Edenic average of seventy degrees. Camden had no ancient and historic missions, like Capistrano—it had no presidential residence, like San Clemente—it had no race track, like Del Mar—and the waves did not crash in high enough to attract hordes of weekend surfers from Los Angeles. Young people thought it was deadly dull, compared to Oceanside or San Diego—and the residents in the retirement center were grateful for that. It was a happy place to call home as the sunset fell on one's life.

Now Caledonia peered through the cool gloom of the lobby, across extra-large overstuffed chairs and heavy oak coffee tables, to the region of that hooded fireplace, in front of which stood a black wrought-iron stanchion. From the stand hung a large, wrought-iron cage—and in the cage sulked a brilliantly colored parakeet, its beady black eyes gloomily fixed on its surroundings with what appeared to be unalloyed pessimism. For all the animation it showed, except when it occasionally turned its head as another resident entered the lobby or passed near to the cage, it could have been a taxidermist's advertisement.

"I hope that thing's not there to stay," Caledonia grumphed, every bit as sour as the bird appeared to be.

"Oh, Caledonia," Emma Grant protested. Emma was tall and spare and rather forbidding-looking, but everyone knew she had a tender heart. "Why be so negative about the poor thing? It's rather beautiful, and it does make a change . . . something interesting, at least, even if you're not fond of birds."

"Don't be so incredibly Pollyanna, Emma," Caledonia retorted. "Just to begin with, it's so dark in this lobby—what with Torgeson refusing to turn on the lights before five no matter what—we'll be lucky if half the old ducks don't walk straight into the stand and bump their . . . there, what did I tell you?"

A jumbled blurt of sound had emerged from across the lobby—half human, half bird, and all annoyance. The Jackson twins, coyly holding hands in a demonstration of mutual goodwill as they traversed the lobby, had walked on either side of the cage without noticing—only to be brought to a sharp halt as their wrists banged the nearly invisible stand.

"My goodness me!" Donna Dee gasped, releasing her sister's hand to rub her own, as the bird let out a confused and raucous chatter of objection. "I do declare, I'm going to raise a welt on that wrist! Sister, there's something there . . ." She groped forward and found the stanchion. "Hard as a rock! This ol' cage is on an iron stand, I do believe!" Her touch set the cage swinging again and the bird retreated to the farthest corner of his perch and glared even more balefully, but made only a weak "chirrk" of protest.

Donna Dee (or was that Dora Lee?—residents had trouble telling them apart, even in a good light) peered through the gloom. "Oh, Sister, do look—it's a dear, wee little bird! Birdie want a cracker? Isn't he just the sweetest little blue boy . . ." The bird's eyes seemed to narrow spitefully, and Donna Dee prudently withdrew her probing finger to about a half inch outside the bars of the cage. But the bird, if it had ever considered attack, thought better of it and merely sank its head down into its feathers, turning its face to the opposite side of the cage.

Caledonia groaned and Angela took on a pained expression. "They're going to drown that bird in all that syrup!" she whispered.

"Good!" Caledonia muttered back. "Wonderful way to dispose of it. Because somebody's sure as God going to break his leg bumping against that iron stand, if it isn't moved. What can The Wart Hog be thinking of? Old people don't see any too well in dim light anyway . . . and black wrought-iron . . . Do you suppose we could get him to put something larger than a twenty-five-watt bulb in one of the table lamps? I know he won't light up the chandelier . . . not unless the Board of Directors visits." Caledonia was referring to their current administrator, Olaf Torgeson.

Torgeson, red-faced and overweight, had permanent dyspepsia from trying to balance his employers' desire for a modest and steady profit with the pressures of inflation and his residents' desire for comfort at an affordable price. His attempts to stretch the budget by cutting corners were notorious, and were responsible for his being, with both the residents and his staff, the least-favorite of all the people in and around Camden. The residents nicknamed him "The Wart Hog" or "The Toad," depending on their mood, and their speculations about his ancestry, his mental ability, and his sex life were many, varied, and scurrilous.

"Did you hear the latest?" chimed in Mr. Brighton, adjusting his weight so that his arthritic hip took a little less as he stood, leaning heavily on his cane. "The Toad has asked the girls in the office not to sharpen a pencil unless the point is almost entirely used up. He says that so much graphite is wasted in the sharpening process, he has calculated that he can double a pencil's life simply by making everybody write with a blunt stub as long as it can make a mark."

"Typical!" Angela snorted. "I couldn't even read the bill

they sent around this month. The carbon paper had been used and reused so often it was hardly making a visible trace on my copy!"

"What do you want to read it for anyhow?" Caledonia asked. "It's always the same."

"Not for long," Emma Grant put in. "I hear they intend to raise everybody's rent another five percent next month . . ."

"Who told you that, Emma!" Mary Moffet asked breathlessly. Mary always seemed to be breathless with surprise.

"Nobody. At least, not at first. I overhead it when I went to the desk to pick up my mail last week . . ."

"Your hearing-aid battery went out last week, Emma," Caledonia reminded her. "I wouldn't rely too much on what you thought you heard before you bought the new one."

Emma was deaf as a post without that hearing aid, and until she'd had it fitted the previous year, had been subject to bizarre misunderstandings because she was too proud to ask anyone to repeat themselves. On one occasion when Mr. Brighton told her he wished he didn't have to walk so much, she thought he'd said he wished she didn't talk so much, and she had been deeply offended until the mistake was sorted out. When Conchita Cassidy, their brightest and prettiest young waitress, had offered pork-rice, Emma thought she was serving more ice for their tea glasses, and refused. That day Emma had unhappily contented herself with only a salad and dessert at lunch, while everyone else dined on an excellent Chinese concoction from the talented hands of their kitchen genius, Mrs. Schmitt.

Today, though, Emma's battery was fresh and her hearing aid was in place, and she answered pertly enough. "I didn't just listen, Caledonia. I asked. Twice. Just to be sure. Torgeson plans to announce it at the residents' meeting next Friday after lunch. You just wait and see!"

"Oh, dear, I don't know if I can pay any more than I'm paying now," Mary Moffet gasped, her tiny face puckered into a frown. "I have barely enough to get by on . . ."

Angela opened her mouth to comment, and the others unconsciously leaned slightly forward to hear. What Angela had to say was often acid, always apropos, and frequently amusing—provided, of course, it wasn't aimed at you! She had once been considered the terror of the retirement center, but in recent years the other residents—with a few exceptions—had learned to tolerate her autocratic ways and to ignore her barbs. Part of their acceptance had to do with Caledonia Wingate, who was "She-Who-Must-Be-Obeyed" to the other residents, and who counted Angela as her friend. Thus, Angela was first tolerated, then accepted. Now the group waited for Angela's comment with pleased anticipation. But the comment never came. Angela stood silent, her mouth open, staring the width of the lobby.

Edna Ferrier, one of their newer residents—at least, new within the year—had been chatting at the desk with red-headed Clara, their weekday desk clerk. Suddenly Edna had slumped to the floor in a heap, leaving Clara momentarily continuing her conversation to empty space.

Like Angela, the residents who were facing the desk stopped talking and stared. That in turn made others turn to stare as well. Conversation halted all around the lobby, and there were small gasps around the room, then silent stares. But there was no movement. If the old hotel had housed any other group but the elderly, someone would surely have leapt forward to pick up their fallen companion. Not so at Camden.

Senior citizens can trip because of poor eyesight or because of plain, old-fashioned, absentminded clumsiness; they may miss a step or suffer a sudden attack of temporary vertigo from lowered blood pressure. Wherever the elderly live, someone is sure to fall, sooner or later. Thus it was that instructions were issued in writing from Camden's main office: "Do NOT attempt to help anyone who falls. Call a nurse at once. You may injure the fallen person or yourself because you are not strong enough to lift them properly." This was the only notice Torgeson ever circulated about which there was not one word of dissent or complaint.

So Edna was left in a heap on the marble floor, while Clara, her face set in a rigid mask of efficient good cheer, phoned for the nurses to come from their little office down the hall in what had been the old hotel's gift shop. Then she came from behind the desk to kneel beside the fallen Edna, to whisper assurances and stroke her forehead, while a buzz of conversational question marks began to sound around the lobby.

Two nurses arrived, walking rapidly and pushing a rolling chair, into which they eased the limp and unprotesting Edna, moving her rapidly out of the lobby's side door toward Camden's own little hospital facility across the side street. There first aid could be administered and a preliminary examination begun while they waited for the center's resident physician, Dr. Carter, to come and determine if a more extensive examination or treatment might be required. And as the little triangle moved out of sight, the lobby's gatherings turned inward again to whisper and speculate.

Angela detached herself immediately from her group and headed toward the desk, where the redheaded Clara was already back at work, sorting the residents' mail into individual pigeonholes. Angela's motto had always been "Lead, follow, or get out of my way!" She had always preferred action to inactivity, especially where satisfying her curiosity was concerned.

"I swear to you," Caledonia had once said to her, half in awe, "if curiosity could turn an electrical generator, they wouldn't need the San Onofre Nuclear Station—you could light up all of San Diego County and sell a little over the border to Tijuana as well!"

But this time Angela's intent was blunted, her curiosity left unsatisfied, as the Westminster Chimes, electronically reproduced, rang their silvery melody across the lobby, and the dining room's double doors were flung open. The tide of hungry senior citizens rolled forward and Angela was swept along with it.

A splendid beef stroganoff, served over crispy chow mein noodles instead of over the customary fat, flat, limp, and tasteless buttered egg noodles (accompanied by a serving of baby carrots with just a whisper of cinnamon, and followed by a Mexican flan), occupied Angela and Caledonia for the next forty-five minutes. So Angela's hunger was satisfied well before her curiosity was.

"Hmph! Nothing! Nothing but a Lane Bryant catalogue," Caledonia trumpeted. Angela and Caledonia had stopped by to pick up their mail, as most of the residents did on leaving the dining room at noon. "Good-looking suit there on the cover. My size, I see—but not my style, of course," she added, sweeping back a flowing sleeve on the caftan she wore. Caledonia had dressed in nothing but caftans for as many years as people (including Caledonia herself) could remember.

"Attractive, comfortable, and I don't have to worry when I gain or lose a little weight!" Caledonia said cheerfully, whenever the subject of her clothes came up. Not that she ever lost an ounce. But it was hard to tell exactly what her shape was like beneath the gigantic folds of loose material; and that very concealment, although she didn't say it, was the major reason she had decided to switch into perpetual desert costume.

The enormously expensive, very long rope of pearls she habitually wore was another form of concealment: one tended to gaze at the pearls—swinging and iridescing and whispering of wealth—rather than to look beyond them at the ample background of Caledonia's massive bosom. The diamonds on Caledonia's hands did the same thing— advertising wealth while busily disguising the fact that the rings surrounded fingers the size of piano keys.

"Clara," Angela warbled, standing on tiptoe to peer around the edge of the desk. Angela was just under five feet tall and had to stretch to see what others could look straight ahead at. "Yoo hoo, Clara . . ." The redheaded desk clerk paused, her hands full of letters and catalogues. "Clara, do you have just a minute?"

Clara looked at the residents flowing from the dining room and through the lobby—one and two at a time, as yet—and decided she did have time. "Well? How can I help you?" She moved, with only a little show of reluctance, away from the center of the desk to the side where they stood; giving out the mail from center stage (i.e., the desk) was usually the high point of her day. But the rush was not on yet. She edged a little closer toward them. "What can I do for you ladies? Mrs. Benbow?"

"Clara, whatever was the problem with Edna? One minute she was standing there, talking to you—the next minute she was lying on the floor. Was it some kind of seizure?"

"Maybe," Clara said, "but I really doubt it. If you ask me, I think it was just shock. The shock of hearing that her friend was dead."

"What friend?" Caledonia rumbled.

"Ah!" Clara beamed. Someone who didn't know the latest gossip was a real find . . . a treat to be savored in a place where every rumor spread faster than mustard on a hot dog. "You know—her friend. Mr. Lightfoot. That fellow she was always talking about. Him who had the cottage up in the old section of town on the hill. Him who used to walk down here to bring her sapotas. Him who was going to propose to her!"

"No!" Angela and Caledonia exclaimed simultaneously, and leaned sharply forward. "Propose? To Edna?"

Clara beamed and took another step toward them. "Oh, my, yes. I was thinking we might be having a wedding . . ."

"Nobody told us," Caledonia rumbled accusingly. "You'd think news like that would have been all over this place!"

"Well, she didn't actually say he was planning to propose," Clara went on. "But she asked me if I thought second marriages worked out . . ."

"Ah!"

"And she was talking to Carolyn Roberts about places to take a honeymoon—well, actually she said 'a two-week vacation' but Carolyn knew what she really meant . . ."

"Ah-*ha*!"

"And she talked to one of the nurses who got married last year after she turned fifty, asking if there'd been any problems for them because they were older. You know what I mean—problems—like problems getting used to each other—like—well—personal problems—you know?" Clara wriggled and winked and both Angela and Caledonia read by those signs that Clara was getting as close to the subject of sex as she could without actually mentioning the word itself.

"And now he's dead?" Angela asked, trying to get to the main point of discussion and away from embarrassing side issues.

"Oh, my, yes!" Clara's red curls bobbed as she nodded emphatically. "They found him this morning down by the tracks . . . right beside the right-of-way. Absolutely squashed flat, they say. Blood everywhere, they say."

"My stars!" Angela gasped.

"Accident?" Caledonia said. "He fell, and the train got him, is that what they think?"

"Maybe." Clara leaned forward and her voice dropped ominously. "And maybe it was suicide! He could have jumped, you know."

"Why would he do that?" Caledonia said. "Was he unhappy about getting married?"

"Or," Angela put in, her eyes glistening with speculation, "maybe someone pushed him! It could be murder, couldn't it?"

"Angela!" Caledonia's voice was sharp with warning. "Now don't get started guessing and nosing around and asking questions and getting involved in things that have nothing to do with us . . . places where we're not wanted!"

But Caledonia might as well have been addressing the parakeet, still glowering at the residents from the cage by the fireplace. Angela had already darted across the lobby to stop Emma Grant and Tootsie Armstrong, as they walked across the lobby. "Girls, girls, have you heard! . . ." Her voice faded out of earshot as she approached her target, but Caledonia could tell by the rapt attention with which Emma and Tootsie were listening that Angela was making it a graphic and horrifying story. Even the parakeet seemed to have edged closer along his perch, and to have cocked his head with interest.

"Thanks, Clara," Caledonia called across her shoulder as she started after Angela. "I think I'd better go try to sit on my little friend."

Clara beamed with affection at the retreating figure, but muttered under her breath, "Gosh, she'd never be the same if you sat on her!" Of course she made sure that nobody could hear the remark; Caledonia was as popular with the staff as she was with the other residents.

"Angela," Caledonia boomed. "Angela, hold up! Wait for me . . . and be careful what you say . . ." But of course the warning came too late. Even the parakeet could have told Caledonia that.

Chapter 2

THE WORLD, alas, seldom goes as we would wish it to. Angela's curiosity burned, and she yearned for information and action (perhaps even in reverse order), but it was nearly a week before anything emerged beyond the initial facts.

First fact: Mr. Alexander Lightfoot was dead—bloodily, gruesomely, unquestionably dead—crushed, mangled, dismembered, and generally strewn along the right-of-way by the steel wheels of the San Diego-to-Los Angeles early morning express. Second fact: Mrs. Edna Ferrier was prostrate with shock and grief, sequestered in her apartment at Camden-sur-Mer and unable or unwilling to respond in more than monosyllables to the callers who stopped by to offer their sympathy and express their concern.

Carmella Riego de Dios was in shock as well and suffering from nightmares, for she had stood by at the request of the police while the body was collected, scraped up, scraped off, and otherwise separated from weed, gravel, fence, and nearby walls and rails, then more or less reassembled and packaged for shipment to the autopsy rooms.

"It was like placing the pieces of a chicken onto one of those little paper-plastic trays they put on display in the meat counter," she kept telling her bosses. "You know— they take the pieces of the raw chicken after they cut it up, and they cover them with clear plastic and they put a price on them? Well, those policemen, they put all his pieces on a kind of a tray—all arranged in order—you know, with top

23

pieces near the top and bottom pieces toward the bottom—and when they had all they could get, they covered the whole thing up with plastic and stuck a tag on it!"

"A price tag?" asked Mr. Contreras, startled and a little confused.

"No, of course not. I suppose it was his name and maybe the date and the initials of the guy who was in charge—something like that." She moaned and clutched her midsection and Dunlop jumped from his chair to fetch her a cup of coffee. Not that coffee calmed a heaving stomach—but he couldn't think of anything else to do.

"Two sugars, Carmella?"

"Three please, Mr. Dunlop. Oh, God, it was so—you know, I don't think I'll ever be able to buy a cut-up chicken on those little trays at the meat counter ever again! I'll always think of them putting his pieces back in order . . . and—"

"Why not get hamburger?" Mr. Contreras said, still confused. "Nobody arranges that; it just sort of *is*, however it happens to fall on the tray from the grinder!"

"Please!" Mr. Dunlop glared at him. "Let's change the subject! Carmella, how about the billing on the Simonetti job?"

Later that week the police came by—not once but three times, much to the annoyance of Contreras and Dunlop. Not that they minded cooperating with the authorities; they'd have been glad, for their part, to be of any help they could. But they felt very protective of Carmella, who got upset every time she had to call up her mental images of Mr. Lightfoot's body. And when Carmella got upset, things in the office got mixed up; and when the office got muddled, the whole of the business slipped back toward that state of utter confusion that had afflicted it "B.C."—Before Carmella—as Mr. Dunlop always called it.

Therefore, when Carmella was upset, and the office got muddled, and the business slipped, Contreras and Dunlop suffered. Mightily. Both of them. And simmered.

The morning after the third police visit in as many days, Carmella was snuffling into a Kleenex, sipping her coffee drearily as she tried to make out an invoice to Koenig Construction. She ran the totals, using her computer as a calculator. "Damn," she said and started over. "Damn," she said again, and began again, reciting the numbers aloud as she entered them. "A hundred and eighty-six fifty . . . Three thousand and no cents . . . Twenty-two twenty-five . . . Forty-three and . . . *damn*!" She thumped the desk and sighed. "Again . . . A hundred and eighty-six fifty . . ."

Contreras looked at Dunlop and raised his eyebrows.

"Damn, damn, damn . . . 'Scuse me, Mr. Contreras, Mr. Dunlop. I can't seem to get these figures right . . . Maybe I'll just get another cup of coffee and calm down . . ."

"Good idea," Contreras said. "And when you come back, maybe I can help a little . . . you read the figures, I'll enter them on the calculator—you know I'm scared of the Macintosh . . ."

Carmella was diverted by his bringing up one of her favorite topics. "If you'd just let me teach you—it's really simple. See, even when you have an account up on the screen, working with it, you can still use the calculator part without losing the document . . . Here . . . let me . . ." She slipped back into her chair and started punching keys.

Contreras met Dunlop's eyes over her head and nodded slightly, rolling his eyes silently to the ceiling to show relief.

Dunlop grimaced back . . . unwound his stubby legs from the rungs of his desk chair, tilted it into an upright position from where he'd been leaning back against the wall, caught Contreras's eye once more and gestured to his watch and mouthed, "Two—" then he shrugged and mouthed again, "Who knows?" He took his battered straw hat from its peg behind the door and left the office.

Ten minutes later he arrived, somewhat winded, in the cavernous and shadowy front lobby of Camden-sur-Mer.

Clara was at the desk, and obviously awash with curiosity. Handling the switchboard, sorting the mail, and answering inquiries from outsiders and residents hardly occupied her mind sufficiently, as a rule, to keep her from being bored. As a result, she had a higher than average interest in the comings and goings of guests for "her people," and that included Mr. Dunlop.

"I'll be obliged if you'd ring Mrs. Wingate and tell her Sam Dunlop is here," he said. She did as directed, and was very disappointed that Caledonia made no revealing comment other than to say, ". . . tell the old goat to come on down here." Clara relayed the message, and watched him all the way through the lobby and out the door to the garden without learning a single thing except that he had a slight limp in his left leg.

His limp was an old injury from falling off a shed roof when he was a little boy back in Edgeley, North Dakota. The ankle had never healed exactly right, but it hadn't hurt for fifty-odd years, so the limp didn't slow Sam Dunlop down as he headed down the garden toward Caledonia's apartment.

The old hotel was built in a U-shape, and when the apartments in the main building had filled up within a year of its reopening, the syndicate that owned it had built a string of bungalow apartments along each side of the garden, extending the "legs" of the U away from the main building toward the sea and ending at Beach Lane. These smaller structures housed one-story apartments, four and five to a building, and slightly more luxurious than the apartments in the main building. The "cottage" apartments had their own kitchenettes and the smallest had a living room and separate bedroom, the largest two bedrooms and a den. Of course they were also more expensive than the main building's apartments, as well as being slightly roomier.

Caledonia had money; in fact, she was probably Camden's wealthiest tenant. And she had been able to afford not just a garden apartment in the cottages, but two apartments, which she had combined by having the connecting wall knocked out. In consequence, she had an oversized living room more suitable to her oversized furniture; a dining ell;

a kitchen with space for a breakfast table; a king-sized bedroom so that she had not had to give up her king-sized bed; and two separate bathrooms.

Dunlop reached her cottage quickly because it was the second on the left as one went down the garden. Before he could ring the bell, the screen door bounced open and he was drawn inside like a dust mote into a vacuum cleaner.

"Sam! Come on in, you old reprobate! Come in! Have you got yourself married again, by any chance? You should, you know—give some lucky woman a break instead of moping because Felicia ditched you. Good riddance to bad rubbish, I said at the time, and I'll say it again! How about a drink? You look absolutely frazzled!"

"No and no . . . that is, no, I'm not married, and you know I don't drink, thank you though, Caledonia."

"Well, maybe not ordinarily. I remember that about you. But you look absolutely shot . . . finished . . . kaput. What's the problem, my friend? You can tell me . . . you and I go way back, remember? To right after I moved here, when I was having this apartment made out of the two separate units . . . and the first contractor messed it all up and overcharged me and falsified some invoices, and . . . well, anyhow, you not only straightened it all out and got the remodeling done in good time, and exactly the way I wanted it, I might add . . . but you undercharged me. You're not only painfully honest you're a moronically bad businessman! But I was grateful, all the same. I said then I'd help you out if I ever could . . . that I considered you a friend . . . and I meant it. So—do you have a problem?"

Sam Dunlop sighed. He had removed his hat and wiped a palm over his scalp through the strands of thinning hair. "May I?" He sat down, when Caledonia nodded, and perched the hat on one knee.

"It's not me with the problem, Caledonia. Or rather, it's me and my partner together. We don't have a problem yet, but we will if the police don't leave our secretary alone. Did you ever meet Carmella? Or, no, I think she came to

us after I took care of this place for you . . . time moves so
fast I can't keep track . . ."

"I don't think I know her."

"Well, she's smart as a whip, capable, energetic—and till
this week I'd have said she could keep her head in any cri-
sis."

"Sounds ideal."

"Um. Well, the problem is, she's the one that found that
man's body by the railway. And she's been an absolute
wreck ever since. What she needs is to be able to forget it
and get on with her life—she needs to get the picture of it
out of her mind—let it get kind of hazy with time . . . but
the police don't seem to want to let her. They keep coming
around and asking questions."

"Well, now, Sam. They have to do that, you know."

"But she doesn't know anything!" Dunlop protested, rubbing his balding head again more vigorously, as though to
ease his frustrations with a massage of the scalp. "She tells
them and tells them, over and over . . . but different guys
come to the office each time. And they ask the same questions. Every time. Each different policeman. Did she see
anything or hear anything? Did she ever see that man
around before? Maybe walking there by the tracks some
other day? Did he ever speak to her? What did he say?
Stuff like that. Listen, she doesn't ordinarily walk along the
tracks herself, let alone see people there. It was just that her
car was in the shop. Well, she's told them and told them . . .
but they just keep on at her!"

"Sam, they've got to be sure . . ."

He jumped to his feet and began to pace the room,
threading his way among Caledonia's antique furnishings as
though the exquisite pieces were piles of sandbags forming
an obstacle course. Caledonia watched him with apprehen-
sion as he stamped and wheeled about. "Listen, Sam, for
Pete's sake . . ."

"You know the police, Caledonia. You've worked with
them before . . ."

"Oh, now, Sam, you've got that a little wrong. I never worked with them . . ."

"Sure you did. You and that friend of yours—the little tub—"

Caledonia loyally stifled a grin. "Angela Benbow, you mean?"

"Yes, that was the name. The other admiral's widow . . . the two of you got in with this fellow that runs things . . . this police lieutenant, Martinez. Couldn't you just talk to him or something? Tell him to give Carmella a break? Tell him she doesn't know anything? Please. She needs to forget the whole rotten thing!"

"Well—" Caledonia tried to let her skepticism show in her voice. "We can try, I guess. I certainly owe you that. It won't do any harm to try. But on the other hand, it probably won't do any good, either."

He fairly leapt to her to grasp her hand. "I'd be so grateful—and Carmella would, I know. And my partner Contreras—"

"I heard you had a partner now. Seen his name on your sign . . ."

"Good man. He's been with me now maybe ten years. But neither of us is worth a damn at the office work part of it, Caledonia. Bookkeeping isn't our strong suit, either one of us. Neither of us can send a bill to someone we know. And if there's somebody who hasn't paid us—listen, it just about kills me! I get ulcers worrying about it. Or I used to. Carmella changed all that. She goes after the slow pays—and she does it so nice they don't even get mad! She phones up people I'd be embarrassed to ask about money, and she usually gets it. And she has the books so organized, Contreras and I can even find stuff, if we need to know something and she isn't around. She's absolutely indispensable, and . . ."

"Okay, Sam, okay . . . I get the idea. You need this girl back on the job. Well, you know there's a limit to what I'll be able to do, even if Lieutenant Martinez were willing to listen to me. I mean, I couldn't interfere with official police business. And even if I could, I wouldn't. And even if the lieutenant agreed to let up on your Carmella, if he had a question that was important, he'd still come and ask her."

"What kind of question?"

"Well, you know, like something he forgot to ask before."

Dunlop sighed. "But maybe they could get their act together so that only one person came . . . just once in a while . . . and they asked each question one time and that was it! Maybe Lieutenant Martinez would come himself. He seems nice—in fact, Carmella didn't even get very upset the time he came."

Thus it was that Angela and Caledonia found themselves exactly where they would most like to be: right in the middle of things! The police investigation had nothing to do with them or, so far as they could tell, with any of the other residents. And without this excuse, there would have been no chance of joining in the excitement.

"Oh, Caledonia," Angela breathed ecstatically when her friend summoned her and told her about their commission. "Oh, Cal, how lucky! How absolutely perfect! I couldn't have planned it better if I'd tried!" On her face was an expression identical to that she'd had the first time she tasted the chocolate mousse served by Camden's cook, a Swiss lady who understood chocolate as only a Swiss can. "Just think! We'll be able to find out things because we're truly official!"

"Whoa up, there! Just a minute. We're not official at all! We have no real connection with this in any way."

"No, but we have a reason—a real reason—a legitimate reason . . . a reason to ask questions and to look up Lieutenant Martinez . . . it's working out so perfectly . . ."

"I'll concede that much. And that's the first thing we want to do," Caledonia said. "Locate the good lieutenant. I expect he'll be in town doing whatever it is one does. We should be able to find him. Now let's see . . . where shall we start looking?"

"How about right outside the door, ladies?"

The women turned toward the apartment's screen door— and there, outlined against the garden beyond, stood Martinez, peering through the dark mesh at them, his handsome olive face split by a broad smile.

"Oh, my goodness!" Angela gasped. "It's Gilbert Roland!"

"So you always tell me, Mrs. Benbow," he responded, bowing just a little toward each of the ladies, as though it were an unconscious motion, something he did as naturally as breathing. "May I come in?"

"Of course," Caledonia boomed, rising in a surge of plum-and-blue flowered chintz, her caftan, which belled out with her movements. "I just put some midmorning coffee on—you'll join us, I hope?"

"Officially I'm on duty. But to tell the truth, a cup of coffee with two of my favorite ladies is not going to hurt a thing. So long as you don't tell my captain."

"Smith? I seem to remember that was his name. Well, I'm not likely to tell him this. Or anything." Caledonia beamed as she tacked away from the door and over to the kitchen to add another cup to the tray, set the coffeepot on as well, and added a plate of cookies, corn curls, squares of cake, tiny bonbons . . .

"Good heavens, Mrs. Wingate! Are you trying to fatten me up for a sacrifice?" Lieutenant Martinez said as she set the overflowing platter down on the coffee table with a little flourish. "I had a full breakfast not two hours . . ." he glanced at his watch . . . "Oh! Well, actually I see it's been over five hours now. I was up so early—I stopped by a diner at six o'clock this morning to eat, because I knew I wouldn't have time once I got up here. Perhaps, after all, I will just try . . ." He took a square of fine white cake with his coffee.

"You like it with cream and sugar, as I recall?" Angela said, smiling fondly at him as she poured.

"Quite right, Mrs. Benbow. How good of you to remember."

At last, with the coffee adjusted to each one's taste and the correct cup put into the right hand—the snacks protested against and finally accepted with a fitting show of reluctance—and the first taste of food and drink taken and found good—the three old acquaintances settled down to business.

"I don't suppose you just happened to drop by because you were in our neighborhood anyway, now did you, Lieutenant?" Caledonia asked.

"No. To my shame." He sighed. "I wish I did have time for friendly calls."

"Oh, Lieutenant, we know you're busy," Angela warbled. "We understand."

He shook his head. "That doesn't stop me from feeling guilty. My mother used to say, 'You don't *have* time, you only *make* time—and you can make time for anything you really want to do.' I listened to that all the time I was growing up and now, if I give the pressures of time as an excuse, I always have a twinge of guilt. It's true I'm busy, but . . . I tell you, the day I retire, I am going to start a program of visiting with a different friend every day . . . and when I finish my list, I'll start over and do it all again. But now . . ." He shrugged regretfully and sipped his coffee again.

"You know," Angela said, "this is a tremendous coincidence, because we were just about to try to see you."

"So I gathered through the screen door just before I knocked. Now let me guess." He held his hand up to stop Angela's interrupting. "Let me see—I'd say it has something to do with the Lightfoot death. Would I be right?"

"How on earth did you know that?" Caledonia said with wonder.

"It's not really magic. Although I've told you before I don't believe in pure coincidence—at least, not ordinarily—this time it may be true. At least, the timing is a lucky accident. There's no accident in my being interested in the

Lightfoot death—that's my job. And your interest is in your nature! The two of you would have to be sound asleep before your curiosity took a rest. One of your residents, Mrs. Ferrier, is involved, so you two would be bound to be standing in the front row, craning your necks to see what was going on."

Caledonia grinned as she sighed, "It figures you'd see right through us. Here we were going to be so-o-o subtle and lead up to the subject gradually. We were going to cajole you into telling us everything you know about Mr. Lightfoot's death. And we were going to work on you in such a roundabout way, you wouldn't have known you were even talking about the subject."

He only grinned and shook his head.

"You see," Caledonia went on, "it's not just curiosity. It's that we want to do a favor for an old friend with a clear conscience."

"She doesn't mean our friend's conscience is clear. Well, it is, of course. But it's *our* conscience she meant! Or rather, you see, ours would be clear if the friend wasn't involved, which would surely mean *his* was clear. No. His *is* clear. I mean, we wanted *our* consciences clear about *you*—I mean, about your saying we'd be interfering. But we wouldn't be interfering, you see, if the friend has a clear conscience. And he does. He . . ."

Caledonia and the lieutenant were staring silently as Angela babbled along. She gradually became aware that they were not responding—not even moving—but rather sitting with glazed eyes and slightly slack jaws, watching and listening.

"Oh, dear. I'm not being at all clear, am I? I meant about the conscience, that it doesn't matter whether or not *our* consciences are clear—except that we wouldn't want to upset a friend—that's you. When Caledonia said 'friend with a clear conscience,' she meant *us*—*our* conscience . . . Of course we certainly hope the friend has. A clear conscience, I mean. I mean . . ."

"Angela, *hush!*" Caledonia commanded. "Hush, settle down, and let me do the explaining. I know the idea you're trying to convey, but even I couldn't understand all that stuff you were saying, and I'm sure the lieutenant was completely at sea!"

"Without a paddle," he said cheerfully. "Yes, Mrs. Wingate, do take over."

"Lieutenant, this morning an old friend came to call on me—Sam Dunlop."

"Of Contreras and Dunlop? Camden Lumber and Building Supply?"

"Exactly. He's terribly concerned about his secretary. You've met her, of course."

"Mrs. Riego de Dios. Of course. She found the body. Not very nice for her."

"To put it mildly," Angela piped up. "We heard it was in a million pieces, spread all over . . ."

Martinez nodded. "Essentially true. Mr. Lightfoot had been crushed and partially dismembered by the train, and the force of the impact had scattered—bits—outward like an explosion. Well, you don't need to hear about that. What was the gist of Mr. Dunlop's concern?"

"That every time you or your people ask his secretary questions, she remembers the sight of that body. It wouldn't be easy at best to erase that image, of course. Anyway, every time she remembers the gruesome details, she forgets her work. And when she forgets her work, Sam's accounts don't get posted, the payroll doesn't get made out, bids don't get submitted—I don't know what-all. So he wonders how long you're going to keep reminding her of it, especially since he believes she's told you everything she knows."

"And of course you volunteered to talk to me about it? To ask me to ease up on her?"

"Now, now, Lieutenant, don't get all tense. I warned him that you'd question her anyway, no matter what I said. But I told him that I would ask if the duplication of effort is necessary. I don't expect you to quit all the questions, just because I ask."

"Very tactful of you and essentially correct. We usually send out several teams, asking questions and gathering information. Sometimes we get our act together quicker than other times. And this appears to be one time we're walking in each other's footsteps—without meaning to, of course. I don't take offense at your mentioning the duplication of effort . . . it's a perfectly reasonable request. I'll get things coordinated—talk to the people involved. That should take care of the duplication, at least. Will that be enough help?"

Caledonia beamed. "That should do it, all right. Thank you. Of course Sam will never believe I didn't arrange it by pulling strings with you."

"That's perfectly all right. As long as *you* don't think you can influence an investigation."

"Lieutenant!"

"And now," Angela said, straightening in her little rose-velvet chair—the only one in the room in which she could sit against the back and touch the floor at the same time, all other pieces having been bought to match Caledonia's giant frame. "And now, what did you come to ask us about?"

"Oh!" Caledonia sat up straighter herself. "I completely forgot. You had an errand here with us?"

Martinez nodded. "I've come to make use of your not inconsiderable talents for observation and your remarkably sharp perceptions about your fellow residents. It's probable, you know, that Mr. Lightfoot's death was an accident. In which case, a lot of our questions and investigation are for nothing. But it's hard to be sure, at this stage."

"You think the man might have been killed? Pushed in front of that train?" Caledonia asked.

"Well," Martinez said cautiously, "or it's possible he killed himself. Suicide by throwing yourself onto the tracks is not all that common—but it's been done."

"Anna Karenina did it, didn't she?" Angela said speculatively. "Of course she was a Russian, and I believe they have a different perspective on such things. Personally, I couldn't kill myself in a way that would cut me up into pieces or mash me or . . ."

"Angela . . ." Caledonia's warning rumbled like distant thunder.

"Oh, sorry. Do go on, Lieutenant. We're really listening, you know. Suicide, murder, or accident, right?"

"Right. And part of our job is to rule out two of the three if we can. Or at least to be able to say one is more likely than the other two. So we need as much information about Lightfoot as we can get—about his frame of mind, about his associates and friends, and perhaps his enemies—about his health, like whether he was subject to dizziness . . . The medical examiner may be able to tell us something about that. If he'd had a stroke, for instance. Although the body was badly banged around. Well, anyway, we need to supplement what little we've been able to come up with so far."

"So how can we help you, Lieutenant?" Caledonia asked. "Neither of us knew the man personally."

"Speak for yourself, Cal," Angela said pertly. "I spoke to him often in the lobby—every time he came by to talk to Edna and I was out there too, he stopped to exchange a few words. He was such a gentleman . . ."

"That reminds me, we need to know about Mrs. Ferrier, too. And his relationship to her. Except for her, he doesn't seem to have had too many close friends here that we can find, and she's the most likely source of information about his family and his activities. But we can't seem to get in to talk to her for more than a moment or two. She cries whenever we do, she hyperventilates and gets the hiccups, and we have to send for your Dr. Carter to give her a tranquilizer each time we try to ask questions."

"They were going to get married, you know," Angela said defensively. "She's bound to be upset."

"I understand. But I can't even verify that story that they were getting married. All I know about the marriage is what

I've heard secondhand, like everything else—so far. But I got to thinking that perhaps you two could help me with Mrs. Ferrier. The very sight of a police identification card sets Mrs. Ferrier's eyes flowing and her nose blowing, but you two might be able to find out more easily than I could."

"Find out what!" Angela pressed him eagerly.

"Now, now, nothing mysterious or spectacular!" He smiled. She was like a hunting dog he used to own that strained to get out of the car door the moment it scented the woods through the tiniest crack in the window. If Angela's button-nose had been a fraction longer, he fancied it would have quivered like that dog's nose had.

"Find out all you can about Lightfoot, of course," he said. "About his state of mind recently, about his general health, who his doctor was, what he did with his spare time, anything! We've got a few odds and ends, and what Mrs. Ferrier says to you will confirm or deny what we've picked up along the way, even if it doesn't add anything new. You see what I mean?"

"Everything, right, Lieutenant?" Caledonia smiled.

"Right, Mrs. Wingate. Well, how about it? Are you two going to be my eyes and ears with Mrs. Ferrier?"

"You know our terms," Angela said, in her most businesslike tones. "We'll do it in exchange for information. And for being treated like adults instead of like frail and slightly weak-minded children who have to be protected. We get so tired of being shielded from the real world! Some people won't even swear in front of us or tell a joke ... just because we're old! Or rather ..." She bit her lips. It wasn't often she admitted that *she* was old, even now that her hair was snow white and her face full of pleats and folds. ". . . we're getting along," she amended primly, and the lieutenant smiled fondly at her.

"In short, you're to remember," Caledonia chimed in, "that we've still got our brains, even if our knees are giving out. Curiosity about one's fellow man is one of the last characteristics to go dormant in the elderly. So you have to promise to keep us posted—and don't pull any punches. And then we'll do your digging for you."

"Ladies, I promise. As time permits, of course. But you're part of the team." The lieutenant smiled at them. "And now—I wish I didn't have to, but I should go back by the railway line. There's a crew doing a final search of the area."

"Search?" Angela's voice was as bright as her eyes. "Search for what?"

"For anything. Anything at all. It has to be done, but frankly, it's rotten work for them, poking through gravel, sorting through trash, digging among the weeds. Maybe even finding odds and ends of that body that we failed to find the first time. And now I suppose, since I assigned them, it's only fair if I go down there and put in at least a token appearance. So for now . . ." and he bowed his way gracefully out of Caledonia's door.

In unison the ladies sighed.

"Oh, isn't he handsome! Isn't he simply—*grand*!" Angela said.

"Grand," Caledonia agreed. "Oops—look at the time! I'll just put these cups into the kitchen and then we should go on up to lunch. It's fresh scallops today, I hear, and that makes it worth getting there on the dot!"

"How did you find that out?" Angela complained. "They never will tell me, when I ask what's for lunch."

"Ah, now, don't forget that I'm officially a detective as of this morning," Caledonia said. "And we detectives never reveal our methods! Come on . . . let's go!" And they went.

Chapter 3

IN THE years when she was Mrs. Douglas Benbow, the wife of an admiral and something of a social leader among her equals, Angela was never less than direct. It had seemed to her, as she often told her adoring husband, that life was too short for taking circular routes. Now at nearly eighty years old—the exact number her fellow residents in Camden could only guess, since Angela, unlike many of the others, remained coy about revealing her age—Angela never took a roundabout way to an objective when the straightforward approach was possible. Furthermore, she never walked anywhere—she darted! Of course she did not really think of herself as old, either. Once in a while, in her private thoughts, she did concede that she wasn't quite as apt to climb the stairs as she had been in her thirties—that she was more likely to settle for the elevator—but she knew she was just as eager to arrive at her destination as she had ever been.

That was one thing that attracted people to Angela: her spry disregard of time and her refusal to give in to its grav-itational imperative—to the force that gradually dragged her contemporaries toward the earth's core, lengthening their noses and earlobes, putting a sag in jowls, breasts, and paunches, shortening spines, and making eyelids droop in the warm California afternoon or during a Sunday sermon. It was not in Angela to sag or to droop. And it was that

39

quality that pulled people to her like a magnet. Angela's life force was a strong current, not an accidental ripple.

Of course, that's the way it was with the people around her whom she liked the best: Caledonia, whose rhythms of life might be slower and more majestic, but who was nonetheless *alive*; Mr. Brighton, despite his painful arthritis; even silly Tootsie Armstrong and childlike little Mary Moffet; and deaf Emma Grant and . . . and whoever showed spark, and whoever refused to admit that their lives were drawing to a close. Those were her family, now that Douglas was gone: the lively spirits that were attracted to other lively spirits . . . They were all indeed growing older, but simply because it was better than any known alternative. They were growing older—but they were not growing old.

So because Angela was a woman of action, rather than returning to her quarters for a nap after lunch as she usually did, she headed to Edna Ferrier's. Edna lived on the second floor, directly above Angela's quarters, which were in the first apartment on the left as you start down the hallway in the South wing. And it was there that Angela stopped her rapid steps and knocked at the door—with authority—the only way she knew how to knock.

At first there was only silence. Then she heard a tiny voice of response, wan and weak and reluctant. "Yes?" came the quavered whisper. "Who is it?"

"Edna, it's Angela. I came by to see how you're doing."

"Fine." There was a pause.

"Well . . . aren't you going to let me in? Are you going to let me stand here yelling through the door?" Angela made her voice deliberately brisk, deliberately injured-sounding. She might feel endless sympathy for Edna in her bereavement, but now was not the time to express it . . . not until she got herself inside.

"Oh, Angela . . ." the little voice sighed. "I don't know . . . I don't feel . . ."

"Of course you don't, dear," Angela said firmly. "But

you can't hide in there forever. A bit at a time you've got to come back to the real world."

"I don't think . . . I'm not ready yet. It's . . ."

"Too soon? Of course you feel that way. Everyone does. But I really do want to talk to you about it." There was another longish, empty pause. "Well—are you going to let me in?"

Ordinarily, Edna was not to be quite so easily bullied as, say, a Tootsie Armstrong (weak of eyes and will) or a Mary Moffet (tiny and naive and overly credulous), but she was obviously not at her most Angela-resistant. After another pause, there was a scraping and a shuffling . . . and then the lock was thrown on the inside of the door, the knob turned slowly, and the door opened just a crack. A puffy, red-rimmed eye peered through.

Quick as that eye could blink its tear-dampened lid, Angela had the door open, pressed firmly to its full width. She put on a cheerful smile and stepped inside the door frame so that Edna couldn't get the door shut again without some act of physical violence, which (the theory went) she would be too ladylike to perpetrate. Angela had learned a great deal from persistent salesmen over the years about their techniques (her own sales resistance was very high, so she'd seen the full range of tricks-of-the-trade)—and one thing she'd learned was "Don't let a half-closed door stand between you and the customer." So she pushed . . . and a surprised Edna let the door swing wide.

"Oh, Angela!" Edna gasped. "Oh, my!"

She was dressed in a tired-looking housecoat and she wore no makeup. She was looking a good deal older than her sixty-five years with her gray-and-brown streaked hair straggling limply around her face. Edna Ferrier could still be described as attractive, although "pretty" was perhaps no longer an applicable term. Features do tend to coarsen with age; after fifty, the princess begins to look more like a peasant's wife than like a courtier's courtesan.

Edna was about 5'4", but that made her taller than

Angela by nearly five inches. And she had kept her figure, though it—like her jawline—was considerably thicker than it had once been. She still had handsome, shapely legs, and ordinarily she dressed simply but elegantly. Many women in Camden no longer bought new clothes, thinking it a waste of money; Edna added at least one new outfit each season.

"She's certainly not at her best," Angela was thinking. And then, in response to a sudden and wholly unexpected pang of jealousy, "Nobody'd tell her today that she doesn't look old enough to be in a retirement home!" She immediately forced the thought into the darkest recesses of her mind and put a sympathetic smile on her face. Time enough later to wish her own hair were not white and her figure not cylindrical. Now she had other things to think about.

"Well, as long as you're here, I suppose you'd better come on in." Edna sounded grudging and infinitely melancholy.

Angela did. She swung the door closed behind her and hesitated, her eye caught—as it had been so often, when she called on Edna Ferrier—by Edna's paintings. Edna did beautiful watercolors of the sea and of California's highland meadows covered by drifts of wildflowers. The flowers, alas, were gone—except in Mrs. Ferrier's mind's eye— fallen victim to the developers who had decided the upland meadows near San Francisco would make the ideal site for a condominium village. No amount of warning from environmentalists or from geological experts could make them change their minds. The meadows were replaced by asphalt streets and narrow, cedar-sided row houses with a lot of skylights and large glass patio doors that stared mutely into sterile concrete atriums no larger than the average living room rug. The only comfort the experts took was that, since one portion of the development was directly athwart the San Andreas fault, the developers would sooner or later face a multimillion-dollar damage suit from irate condominium buyers. Small comfort, really, for vanished fields of wildflowers.

Angela admired both the artwork and the subject, and a tiny sigh escaped her for the lost beauty of California as she and Douglas had first seen it when he was a lieutenant, stationed near San Francisco before the boom days. But she brushed the regret aside. Angela was not a dweller in the past, any more than she was one who feared the future. She was one of those admirable people who can live entirely in the present—not without memories, but without grief.

"Now, dear, tell me all about it," she said, as she sat down on a little chintz-covered love seat. Nothing specific, but the invitation to a confidence was enough as a rule to start people talking . . . and it worked this time, just as well as it usually did.

"Oh, it's so dreadful . . ." Edna's voice quavered and tears welled up in her eyes. She seated herself in a comfortable chair next to Angela, slumped back between its overstuffed arms, pulled a fresh tissue from the decoupage box on the lamp table, and blew her reddened nose very noisily. "I don't think I'll ever be the same . . ."

"Of course, of course," Angela muttered. Experience had shown her it didn't matter exactly what you said as long as the tone was right. "Do tell me all about it," she breathed, trying to sound sympathetic instead of eager.

"We were going to be married next month. Did you know that?"

"No!"

"Alex had been married long ago, back in the East, before he moved here. She died . . . tragically, I think. He didn't like to talk about it. But then, I didn't like to talk about my Horace, either. Not that our marriage was so ideal, but I did miss the silly man, after he drowned in that storm that capsized those boats on Lake Mead . . . I told you about it, I think . . ."

"Well, no, but . . ."

"It was so long ago anyhow. And since then I've been on my own. Really didn't try very hard to find someone, you know. My Horace wasn't everybody's ideal—he was a small man and not very muscular . . . that's one reason he drowned in those waves, when others were able to stay afloat, I suppose. And maybe people would think he was a little dull; bookkeeping in a big law firm isn't—it isn't—"

"Swashbuckling?"

"Exactly." Edna sighed. "But he was interested in me, he enjoyed my company, and whatever I wanted, he wanted for me. And he thought I was pretty. That's—that's endearing, you know . . . I wasn't bad-looking, but I wasn't ever a beauty. Except to him. And that made him better-looking to me than a lot of other men would have been."

Angela nodded wordlessly, thinking of how her Douglas had adored her throughout their marriage. And how much she missed being petted and loved and spoiled. In unison, the two women sighed.

"And then I met Alexander . . . Alex . . . so different. He was still quite good–looking, you know."

"Well, it really was hard to say. Every time I saw him, he had that beard, and . . ."

Edna smiled sadly. "He was going to shave it off, he told me. He teased me—said I might change my mind about marrying him, after I saw his real jawline. Such a tease, always. There wasn't anything at all wrong with his face, of course. I mean, he had a strong jaw . . . well-formed mouth and teeth . . . no scars . . . I could see what his face was like, even through that beard. Maybe because I paint, I can see things. I don't know, but I just didn't think it made that much difference to his looks. It was just—well, I wasn't all that fond of—" She hesitated. "You know, when he kissed me—it kind of scrubbed! Prickled. So he said he'd take it off."

"Yes, of course. Obviously very sensible. Well, anyhow, what do you think happened to him? I mean, why did he

fall under that train? Was he subject to fainting spells? Did
he have heart trouble?"

Edna shook her head. "Definitely not. He was—Angela
don't tell any of the others this—he was a little younger
than I am. Maybe five years or even a bit more. And even
healthier, so far as I know. I don't think he got dizzy and
fell, if that's what you're asking. Of course, they'll find out
more when they . . . they're going to . . ." She stopped,
helpless to complete the thought.

Angela cleared her throat hastily. She was not entranced
herself with the subject of the autopsy. "Oh. Yes. Well. I
see." She plunged ahead. "So . . . no heart trouble that you
know of. Okay. Had he ever lost his balance when you
were with him? I don't mean figuratively—I mean literally."

Edna didn't smile a quarter-inch in response to the feeble
little joke. "Never that I know of. I don't believe he fell because he was sick or anything."

"He wasn't accident-prone, was he? I mean, did he ever
trip over his footing? Bang into something because he
wasn't looking carefully?"

Edna just shook her head.

"What about depression? Was he moody?"

Edna shook her head again. "He seemed cheerful enough
most of the time. He had a temper—quite a quick temper—
but it went away almost at once, or else he was able to
master it. And I don't think you commit suicide in a fit of
anger, do you? And that's the only thing I ever saw in him
except the most sunny, hopeful . . . I don't believe he killed
himself."

"But you do see what you're saying then, Edna. If he
didn't lose his balance and fall, and if he didn't have a
heart attack or a stroke or an attack of dizziness, and if he
didn't kill himself in a fit of depression—well then, someone must have pushed him. That's the only other thing I
can think of. Someone killed him."

"I know. That's what I think."

"But why? Did he have enemies?"

"Of course not." Edna was indignant. "Everybody liked Alex. He met a few people up here, you know, on his visits. We played cards a couple of times with the Graingers—that retired pediatrician and his wife who moved into the cottage apartment opposite Caledonia, you know? We went to a couple of concerts together, the four of us . . ."

"I see. And?" Angela encouraged her.

"And I brought Alex here or had him meet me here fairly often because I liked showing him off. And honestly, everybody liked him. Everybody! Dr. Grainger, for instance, invited him back twice on his own—I mean, without me. They played golf or something once, I think, and once they went walking down along the beach . . . I don't know. Anyhow, they liked him. And everybody did."

"Well, he could be popular and well liked and still make someone mad at him, couldn't he?" Angela insisted.

"I suppose so. But everybody seemed to take to him right away. People—I don't know—people trusted him. He had a way with him . . . even dogs and children. I wish you could have seen him the day we went with the Graingers to the San Diego Zoo. Alex had a circle of children around him like a department store Santa Claus does. He'd spotted one youngster fussing and tired and bored, and he asked us to excuse him. He went over, sat down next to the child and began to talk to her. In about two minutes she was laughing and happy. Then other children drifted over, and pretty soon he was telling some fantastic story and they were thoroughly engrossed. And he was happy, too, gesturing and acting out those stories . . . The Graingers and I were fascinated. Dr. Grainger couldn't take his eyes off Alex. And the kids' parents were all standing around beaming . . ."

"They were grateful for a moment's peace, I bet," Angela said sourly. She and Douglas had never had children, and though she was fond of other people's children in ones and twos—for a limited time and so long as she was

not expected to care for them—her idea of Hell would be
to be put in charge of a nursery school or kindergarten.
Even thinking about it made the vein in her temple start to
throb.

Once, years ago, when she and Douglas had been stationed in Charleston, she tried to act as leader to a troop of
Brownies. Douglas had urged her to get more active in the
community—to do something with the families of enlisted
men. It had seemed to her that group baby-sitting (the term
she used for her stint as head of the little troop) was the
most painless way to fulfill what Douglas seemed to regard
as her duty. (Angela might believe herself *noblesse*, but
without the admiral's urging, it never would have occurred
to her that she was *obligé* about anything.)

There had been a fire in the next building one afternoon
while the girls were playing "Musical Chairs." It wasn't until the troop meeting was over and they all went outside
sometime later that Angela realized the Charleston fire department had been busy doing its thing not thirty yards
from where she had been trying to introduce order into the
game, which had degenerated into hilarious chaos. She
hadn't heard a bit of the activity outside—not even the sirens!

After two weeks, she had resigned, her patience and her
supply of aspirin exhausted at about the same time, leaving
the Brownies to the vigorous leadership of the outdoorsy
wife of a lieutenant (j.g.). Angela might have been a strong
woman by nature, but the *joie de vivre* of eight-year-olds
had come as a surprise. So much for civic responsibility.

"He seems to have been a saint on earth," Angela reported to Caledonia, when she had finally disengaged herself from Edna Ferrier and joined her friend in Caledonia's
apartment in the late afternoon. "Alex Lightfoot was handsome, friendly, popular, and nice to children. He didn't
have heart trouble or high blood pressure or fainting spells,
and he was never depressed. Since he didn't die by accident, he didn't kill himself, and nobody had anything

against him, so he wasn't killed for vengeance—then the only thing I can think of would be that somebody shoved him under that train because he was in their way."

"What do you mean, 'in their way'?" Caledonia asked, sipping her evening sherry from the elaborately patterned, cut-glass stemware she used as casually as though she had picked it up in a K-mart "Blue Light Special."

"You know—like he saw something he wasn't supposed to see. Say he witnessed another crime, and they killed him so he wouldn't talk."

"Oh. Sure. Makes sense—but what?"

"Well, I don't know that. That would be what the lieutenant would try to find out."

"Of course there's always—suppose someone wanted to rob him? To take Lightfoot's wallet? And there was a struggle? The thief could have pushed him, and he went under the train by accident—"

". . . or someone could have robbed him and then pushed him deliberately—to avoid his identifying them later . . ."

"Well," Caledonia said, heaving her bulk off the chair in a billow of jade-colored satin, as her caftan belled out around her. "That could mean Lightfoot was being robbed by some person he recognized, couldn't it?"

"Yes. It probably was his paperboy, or his yardman . . . someone he would know and be able to identify as being the thief . . . We could start asking about anybody who worked with him . . ."

"Of course it could also be the butcher, the baker, or the candlestick-maker! Almost anybody! Not necessarily someone that worked closely with him. His doctor . . . his lawyer . . ."

"Oh, Caledonia, be serious. Doctors and lawyers don't steal wallets from people out for an early morning stroll. And someone with a steady, good-paying job—like a baker—wouldn't need to be a thief, either, now would they?"

"Of course not. But you're making a broad assumption—that the person was going after his wallet."

"Certainly." Angela shrugged her little shoulders. "We don't have any other information. Yet. I mean information about anything else he might have had that was worth stealing. And till we do, we can't jump to conclusions."

Caledonia threw her head back and barked with loud laughter. "That, coming from you, is hilarious. That's all you do for exercise these days—jump to conclusions! But I think you have a point. If you think of theft, you have to think of money—and someone in need of money. There's plenty of that going around, these days, with kids into drugs and needing money . . ."

"And not just kids, of course."

"Right."

"If we get more information, of course, we may find out he was carrying a will that would disinherit a young relative—the only copy—" Angela was warming to her speculations. Her eyes blazed. "Getting rid of Lightfoot cleared the way for this young man to inherit the whole works . . ."

"Whoa, Angela. Whoa! That's going pretty far. Just for starters, I don't think he was especially wealthy, was he?"

Angela was crestfallen. "Oh. I guess not. Edna would have mentioned . . . Well, how about the secret papers?"

"What secret papers?"

"Spying stuff. Secret plans to a new aircraft."

"Where would he get things like that? He was retired. He didn't work in a high tech industry even before he retired. Didn't someone tell us once he used to be a real estate salesman or something?"

Angela jumped to her feet. "If you're just going to find fault with every idea, Caledonia, we'll never get anywhere at all. You have to make some assumptions . . . you have to have somewhere to start. And if we don't assume the man was killed by someone else, where's the fun?"

"Fun? Angela! You shock me."

Angela peered up at her huge friend and smiled serenely. "No, I don't. You think exactly the same. If the poor fellow had a heart attack, or stumbled on a rail, it's sad and shocking. But if it was murder . . ."

Caledonia allowed herself to smile back. "Yes. I do see. And I do agree, of course. We never have had so much fun in our lives as the times Lieutenant Martinez has been here investigating . . ."

"And we have been investigating."

"Even the times we got in deep trouble . . ."

"Oh, Caledonia, don't mention trouble! That's no way to start out on an adventure, to think of things that could go wrong."

Caledonia grinned. "Well, I did promise Sam Dunlop I'd help if I could—and I can't be any help at all if this is a random killing by a casual mugger . . ."

"Or if it's accidental. Or the result of something like a stroke. So we'd better go on the assumption there's a reason behind it all, hadn't we? Now, let's think. What next?"

"Well, I hadn't got that far, but suppose we talked to some of the other people Lightfoot met here? How about that?"

"Wait a minute, Cal. What are we trying to find out?"

"Anything, girl. Absolutely anything. Because anything is better than nothing—and that's all we know now. Nothing."

But neither of them could go further. They wrestled with ideas until supper without success, and the next morning, Angela returned to Caledonia's apartment just before lunchtime to begin the discussion all over again.

"Who should we talk to first?"

"Well, how about if we start with staff here?"

"That's not much use, Cal. Martinez will have talked to the staff already."

"Maybe so. Anyhow, it's time to eat. You have breakfast, but I don't and I'm starving. So how about if we go on up to the main building now?" Caledonia started for the door, with Angela pattering along behind.

"You know, I just thought, there is one person we can ask," Angela said. She was puffing a bit as she trotted along, trying to walk beside Caledonia. Angela moved fast, but she was so tiny that she had to step lively to keep up with the free-flowing stride of her giant friend. And these days she frequently found herself winded by the effort.

"Who's that?" Caledonia said, huffing along steadily like a steam locomotive pulling up a one-in-six grade. "Who can we ask?"

"How about Edna's brother-in-law? You've met him, I think. Mr. Something-or-Other Clayton?"

Caledonia stopped so abruptly Angela— hurrying without really looking where she was going, a frequent fault of hers—almost slammed into Caledonia's broad back. "Clayton? You mean that funny little man with the large Adam's apple and the thick, steel-rimmed glasses and the lank, thin, gray hair he parts in the middle? The one who looks a little like Calvin Coolidge would have, if he had worn glasses?"

"That's the one," Angela said. "You remember that Edna introduced us? Wallace—yes, that was it—Wallace Clayton lives somewhere around here, I think . . . I'm not sure if he's right in Camden, but anyhow he's close enough to visit Edna frequently. He stopped by three days ago—I suppose after he heard Lightfoot had been squished—"

"Angela! Please! Don't be so graphic! Not when we're just going in to eat lunch . . ."

"Sorry. But I think he came to pay his respects to Edna . . . comfort her, you know. Not that that skinny little chap would be much to lean on . . ."

Caledonia let out a snort like the trumpet of an elephant calling to its mate across the veld. "Not for such as me, anyhow. But you're right. We should certainly talk to Clayton. I wonder how we can get hold of him?"

They didn't have to wonder long, for, to their delight, Wallace Clayton was standing just inside the front doors of the lobby, as they entered from the garden. He was in earnest conversation with Camden's resident sot, Mr. Grogan. At least, Grogan was earnest—Clayton just looked pained. As Grogan talked, Clayton leaned away . . . listening, or appearing to listen, and trying to evade the famous Grogan whiskey-breath, which seemed to be more than usually offensive this evening, judging by Clayton's pinched expression.

"Here," Caledonia said. "Let's do our good deed for the week. Let's rescue the man, and it will give us an excuse to ask him a few questions. Mr. Clayton . . . Mr. Clayton . . ."

Caledonia plowed through the lobby among the groups of residents rather like a powerful liner gliding through a harbor filled with smaller ships. She moved majestically, oblivious to impediment, and the others bobbed nervously aside, scurrying for cover as she sailed serenely toward her objective.

"Ah! It's Mrs. Uh—Mrs. Uh—yes . . ." Mr. Clayton was overcome with delight at the appearance of what he hoped to use as a rescue party, but in the pressure of the moment, whatever memory he had of the name of his huge deliverer deserted him.

Then Angela emerged from Caledonia's wake, bobbing into sight quite suddenly. Clayton gulped with mild surprise. "Oh! And your friend, Mrs. Uh—Yes, indeed. I remember you very well, Mrs. Uh—" He bowed slightly to Caledonia. And as Angela pulled up beside Caledonia, he nodded again saying, "And you, too, of course. My sister-in-law introduced us at the uh—day, you know . . . the— uh—about a year ago . . . Mrs. Uh—Yes." He gave up and looked hopefully at the two of them.

"Ho!" Grogan shouted jovially, focusing briefly on the newcomers, but long enough to make out their identity. "It's Laurel and Hardy! Mrs. Wingate and Mrs. Benbow, of course. Good evening." He tried to sweep an elaborate bow, overbalanced, and would have pitched forward into Caledonia's arms had she not steadied him with a single great hand against his chest.

"Grogan," she said sternly. "You've been at the bottle again."

Standing, as it were, on the bias, he beamed upward at her sideways and agreed in a surprised voice. "Yes, I suppose I have. Perceptive of you to notice. Just a wee dram or two, of course, Mrs. W. Not enough to worry about, really . . ."

"We aren't worried," Angela said coldly. She still had trouble forgiving him for not allowing her to reform him, some months before. He had tried to be good, but he had backslid with such a resounding thud that he had stayed in a stupor for a week after falling off the wagon. "Mr. Grogan, go into the dining room . . ." she gestured at the doors that had been swung wide, through which most of the other residents were moving now, ". . . and get something to eat to absorb the alcohol. Try to sober up."

"You're disgusting, Grogan," Caledonia said cheerfully. "Your breath smells, your clothes are dirty, you haven't shaved . . . Get away from Mr. Clayton. You're embarrassing the poor man. Get yourself fed and washed and then perhaps decent folks will talk to you."

"Oh. Surely. Right," Grogan said, and added, with a tattered remnant of dignity, "I can see that I'm in the way, of course. Ladies—" He bowed uncertainly, straightened himself with difficulty, and tacked in wide, swooping curves toward the dining room doors.

"I suppose I've hurt his feelings," Caledonia said. "But it serves him right. Now . . . Mr. Clayton . . ."

Chapter 4

"IF YOU want to know the truth, I didn't like him much," Wallace Clayton said, using his napkin to wipe the tears from the corners of his eyes and giving a final, feeble cough. He was seated with Angela and Caledonia at their table in the dining room. Since he had, as he told them, come to visit his sister-in-law, it had taken some persuasion to get him to join them for lunch to discuss the late Mr. Alexander Lightfoot. In the end, it was flattery that did the trick.

"Oh, Mr. Clayton," Angela had sighed, moving close beside him, so that she was looking up at him, even short as he was. "We do need your council and of course you are the only one who knows Edna well enough—we just don't know what to do to help her, in her distress. But you . . ." She fluttered her eyelashes slightly, and Mr. Clayton capitulated.

"Mind you, I won't linger long," he insisted. But he allowed himself to be escorted by the two women, one on either side, to their table, where an extra place was hastily laid.

The interview had started reasonably well, but when Angela repeated her assertion that it would seem Mr. Lightfoot had been next up for canonization, Mr. Clayton had choked on his tomato surprise. He recovered rapidly enough, with Caledonia pounding his back and roaring into his ear, "Cough it out, man. Cough it out!"

Now he cleared his throat and repeated, "No, I honestly can say I didn't care for the man."

"Edna thought everybody adored him," Angela protested.

"She would," Clayton said, buttering a walnut muffin with dainty, precise swirls of his knife. "Everyone thinks Edna is such a staid, sensible, practical woman. She's just a little girl in the ways of men, and she needs protection." He regarded the buttered muffin's surface with satisfaction, then popped the finished product into his mouth and reached for another muffin.

Angela and Caledonia were not of a generation of women who could be said to be liberated, nor even moderately assertive in the matter of women's equal rights. But their eyes met across the table and they registered similar expressions of horror and distaste. ("That—that *pipsqueak!*" Angela raged, as they discussed it later. "That appalling little mouse, assuming the poor little woman needed protection! His protection!")

"Ladies," Clayton went on, splitting his second muffin and inserting his knife into the butter for a generous dollop. "Ladies, my late wife's sister's late husband, Horace Ferrier, knew this. He provided in his will that Edna's estate would be held for her in protective and capable hands, but that she could not touch it directly herself. She has the income from the estate, but not the management of the estate. Horace knew money and he knew his wife. Her judgment . . ." he waved the butter-covered tip of his knife in the air to emphasize his point, "her judgment is not to be trusted, and especially in such worldly matters as money management and men."

"I hardly think," Caledonia rumbled threateningly, "one follows the other. I mean, suppose one weren't a good money manager. One still might not need a keeper in one's personal relations."

"Ah, but that's the point," Clayton said, bringing the knife down through the air in a gesture so sharp that the blob of butter flew off the end and splatted against the garden window next to which their table sat. Angela watched in fascination, unable to decide whether to wipe it off or leave it—which would be more embarrassing to the man? He half rose in his chair, grabbed his napkin, and wiped the blob of butter clear from the pane himself, without missing a conversational beat—obviously not nearly as concerned with the social blunder as Angela had been.

"In her case," Clayton said, retrieving the butter and giving a little circular swipe to the grease spot on the window, "they do go together. And her attraction to this Lightfoot only proves how wise Horace was. She has no notion of budgeting, her checkbook stubs never add up, she overdraws her checking account constantly—and with Lightfoot hanging around, she was spending far too much. Her available cash resources were dwindling alarmingly. You don't want to touch the principal, of course . . ." he added smugly, seating himself and dipping fresh butter for his muffin in the same instant.

Angela looked dazed. Caledonia looked bored. This was not the kind of thing they enjoyed finding out nor what they'd had in mind when they began their discussion.

"Look here, Clayton . . ."

"Wallace." He smiled, and took another half-muffin into his mouth in one bite. "Please."

"Okay, Wallace-Please," Caledonia growled. "Let me try to get the essentials—the bottom line. You didn't like Lightfoot, you think Edna is a financial babe in the woods, you think her late husband provided for her wisely by putting her estate into the hands of . . . Say, Wallace-Please, you aren't by any chance the one who manages her money, are you?"

He nodded smugly. "Exactly. My brother-in-law was himself an accountant—as I am—and we saw eye to eye on financial conservatism. I was named executor and trustee of his estate. For a small fee, of course; I am, after all, a professional!" he said proudly. "We also saw eye to eye on our wives' lack of worldly defenses. I had made similar provision for Horace, had I predeceased him, to care for my wife's welfare. She did not, alas, live long after we made the agreement. But Horace would have watched after her, had it become necessary, as I care for Edna now on his behalf."

"Ah." Angela was somewhat enlightened. "You got together and decided the best way to take care of the ladies . . . but what if you both died? Either together or about the same time?"

Wallace Clayton peered unhappily under the napkin into the empty muffin basket. "Will they be bringing the main course soon?" he asked hopefully. "To answer your question, Mrs. Uh—Benbow Uh—" (Angela knew perfectly well she was expected to say "Angela. Please call me Angela," but she absolutely refused! First-naming someone on short acquaintance was bad enough. So gauche. So Madison Avenue! So Hollywood! And of course first-naming someone you had taken a dislike to would be . . . she shuddered . . . unthinkable!)

When it became obvious to him that the desired familiarity would not be offered, Clayton shrugged in a tiny gesture of dismissal and went on. "To answer your question, that is one reason Horace and I never traveled in the same airplane, although we and our wives spent many vacations together, and Horace and I went to the national convention together for two years . . . We hoped to avoid a common disaster."

"But if it had happened! Oh, say there was an outbreak of bubonic plague . . ." Angela, in her impatience, had gone overboard, as usual.

Clayton looked startled, but he was equal to the challenge of the question. "The Farmer's National Trust held our wills—back in Wichita, where we lived and worked till Edna and Horace got this mad idea to retire to the West . . . a decision, I believe, that cost Horace his life. He hated boating—and the idea of going with a group out onto Lake Mead . . . I really have felt that Edna's lack of practicality showed throughout in all they did after Horace retired. He couldn't say no to her, and she was surely the one who wanted to come to California, and to join those silly clubs for retired persons . . . like the one that went on that fatal outing . . ."

He shook his head, and in doing so caught sight of Chita Cassidy, the prettiest of their waitresses, bringing in the plates on which rested a breast of chicken marinated in tarragon mustard and baked toasty brown, a pile of baby limas, three or four tiny boiled new potatoes in their jackets, and a few slices of pickled beets for color. Angela didn't care for beets and was about to comment on the foolishness of those who did, when Wallace piled into his plate, beets first. So occupied with food was he that he held his peace through most of the remainder of the meal.

In fact, he didn't begin talking again—on the subject of Edna and Lightfoot, Edna and Horace, or anything else!—until after dessert, a fresh fruit trifle, had been served. Dipping his spoon sensuously into the custard sauce, he picked up the discussion where he'd left it.

"I started to tell you, ladies, that Horace realized Edna was what you'd call a 'soft touch.' She had simply no sense about people at all, and sometimes picked as friends individuals with no social position, no influence, no special talent or grace—She got quite stubborn about them. Horace couldn't approve, but he couldn't bring himself to say no to anything, where she was concerned. He could, however, stand guard, even after death, to see that she didn't squander her income giving gifts to indigents or taking up with cleaning women . . ."

"Taking up with cleaning women? What exactly do you mean?" Caledonia was ominously autocratic as she asked the question. She, like Angela, did not gladly tolerate fools, and least gladly of all those snobs who chose their friends on the grounds of social class. And she was obviously beginning to see Clayton as that sort of fool.

"Well, it was just an example," he said hastily, sensing

that somehow he had put a foot wrong. Could this appalling Valkyrie have worked as a cleaning woman at one time? He looked at her meaty arms and shoulders and thought it likely—or perhaps as a stevedore!

"I mean—well—you see—one time our cleaning woman in Wichita told Edna her daughter needed a new coat for school that winter, and Edna went out and bought the child a full winter wardrobe. Completely overboard! That woman knew better than to ask Horace or me, of course. She went straight to Edna. All kinds of people with all kinds of sad stories . . . Edna just attracts them! Like a magnet! That's all I meant by the remark!" His apology didn't seem very successful, and he stumbled on.

"I considered Lightfoot something of the same caliber of person . . . he probably needed money and thought he would get some from her. Well, after all, he was only about fifty or so, wasn't he? And Edna is . . . a mature woman of sixty-five. Now why would a young man like that be interested in an older woman? Unless of course she has money. As Edna did."

"Was there anything else?" Angela asked, her voice sharp with annoyance. His implication that older women could not be attractive galled her more than she would have cared to admit. "I mean—was there anything special about him that made you dislike him? I mean, what was he like?"

"Like?" Clayton said blankly. "Why, like any man at all, I suppose. Not fat, not young, not short . . . he just sort of *was*."

"Then why did you dislike him so much? Was it just that you got suspicious he was after Edna's money?"

"Yes." Clayton looked at his rapidly emptying dessert dish and sighed. "Or rather, no. It was more than that. Something about him personally . . . For one thing, I thought he was false. Overly hearty, overly charming, overly interested in people . . . I thought it was all put on. Edna didn't, of course . . ."

"And apparently others didn't, either."

"I know," Clayton said spitefully, dropping his spoon onto the dessert dish with a clank that was apparently meant to express disapproval. "But then there are often people who want to be deceived—to think others find them attractive or interesting. His overly friendly manner might fool them, all right. It didn't fool me for an instant. He wasn't what he appeared to be, that man. And Edna is well out of the engagement."

"But, Mr. Clayton," Caledonia protested, refusing as Angela had to indulge in first-naming. "Edna certainly doesn't feel that way."

"Now, perhaps." He pinched his lips together. "In my opinion, she will be grateful the marriage never took place, once she finds out the truth about the man."

"What truth?" Angela persisted. "Finds out what?"

"That we don't know, of course," he said smugly. "But you can bet there was something. And it will all come out, in the end. Virtue will triumph . . . my judgment will be vindicated." He rose from his place. "Well, now—this has been very pleasant, and I thank you for the lunch, but I did come here to talk to Edna. And I must go to her room . . . I rather expected she might come in to lunch. But I haven't seen her. Unless she came in after I was seated, perhaps?" He had his back to the door, and as he spoke he craned around, as though he might see her coming in behind him.

"She's still having trays in her room," Caledonia said.

"If she eats anything," Angela added. "She's really depressed, you know. And the maids told me she hardly touches her food."

"Well," he said, pushing his chair back. "I really must see what we can do about that. We must get the roses back into those cheeks, mustn't we? So, if you'll excuse me . . ." and he exited the dining room at a brisk clip, a half-smile of anticipation on his face as he headed across the lobby, presumably to call on his sister-in-law.

"Get the roses back in those cheeks? Virtue will triumph?" Caledonia said wonderingly. "I don't believe I've heard anyone talk like that since the last Shirley Temple movie I saw on Saturday afternoon TV! That man is a throwback to another decade!"

"I don't like him, Cal," Angela said. "I can't tell you why . . . I just don't like him!"

" 'I do not like thee, Dr. Fell; the reason why I cannot tell . . .' " Caledonia recited. "Except it's 'I do not like thee, smirking Wally; with you I will not dilly-dolly!' "

"Dilly-dolly? Don't you mean dilly-*dally*?"

"No, I meant what I said. Dolly to rhyme with Wally. Don't make a face at me, Angela. It's all I could think of on the spur of the moment. Besides, there's just no decent rhyme for Wallace, is there?"

"You know, Cal, I don't think in all his life anybody ever called that man Wally. Or Wall, or Will, or Willy . . ."

"Or Clay, or Claytie . . . You're right, Angela. The man is a full-blown, unmitigated Wallace if I ever saw one. I mean, no pet names for that one—not ever! He looks like he ought to be teaching dead languages in some academy . . . Or like the stereotype of an accountant. Can't you see him in a celluloid collar, perched on a stool at a high, slanted desk, wielding a quill pen and entering figures into a giant ledger . . ."

"Talk about stereotypes! Accountants work with computers, now, Cal. He'd be sitting in front of a little green screen typing figures in and letting the computer whir away doing all the calculating . . ."

The ladies rose from the table and started for the lobby. About halfway down in the gloom there was some kind of commotion—over by the fireplace, a little knot of people, and from the group Grogan's voice rose loud and clear: "I'll wring the little perisher's neck! He bit me! Bit me right on the finger! All I did was try to chuck him under the chin! What kind of place are they running here, where the decorations attack the residents!"

They heard the soft voice of Mr. Brighton: "Let's see the

finger, Grogan . . . Man, the skin's not even broken! He only pinched you."

And one of the Jackson twins was protesting in a lilting, magnolia-scented voice, "Well, he's just bound to be nervous with all the people around the cage and all. You mustn't blame our darling little bird. I declare, he wasn't to know you meant no harm, now was he . . ."

"Come with me . . . we'll take a walk down and look at the ocean, and talk as we go," Caledonia said, steering Angela toward the door that led to the patio, and thence to the gardens, with a commanding hand on Angela's elbow. "Now," she said as they got away from the ears of the other residents. "Where should we look for information next? We haven't found out diddley-squat, so far."

Angela sighed. "I know. Clayton was pretty much a washout. Except . . . There was something . . ."

"It's his eyes. They're too close together."

"What?"

"Never trust anybody with eyes that close together!"

"No, I didn't mean his eyes. Although you're right—they look like they're trying to link up across his nose! No, I meant something he said. About Edna's money. She's not incredibly wealthy, according to him, but she's comfortably off. And he manages it all. Now, what would have happened to her money if she got married again, to Mr. Lightfoot?"

"I suppose he'd have control of it. Her new husband. Through her. That was kind of what Clayton was talking about there, wasn't it . . . that he didn't trust Lightfoot and thought he wanted control of Edna's money . . ."

"Ah, but suppose there wasn't any."

"Wasn't any?"

"Money! Suppose our foxy-eyed Wallace has been dipping into the till? Suppose he's been taking money from Edna's securities or investments or whatever it is he manages for her. And of course when Lightfoot got hold of the books, he'd find out, and then it would be all up with Clay-

ton! I know you're going to say I'm just making this up out
of whole cloth, but I saw almost the same identical plot on
the late-night movie last week. This guardian had control of
this girl's fortune and he tried to kill off every fiancé she
got, because when she married she'd get control of her own
money. But he'd spent it all, and . . ."

"Wait, wait . . . I don't want to hear about one of your
movies. I want to think about Wallace Clayton. He's an accountant, and he's trustee of her husband's estate, on Edna's
behalf . . . he kind of manages her money, isn't that what
you gather?"

"Right."

"Now other than the movie, what makes you think old
Unmitigated Wallace could be an embezzler who's dipping
into his client's money?"

Angela shrugged. "Well, of course there wasn't anything
obvious, you know. It was only that I wouldn't put it past
him!"

"Just because of those close-set eyes? Martinez isn't going to be able to take that kind of evidence into court, you
know."

"Of course he can't, Caledonia . . . so what I propose we
do is to find out more facts! To uncover the truth!"

"Sure. I agree that's better than guessing any day. But
now the big question—how?"

"How?"

"I asked you first. I mean, neither of us knows the first
thing about accounts and bookkeeping, or even how to run
a computer."

"Computer?"

"You're the one who said it, Angela. You said modern
accountants have computers. About all I could find on a
computer would be how to turn on a switch! As far as finding someone's records and checking balances . . . I'd be
lost! And you would, too."

"Well, it can't be that difficult, can it? I mean, quite ordinary people run computers and keep account books and

. . . well, what I mean is, we never really know we can't do it until we try! You see what I mean?"

"I sure do. Angela, what you're saying is, let's go nosing around first and figure out whether we can get the information later . . . And for once I agree with you."

"You do?" Angela was a little surprised, but rather pleased. Caledonia didn't often approve her ideas without an argument.

"Sure. I can see that Wallace certainly won't give us the information of his own free will . . ."

"Well, what shall we do first?"

"I'd say we call on him and try to get a feeling for his finances and his state of mind and . . ."

"And," Angela went on gleefully, "if he weren't even at home when we came to call, so much the better!"

'Oh-oh . . . I should have known you'd get around to suggesting breaking and entering."

"Well, no, just waiting for him till he comes back. But if we happened to look at things on his desk . . ."

"Or in his desk?"

". . . while we were waiting . . . You do see, don't you, Cal? Now, the first thing is to find out where he lives."

"He lives here, does he?" Caledonia asked as they moved back toward her apartment. "I thought he disapproved of California. He talked as though it was the Wild West, and civilization stopped at his beloved Wichita!"

Angela snorted. For her, with her own brand of snobbery, civilization was confined to the two coasts. In between lurked the great American wasteland, with a small pocket of civilized folk locked tragically into Chicago, another lost in the swamps at New Orleans, with perhaps a scattering in frontier outposts that contained tiny enclaves of the cultured—places like Atlanta and Houston and Cleveland, which, after all, did support symphony orchestras.

Between such isolated urban centers, there were in Angela's mind only vast open spaces given over to gambling casinos, dude ranches and sagebrush, rippling wheat and range cattle, and a series of very small towns with dirt roads, one main street, and a handful of residents who drove pickup trucks and sucked on straws or chewed tobacco. And where there was absolutely nobody who had ever heard of Degas or da Vinci or Debussy or Dvořák! The notion that Wallace Clayton considered Wichita more sophisticated than San Diego and its environs was too ludicrous to be taken seriously!

"I really can't say what that man thinks, his notions are so bizarre," Angela said loftily. "I only know he visits Edna often—you've seen him going through the lobby yourself . . ."

Caledonia nodded.

". . . and obviously he was on the spot the instant she needed comfort, after Lightfoot died. I just assumed he lived around here now . . . and I was right, wasn't I?"

She pointed to the phone book Caledonia produced . . . to the entry for Wallace Clayton. "Oh, look . . . this is interesting," she said, peering closer. Caledonia leaned to look over her shoulder. Wallace Clayton was listed as an "Acct" with both a "Res" and a "Bus" phone. "How about that!" Caledonia said. "He maintains an office here in town! He's not retired at all!"

"And," Angela said, "it's an 'Acct' office at that! So his books and accounts will be there, not at his home!"

"Of course. What else?"

"Well, I only meant that if he were a grocer, or a doctor, or a teacher by trade, the information on Edna's estate might be in his desk at home because it wouldn't have any connection with his profession. But seeing as how he's working as a professional accountant, the chances are, he keeps all his accounting information at the office. Let's see . . . why, it's just about three blocks over—on Garfield Avenue. It's just number 321, hardly even three blocks. Caledonia, we could walk over."

"Oh, Angela—" Caledonia groaned. "Right this minute? Must we?"

"Well, there won't be a better time. We know Unmitigated Wallace is with his sister-in-law, presumably bringing the roses back to her cheeks. It's a perfect time to go by the office and at least get the lay of the land. You don't have to come if you don't want to," Angela added, knowing that was the spur that would make Caledonia get to her feet.

It did. And together they walked the three blocks, Caledonia complaining mightily the whole time. She hated walking with approximately the same intensity with which Ahab hated Moby Dick! But this was, after all, a special occasion.

When they arrived at 321 Garfield, they found it was an appliance store. But beside the store's last show window there was a door marked 321-B that led to a flight of narrow steps. Caledonia glared at Angela. "Steps!" She spit the word out. But there being no alternative except to back out of the expedition, she followed her smaller, spryer friend up the stairs, pulling heavily on the rail as she hoisted her bulk up, and pausing after about every fifth step to inhale deeply—a noise that was reminiscent of a whale surfacing to blow.

"Omigawd," she groaned at the top. "I hope I never have to do this again! Just a minute . . . let me catch my breath . . ."

Angela was already halfway through the outer door on which the gold lettering read WALLACE FAIRLEIGH CLAYTON, JR.—TAX ACCOUNTANT AND FINANCIAL ADVISOR. Caledonia stumbled in after her.

Behind the desk sat Margaret Hamilton—at least, that was Caledonia's first impression, seeing, as she did, through bleary eyes, clouded with sweat. ("Probably her sister, the Wicked Witch of the East," Caledonia confided to Angela later. "Don't be silly," Angela retorted. "Everybody knows that sister got sat on by the house!")

"Something I can help you with?" the Witch of the West asked, with a forbidding glare.

"We were thinking . . . we wanted . . ." Angela was so

taken aback by the uncanny resemblance to the late actress that she could only stammer. Usually she was quick with the excuse or the manufactured story, but for a wonder, this time it was Caledonia who came to the rescue.

"We were thinking of hiring an accountant," Caledonia said. "And Mr. Clayton had been recommended . . ."

"Yes?" The receptionist was not being very helpful.

"Well, what are his hours? Can we just come in when it's easy for us? Or does he prefer new clients to make an appointment?" Caledonia was still carrying the conversational ball. Angela had turned her attention to the rest of the office, her eyes focusing on the door to the inner office, behind which, presumably, Mr. Clayton kept his own desk and his personal papers.

"It would be much easier, of course," the Witch replied mildly, "if you'd make a firm appointment. Mr. Clayton customarily spends only a part of the day in the office— usually in the morning. He is here by eight or eighty-thirty, but he usually leaves at eleven o'clock or so. He's semiretired after a successful career in the East . . ."

("The East?" Angela said scathingly later. "Since when is Wichita 'The East'? It's east of Salt Lake City—east of Las Vegas—east of California . . . sure! But 'The East'?"

"Which just goes to show," Caledonia remonstrated with her, "that you're not a true Californian yet! Everything's relative. When you were living in Washington, I bet you thought Ohio was 'The West.' You should know that to a native Californian, everything beyond the San Bernardino Mountains is 'The East.' ")

". . . but of course," the Wicked Witch continued, eyeing Caledonia's incredible pearl necklace and her diamond rings, "he would come in during the afternoon, if that were necessary for you. He does make an exception when that's all a client can arrange. We try to be helpful. After all, that's what we're in business to do."

Angela seemed to wake up at last. "How does it happen

you're here this afternoon, then, if the office isn't open?"
she asked.

"Oh, but it is. I keep the office open a full day," the
dragon replied, pleasantly enough. "I'm Miss Stoner, by the
way."

"How do you do," Angela said, without responding with
her own name. "Now about our appointment . . ."

They settled on a day in the following week and on a
morning hour, after an urgent protest by Caledonia, who—
arguing heatedly, with all the conviction of a genetically
programmed late riser—seemed to forget that, since they
had no intention of actually keeping the appointment, she
would not actually be expected to rise in time to make a
9:00 A.M. business date.

"What name shall I put down?" Miss Stoner said.

Angela and Caledonia hesitated and looked at each other.
This time Caledonia appeared to be without inspiration, so
Angela took charge. She removed a dainty linen handkerchief from her little purse and coughed into it delicately as
she talked. "Mrs. Win-[*cough*]-sdge . . . and . . . I am Mrs.
[*choke-gasp*]. . . Bing-[*sniff*]-brl," she said, giving a genteel
snuffle.

"Winsludge and Bingball?" Miss Stoner said doubtfully,
writing in her book as Angela looked on.

"Uh-uh . . ." Angela corrected, her voice muffled by the
handkerchief. "That's an *E*. There's no *U*. It's Win-[*cough*]
and Bing-[*sniffle*]." She cleared her throat delicately and put
the hanky away again.

Miss Stoner diligently erased the entry in her book mut-
tering, "Win-sledge."

"Well, Miss Stoner, we'll see you next week, then. Unless of course something comes up and we have to
cancel . . ."

"Oh, dear," Miss Stoner said. "You will let us know if
your plans change, won't you? Mr. Clayton would be so
annoyed to clear a space on his calendar and then have a
cancellation—unless you called in, of course. We under-

stand that things come up—but we would like some notice."

"Of course, my dear Miss Stoner," Angela said sharply,
without a sign of the cough or the sniffles. "Of course.
Now ..." she put a hand on Caledonia's arm and gave a
little tug in the direction of the door, ". . . we certainly
thank you for your time. You've been most helpful."

They clattered down the stairs without exchanging a
word, while the office door eased itself painfully shut,
pushing effortfully against the pneumatic stop and sighing
as it swung to.

"Now, Angela, what was all that about Winsludge and
Bingball?"

"False names, of course. I suddenly thought—what if
Unmitigated Wallace is an embezzler? Or worse still, a
murderer? You don't want him knowing we're poking
around in his affairs, do you?"

"Oh. Good thinking, girl!" Caledonia gave a large nod
and Angela turned bright pink with pleasure at the unaccus-
tomed compliment. "But why on earth did you come up
with Winsludge and Bingball?"

"Win*sledge* . . . remember? I corrected her," Angela reminded her friend. "Nobody would believe 'Win*sludge*' after all. I made it more believable by changing it to . . ."

"Listen, come on in here . . ." Caledonia pulled Angela
into Home Folks—a small cafe with bright blue-checked
cloths and fresh flowers on every table, where they served
sinfully delicious baked goods. It was a place the women
from Camden tried hard to bypass on their trips to town,
lest they hear (as Snoopy puts it) a chocolate-chip cookie
calling their name!

"Waitress . . . two of those big cookies and two coffees,
please. Well? I'm waiting . . ." Caledonia addressed the last
half of the remark to Angela. "Of all the unlikely . . . He'll
surely know those are phony names. There are no such
names!"

"But they're enough like our own that, if he does find

out it was us, it'll seem like an accident—like The Wicked
Witch took 'em down wrong. But if he ever asks us, I can
say she probably garbled 'em because I was blowing my
nose at the time!" she finished triumphantly.

Caledonia's hoot of laughter made other customers'
heads turn toward them with curiosity. Caledonia lowered
her voice a few decibels. "Well, all that aside, I don't see
that we've accomplished much today. We haven't learned
one thing except Wallace's secretary's name, and that isn't
important—even though it is appropriate to her! I mean, the
Great Stoner Face, and all that. We've made an appointment we have no intention of keeping . . . we have given
false names . . . and we know not one more thing about
Clayton's business affairs than we did before."

"But we know when we can find out!" Angela said triumphantly. "Because while Miss Stoner was writing down
our appointment, I walked over and peeked over her shoulder into the appointment book—and he doesn't have one
single thing on for tomorrow afternoon. So he won't be at
the office at all, after lunch, and we can look around then."

"Mmmm . . ." Caledonia was letting the chocolate-chip
cookie melt in her mouth . . . "How?"

"How what?"

"How do we get past Stoner?"

"I'll think of something . . ."

"And when we do, how do we know if we've found
something important or not?"

"What do you mean?"

"I mean, I wouldn't know a credit from a debit. I
wouldn't know double entry bookkeeping from double vision. Figures mean absolutely nothing to me. And I thought
you were the same! I mean, you claim you can't even balance your own checkbook!"

"Well . . ." Angela was more capable of simple arithme-
tic than she liked to admit. Her pose of fiscal incompetence
had saved her frequently from being elected treasurer of the
Officers' Wives' Club, and it had become habit to claim

that, where numbers were concerned, she was nothing short of learning disabled. But the truth was that accounting procedures were indeed beyond her.

"We're going to have to think of something that will help us, that's all," Angela said airily.

And then, as an afterthought, she said, "Listen . . . it's still early. Do you suppose we could each have another of those wonderful cookies without spoiling our supper?"

Chapter 5

"MISS STONER is not going to be easily distracted," Caledonia told Angela that evening over their customary predinner sherry in Caledonia's apartment.

"Well, she goes out to lunch some time or other, doesn't she? Maybe we can get into the office while she's gone."

"She almost certainly locks the outer office while she's away. Maybe the inner office, too. Will you have another sip?"

"Thank you. I might just have a little bit more," Angela said. Flushed both with her first sherry and with the afternoon's success, she extended her dainty, cut-crystal glass. "Is it rather warm this evening?"

Caledonia smiled and said nothing, but she opened the window to let the ocean breeze sweep through the room. Pouring out more of the lovely golden sherry she said, "I don't fancy trying to break down the door. I think we certainly want to sneak in for our information. I don't believe we want to tip off the Unmitigated Wallace that someone is nosing around his affairs. It would hurt his feelings if he's innocent . . ."

". . . and scare him off if he's guilty!" Angela cried gaily. The sherry was certainly making itself felt . . . she was positively giddy with her sense of purpose and importance. "We have to think of something else. Let's see . . . what shall it be?"

But their best efforts produced not the first brilliant idea.

72

At least, not before dinner—a rather heavier meal than Mrs. Schmitt usually made up: a stuffed pork chop, spicy and golden brown; a small pile of wild rice that had been cooked with thin wedges of sweet-tart apple mixed in; a spear of broccoli dipped in lemon; and a sliver of velvety pecan pie to follow. Sighing as they walked out to the lobby, the women strolled toward the far end of the huge room to pass a few pleasantries with the little group gathered there: Tootsie Armstrong, Mr. Brighton, Emma Grant, and Mary Moffet standing near, to Caledonia's displeasure, the bird cage.

Emma Grant was putting bits of leftover broccoli into the bird's food dish, maneuvering the shreds very delicately to avoid dropping them into the water dish below. The bird was standing on its perch, frowning with a terrible concentration at her fingers as they moved in and out between the bars. "He's not biting me," Emma boasted. "I wonder what Grogan did to get him so excited?"

"Oh, dear," Mary breathed nervously. "I just wish he wouldn't glare so hard. He looks like he is putting an ancient bird-curse on everybody!"

"Nonsense," Tootsie twittered. "I may not know a lot of things, but I know better than to think there's any such thing as a bird-curse." Although, in her addled way, she didn't sound very sure of herself.

"Hell in a basket!"

"What did you say?" Emma asked, looking quickly at little Mary Moffet.

"I didn't say anything," Mary answered nervously. "Not a word."

"Hell in a basket!"

"Lord, Lord—it's the bird!" Mr. Brighton breathed. He alone had been watching the cage while the women talked and looked at each other. "He's talking!"

"What's that he's saying!" Emma pleaded. "I can't make it out."

"Hell," the bird repeated very clearly, *"in a bas-ket!"* He

wagged his head threateningly. *"Same to your cat!"* he added venomously.

Brighton laughed. "I do believe he's swearing ... at least, it seems to be an exclamation of grave displeasure! Fancy that ... there is such a thing as a 'bird-curse'— though not as you meant it, Mrs. Moffet. Ah, Mrs. Wingate—Mrs. Benbow ... come over and listen to our bird talk."

But the bird turned its back on the group and huddled down into a corner of the perch and said not another word.

"Well, perhaps he's out of the mood again," Tootsie Armstrong said. "He wasn't talking nicely anyway. It's just as well. Someone should teach that bird some manners, if you ask me!" And she pivoted on her little high heels and moved toward the elevator that would take her to the second floor and her own apartment. "Good night, everybody."

" 'Night, Tootsie," Caledonia said absently. Then to the others she said, "Any news? Anything I don't know about that's happened today?" Just before and just after meals were the times when gossip was exchanged and everybody caught up on all that had happened to their fellow residents recently.

Emma Grant shook her head. "Except that, you mark my words, we're going to have another rate increase announced at the meeting Friday."

"Oh, dear," Mary sighed.

"So you said, Emma," Angela reminded her. "We'll wait and see if rumor is accurate."

"Emma, are you walking down the garden for your evening exercise?" Mary Moffet said. "I could use the company on the way home." Mary's apartment was in the last cottage on the right, directly on Beach Lane, and sometimes it frightened her that outsiders—strangers—people who were not residents—seemed always to be walking past her windows.

Mary had just last week requested to be moved to the main building at the first opportunity, following an evening during which two rather amorous teenagers standing directly outside her bedroom window had discussed whether or not they would spend the night in the backseat of the young man's car, and what the girl's father would do if he found out. Mary, for all her advanced years, was naive and simply would rather not face real life if she could avoid it. In the main building she would be sheltered from sharing knowledge of teenage exploits, sexual or otherwise, and Torgeson, she told the others delightedly, had agreed to put her name at the top of the waiting list for a move.

"Yes, Mary, I'll walk you home," Emma said good-naturedly. "You'll be safe enough with me, I imagine."

"Oh," Mary denied, a little embarrassed, "I wasn't really worried, you know. I was just thinking of the company. Someone to talk to, you know. Well, 'night all . . . Mr. Brighton—Angela—Caledonia . . ." and she and Emma left.

"Ladies," Mr. Brighton yawned to them. "I should be turning in as well. I delayed going up those five little steps to our hall," he bowed toward Angela, whose room was the first on their corridor, as Mr. Brighton's was the fifth on the opposite side. "I delayed those steps because of my arthritis. It's giving me the very devil tonight, and . . ."

"The devil you say!"

"It's the bird," Angela exclaimed. "You were right! He can talk."

"The devil you say!" the little creature exclaimed again, advancing on his perch toward them.

"He doesn't seem as frightened, now there are only the three of us," Brighton suggested.

"And nobody's poking fingers in the cage," Angela added. "He may perceive that as a threat."

"If he could read my mind, he might back off again," Caledonia said, but her tone was light.

"I don't believe you really hate birds, Cal," Angela suggested.

"Ah, but I do! Hate them with a passion. Well, not that I'd ever harm one or let one get hurt. But I'm really not a pet person, you see."

"Mr. Brighton . . ." Angela began.

"Add it up!" the bird interrupted, cocking its head and looking interestedly out at them. *"Add it up! Add it up!"*

"Well," Brighton laughed, "the bird is something of a clairvoyant. Or a historian! That is an odd coincidence . . . for him to hear my name and then to come out with my profession."

"Profession?"

"Yes, before I retired, I was an actuary. That's how I made my living—adding up, so to speak."

"Add it up," the bird called to him cheerfully. *"Same to your cat!"* he threw in for good measure. *"Chirrk!"*

"Wait a minute," Caledonia said. "Is an actuary an accountant?"

"Well, some are and some aren't. Mostly we're statisticians. I had a few courses in accounting when I was in college . . . but I wouldn't say . . ."

"Oh, Mr. Brighton, you're the answer to our prayers!" Angela exclaimed.

"Wait a minute . . ." Brighton put a hand up. "I haven't worked with ledgers and accounts for years, if that's what you're looking for. If it's something about taxes, or setting up a bookkeeping system . . ."

"No, nothing like that," Angela assured him. "It's . . . Cal, how are we going to explain this?"

"Look, Tom, let's talk a minute," Caledonia said, taking him by the hand and leading him over to a couch, where the three of them could sit together, Tom Brighton sandwiched between the ladies.

He eased himself down with obvious pain, but once in place, sighed luxuriously. "Ooooh, that feels good, getting the weight off that joint. I really am going to have to see about replacing that right hip . . . it's just—well, you know, you hate to voluntarily have a part of yourself cut off or cut out, because there's certainly no going back, if you don't like the way the new part works. If only there were a way to try those things out beforehand . . ." He sighed again . . . and

then laughed out loud as the bird in its cage let out a dupli-
cate of the sigh . . . looked at him with its head turned sideways, and sighed again. "Well, there's no mystery about
where the little fellow learned that noise . . . I must make it
twenty times a day! Now, ladies . . . what is this request of
yours? I must warn you that if it involves walking . . ."

Caledonia and Angela looked at each other. "Well, it
does, I'm afraid. That is, the building is only three blocks
away, but we can get you there in a car . . . no problem
about that. It's the stairs . . ."

"Stairs?"

"A full flight, and quite steep—they made me huff and
puff, I can tell you," Caledonia asserted.

"Well, let's talk about the task and not about the problems," Angela said.

"But if the problems are too great?" Caledonia suggested. "Maybe Mr. Brighton would rather not know our
scheme, seeing as how the ethics may be questionable, and
even the legality is borderline."

Brighton smiled benignly. "I'm too old to worry about
what's legal and what's illegal, if helping a friend is involved, dear ladies. Now morality is something else . . ."

"Nobody said 'morality,' " Caledonia corrected him. "I
said 'ethics'—and I meant 'business ethics,' and that's a
whole 'nother kettle of fish!"

"Well, all right then! Now, at least let me hear about it,
why don't you? I'll decide whether it comes within the
realm of the possible for me, or not."

"Briefly," Angela said bravely, "we intend to enter the
private office of a professional accountant and look over a
particular financial record to see if there's any evidence that
he's been taking his client's money."

"Oh, boy!" Brighton shook his head. "I'm not sure I'd
know that kind of evidence if I saw it. You may really want
to hire another professional accountant to look at the figures."

"There's the rub," Caledonia said. "We don't mind

breaking and entering ourselves, for the sake of the information. And a friend might risk it with us for a good cause. But if we hired somebody for the job, I'm sure he'd feel differently."

"You see," Angela bubbled, "what we're planning to do—we're going down to Wallace Clayton's office over on Garfield Avenue tomorrow while he isn't in. And we're going to lure his secretary away, and then we're going to go in and look over his records on Edna Ferrier. He's the trustee of her husband's estate, and we think he might have been taking money from the fund . . ."

"We think no such thing, Angela!" Caledonia interrupted. "That was just a suggestion. We need to know as much as possible about her affairs, because of her association with Alexander Lightfoot . . . it's really Lightfoot we're looking into, you see . . ."

"Ah," Brighton said wisely. "Now I see. You think Lightfoot's death might not be accidental?"

"Possibly not . . ." Caledonia said cautiously.

". . . and you are looking into his associates and friends—and his soon-to-be-wife?"

"Right again."

"Oh, well," Brighton said briskly. "Count me in! It's to help somebody who's one of *us*. That makes it okay. All in the family, so to speak."

"Now, Tom, are you sure?" Caledonia said gently. "We're not strictly within our legal rights, poking through his office, as we plan to do . . ."

"My dear, dear ladies," Tom Brighton said happily, "you two have more fun—you get into more mischief and seem to keep more active than any ten of the rest of us put together! Everyone here envies you your energy—your drive. The chance to have a part in one of your adventures is something nobody could resist! And me least of all. I don't know how much help I can be, but . . ."

Thus it was that at about 11:30 the next day, the three conspirators were gathered in front of the appliance store on

Garfield Avenue, their heads together as they conferred, apparently sharing serious concerns about a washer and dryer combination in the window that had a huge SALE sticker on it. Any passer-by might have concluded they were arguing the merits of the single unit over two separate machines, or whether to buy the "harvest gold" model or go all out for one in "poppy red." Actually, they were mapping strategy, having decided on nothing useful before they left on their mission.

They had taken a ride with Camden's little van, which was going downtown anyway to drop Janice Felton and Sadie Mandelbaum at the bank. Caledonia insisted the van drop the other two first . . . "We just tagged along . . . The van was scheduled so it could take you to the bank, and we don't want to delay you on your errand," she insisted. "We'll drop you off, and while you're doing your business we'll have the van take us down the way. Then we'll send it back for you . . ."

"That's really very nice of you," Janice had said. "It's not necessary, but . . ."

"Nonsense . . . nonsense . . ." Caledonia said airily.

As soon as she and Angela had helped Tom Brighton from the van, and it had disappeared around the corner, Caledonia hissed to them, "The fewer witnesses the better. See what I mean? This way only the van driver knows the corner we were dropped at."

Angela skipped toward the door marked 321-B. "Here . . . over here . . ."

Caledonia held up a warning hand, then beckoned imperiously with both hand and head. "Sssst . . . Angela . . . don't go up to the office yet. C'mere! Let's figure out what we're going to do first."

While apparently gazing with every evidence of interest at a cardboard sign that bore the legend OTHER WONDERFUL BARGAINS INSIDE, Brighton said, "I thought a lot about this, last night after we went our separate ways. If I'm to be of any help, you have to give me quite a bit of time. For one thing, I'll need time to recover from those stairs before I even begin! I will also need time to find the right accounts, time to study them . . . you need to come up with a scheme that will give me about an hour."

"An hour!" Angela was clearly dismayed. "I thought maybe I could just ask Miss Stoner to help me fix a broken slip-strap, and we could go to the ladies' room so she could pin me up . . ."

Caledonia shook her head. "Very ingenious, but that'll obviously take closer to three minutes than to an hour."

"Well, another idea I had was that we could put chloroform on a handkerchief, and go over behind her while she was working at the desk, and we'd put the handkerchief over her nose . . ."

"My Lord!" Brighton was clearly appalled.

Caledonia laughed out loud. "Colorful. Very colorful. But there are several problems with that idea. I'm sure you've thought of them. For instance, where do you propose to get a bottle of chloroform? A doctor or a pharmacist would want a reason, I think . . ."

"Well . . . I could think of something that—"

"And then we can hardly put a handkerchief over Miss Stoner's nose without her noticing it! We don't want her to be able to point an accusing finger at us later, so any form of physical assault is definitely out!"

"Could we maybe hire someone to . . ."

"Angela! No! No rough stuff!"

"Well, I know that." Angela was defensive. "I actually threw that idea out myself. I was just telling you, that's all—"

"For Pete's sake! Don't bother with the schemes you threw out. Let's talk about the more practical ideas."

"I thought of one," Brighton said. "It's probably not very good, but—is there a closet in the office? A supply closet perhaps?"

"I think there is," Angela said. "Yes, I recall . . ."

"Because," Brighton continued diffidently, "if she went

into the closet for something, you could slam the door on her and lock it. She might think it happened accidentally . . ."

"But not if we were in the office when it happened and didn't help her after she got stuck in there," Angela said glumly. "I mean, picture it! We're sitting there innocently, she gets stuck in the supply closet, she hollers, 'Help me get out of here,' and an hour later we turn the key and release her. Now, she's bound to be suspicious of that!"

"Well, perhaps we should wait outside till she goes to the closet for something," Brighton said. "Then she wouldn't know we were there at all."

"And we wouldn't know when she went into the closet!" Caledonia said. "I don't know about you, but I can't see through a solid wooden door . . . and that's all there is from the hallway to the office."

"And even if it were one of those glass doors," Angela said, "Miss Stoner'd be bound to notice three people lurking around in the hallway peering through at her every time she got up from her desk. The supply closet is a good idea, but I don't see how we'd do it and still escape suspicion."

A salesman within the appliance store strolled by the window and catching sight of the three of them, raised his eyebrows in an expression of bright invitation. Caledonia sighed, shook her head in a show of mild regret, and steered her companions to the next window, where several vacuum cleaners stood, their hoses intertwined like a nest of snakes. Inside the store, the clerk edged unobtrusively along, closer to their new position, trying to look nonchalant and inviting at the same time.

Caledonia waved her hand toward the window display in pretended interest, and all three turned their eyes dutifully toward the nozzles and brushes and disposable bags. "You can only look at an enameled agitator or a collection of revolving brush attachments for so long without making someone suspicious, I guess. We're getting a bit conspicuous. We need to move now and then to keep credibility. Well, any other ideas?"

"We could call 'Fire' and ring that alarm in the box . . . there's an emergency box on the wall beside the stairwell," Angela suggested.

Brighton shook his head. "Sorry, Mrs. Benbow, but I couldn't go along with that. I used to serve on the amateur fire department back home in Nebraska, and to me a false alarm is nothing to fool with. I really must insist that you find some other way."

"Well, suppose we don't ring the alarm, but just—oh, maybe set a fire in a wastebasket and let the smoke drift into the office . . . then when she comes out into the hall . . ."

"Yes, Angela? When she comes out into the hall, what? She'd ring the alarm herself, if she didn't see first that it was just a trash can fire. No good." Caledonia pretended to point at the next window down and moved the other two along with her to stand at a display of trash mashers, dishwashers, and garbage disposals. "Tasteful—not gaudy—I wonder who decorates their windows?"

"Oh, Cal, don't be sarcastic . . . be helpful!"

"I'm trying, but frankly, trash mashers and vacuum cleaners don't bring out my best thinking. And my feet are starting to hurt."

"Well, I tell you what I'm going to do," Angela announced. "I'm going on up there and talk to Miss Stoner in person."

"Dear lady, about what?" Mr. Brighton asked.

"I don't know yet. But I can usually think of something."

"But why? I mean, why go up and talk to her? Do you think she will present you with an idea for her own kidnapping?"

"Yes, I do," Angela said loftily. "Or rather, I expect something in our conversation will give me more inspiration than . . ." She pointed at the window display and shuddered. Domesticity—at least the practical side of homemaking—had never been her long suit. It had made conversation difficult when the officers' wives got together for a coffee; the other women talked of new detergents, reliable diaper services, and how to get rust stains out of teakettles ... while Angela yawned and daydreamed about her collection of tiny antique boxes, or about the art show at the museum, or about the elegant dinner party she and Douglas were hosting—with the help of a catering service, of course. She simply had nothing in common with housewives and mothers ... and it had never bothered her in the least!

Now she turned her back abruptly on the enticements offered in the name of neatness (pronounced, in Angela's book, "drudgery") and, chin thrust high, marched briskly toward adventure. Inside the appliance store the salesman, who had been watching with hopeful patience, sighed deeply and turned away himself ... not to adventure, but to pimento cheese, a banana, and whatever else his wife had put in his lunch. Food soothes disappointments.

"What shall we do while Mrs. Benbow's up there?" Brighton asked. "Would it be best if we waited out of sight, perhaps? I mean, she might take a notion to throw that Miss Stoner out of the window or something."

"Well, nothing quite so drastic, I'm sure. Or rather, no, with Angela one can't be absolutely sure, but I'd guess that nothing like that was going to happen. On the other hand ..." Caledonia put an arm under Mr. Brighton's elbow and steered him toward the next shop down, a bookstore where they could step inside the deep entrance and examine books on the sale table (NO TITLE OVER $3) while they waited.

And it seemed as though they waited forever, thumbing through outdated photography manuals, a collection of Zen sayings about stamp collecting, the illustrated memoirs of an industrialist, and the ghostwritten autobiographies of two Hollywood has-beens and one never-was. Then Caledonia looked up to see Angela, arm in arm with Miss Stoner and chatting with animation, strolling by the door of the shop.

Caledonia lifted a book of modern children's verse (a Mother Goose that featured off-road racing, computer games, and punk rock) high in front of her face and peered around it with one eye to watch Angela and Miss Stoner as they went past. She was convinced she had evaded detection till Angela looked back at her, behind Miss Stoner's shoulder, and made an "OK" sign with her thumb and forefinger . . . then jerked the thumb in an upward gesture that apparently meant . . . "Go on up!" The two women, Angela still talking a blue streak, disappeared around the next corner. Caledonia's last sight of Angela was her hand signaling with a waving forefinger and mouthing silently something that looked like "One, now!" or "One hour!"—it really didn't matter which.

"Let's go," Caledonia said, seizing Mr. Brighton by the elbow and propelling him toward the entrance marked 321-B. Fortunately the day was warm and dry, and Mr. Brighton's arthritic joints were not especially painful at the moment, so he was able to move rather briskly. The stairs were another matter, and it took him a good five minutes to haul himself to the second floor, stopping to wince and groan with each step. Five precious minutes gone from their slim allotment, but it couldn't be helped, of course.

"I haven't the least notion how we're going to get into a locked office," Caledonia said as Mr. Brighton made it onto the last step, shaking his head and drawing his breath sharply inward. The problem, however, solved itself. Or rather, it had been solved in advance. Caledonia turned the knob of the office door, pushed, and the door opened easily. Across the latch, holding it from sliding into the lock, several lengths of Scotch tape had been fixed . . . Angela obviously had not wasted the time she spent in the office.

They went in, removing the Scotch tape so the door would lock behind them.

Chapter 6

THE ROOM was, as expected, deserted. "There's something gloomy about a clean desk and filing cabinets with no ornaments on top of them. It's—it's just work space," Brighton observed in a whisper. "It's so sterile looking! When I had my office . . ."

"No need to whisper," Caledonia said aloud. "There's nobody else on this second floor—no other office. Though I wouldn't shout either. Because if they were to come back for any reason, and we were talking aloud, they'd probably be able to hear us right through the door. Well, let's look into Clayton's private domain, and . . . Hey! How about that!"

There was no lock at all on the inner door. Either Wallace Clayton had a clear conscience, or the outer lock was considered sufficient.

"Or there's a safe and he's got everything important locked up in it," Caledonia muttered aloud, as she swung the door wide. "Damn it . . . I . . . *Ahhhh*, well, now that's better!"

There seemed to be no safe—and no filing cabinets, either, although there were a couple of leatherette guest chairs, a couch with an end table on which stood a brass lamp and five leather-bound books held up by white marble statuettes (a reproduction of Michelangelo's *David* and one of the *Venus de Milo*), a coffee table with four copies of *U.S. News & World Report*, and an executive desk. Just behind the door stood a brass umbrella stand, displaying a polished wooden cane and a dignified black umbrella and, surprisingly, what appeared to be an oversized golf umbrella showing a touch of light blue in its folds. The only other accents in the room that were not coldly austere and businesslike were a luxurious potted fern that hung on a brass chain in one window, and one of Edna Ferrier's paintings of the California hills, in a narrow silvery frame on the wall above the couch.

Over in one corner, there was, to Caledonia's dismay, a small computer on a specially built desk, with a dot matrix printer beside it on a rolling stand. Except for a tangle of sheathed cable sprouted from the back of the various computer components, the room was painfully neat—the books were lined up between their marble bookends according to height—the magazines were laid one on top of the other, each showing a careful inch of the top and one side of the copy beneath. Except for that jumble of wire, the room simply had no warmth. "Not that a bunch of electrical wiring dangling around is warm and cozy," Caledonia muttered. "But at least it's a change from this fussy-neat . . . Oh, Lord! I just thought! I hope I don't have to fool with the computer. Brighton . . . Hsst . . . Tom Brighton! Hssst!"

Mr. Brighton had gone to the executive desk and opened the file drawer and was thumbing through its contents. He looked up inquiringly.

"There's a computer . . . do you know how to handle one?"

He shook his head. "Never touched one. I suppose I could learn . . ."

"We don't have time for a course in programming right now. And I suppose everything important is in that dreadful little machine! Damn! Well, we can hope. I'm going to check the files out there . . ." and she headed back to the outer office to attack the file cabinets.

She found folders marked FERRIER (EDNA) and FERRIER (HORACE) with no trouble at all. She also found a small copy machine on a table in the supply closet. It seemed simple enough, even to her eye, and it seemed to have no counter which would number the copies made—that is, if she used it, she thought it would probably leave no record. So she set out to copy both Ferrier files . . . even including a personal note *(Wallace: Got your letter and will be looking forward to lunch the day you arrive from Wichita. We have a lot to tell you—and we'll be returning from a trip to Lake Mead, so we'll have pictures to show off. In friendship, Horace)*. She wondered if that was the last thing Wallace had heard directly from his brother-in-law. Poor old Horace!

The files were relatively slim, and Caledonia was able to return them to their place without difficulty within about ten minutes. She let her fingers do the walking through the rest of the file folders, but none of their labels looked at all promising to her. She sighed . . . she really wouldn't know if some Billy Sol Estes had left records here of all his transactions . . . reading the chaste, typed labels on the files really told her nothing. Perhaps she was missing the most important kind of evidence of corrupt and dishonest practices, but she rather doubted it. It all looked useless and boring to her—a complete waste of time.

"How are you getting along?" she called in the general direction of the executive desk as she returned to the inner office. But there was no one at the desk. Instead, Tom Brighton was seated at the little computer, his face alight with interest, as he punched keys and listened to the machine whir and watched the screen change its display.

"Mrs. Wingate, do come and look at this!"

"You told me you couldn't run a computer!" Caledonia accused him.

"I can't. I mean, I couldn't. This little thing runs itself! Well, almost. I didn't find anything, so I thought I might as well see—anyhow, I just turned it on, and it made some whispering noises, and pretty soon a title came onto the screen. And guess what it said?"

Caledonia made a face. "Please!"

"Sorry. I'm just so tickled with this, I can't ... It said CHESS GAME."

Caledonia peered over his shoulder. On the screen in black and white there was indeed the pattern of a chess-board with tiny chessmen pictured, half in solid white, half in black outlined in white. "Okay ... I get the idea. So then what?"

"Well, it had the instructions right there. Or anyhow, it said FOR INSTRUCTIONS, PRESS SPACE BAR and I did. And it lists on the screen how you're to do moves. You can move the piece with this little rolling ball affair. I believe it's called a mouse—and before you ask, I haven't the faintest idea why. Anyway, it works like one of those remote arms in the fair, the claw thing that grabbed the cheap jewelry and the gumballs out of the machine while you turned a knob ... remember? Something like that. But different. Anyway, it's easy enough to figure out. And then, after you've moved, the computer comes up with a move of its own."

He moved the mouse slightly, and the picture of a hand appeared beside the white bishop. Brighton pushed and moved the mouse again, and his bishop moved to a new square. There was a pause, and then a little whir, the display flickered, and Mr. Brighton's white queen disappeared, replaced by the black queen! At the foot of the screen a legend was displayed: CHECK!

Brighton laughed out loud. "Damn! I wasn't watching what I was doing. I was so busy demonstrating the computer, I forgot about playing chess. It's got me beat!" He reached up and patted the side of the monitor. "Isn't that the cleverest little machine? I mean, just look at that move!"

Caledonia shook her head. "I'm not a chess player, Tom. I can't appreciate the niceties of the game. And I'm not a computer lover, so I can't marvel at how wonderful it is that a machine can play a game ..."

"... and a very creditable game, Mrs. Wingate. Very creditable!" Brighton amended.

"Yes. Well, that doesn't seem very much to the point, Tom. Did you find out anything about Edna Ferrier's accounts? Or are we going to have to take a quick computer course and go through that?" She waved her hand at a box of labeled computer disks in a smoke-gray case of translucent plastic that stood beside the machine.

"I don't think you have to go through them," Brighton said. "Look."

He flipped open the plastic lid and showed her the labels. COMPUTER PINBALL, SHOOTING GALLERY, SPACE CADET FLIGHT, GUESS THE SECRET NUMBER, and CROSS-WORD CRAZE.

"But they're all games!" Caledonia said. He nodded. "Where's the serious stuff?" she asked.

"Not on the computer, apparently," Brighton said. "I actually found an old-fashioned ledger over there ..." He gestured at the desk, and she saw that on the otherwise neat surface, a thin black leather-covered ledger had been laid out.

"Anything to photocopy?" she said. "There's a copy machine out there."

"Yes, if you don't mind. I think I know everything from looking at the records a short while. They seem very simple. But if you'd just make copies, so I can have a little longer to examine ... There aren't many pages," he added apologetically.

"No problem at all," she said, swirling across to pick up the book and head for the outer office. "But while I'm doing that, you'd better tidy up in here."

"Mmmhmm," he said absently. "Now, let's see. How can I start the game again? Well, if I just ..." He reached for the On/Off switch—an old repairman's trick: if you don't know how to run something, just start all over and see if that works. As Caledonia left, she saw the screen flicker to black and come back to life as he settled back in his chair. He moved the mouse slightly, and CHESS GAME appeared on the screen in ornate letters. Caledonia went off to the copy machine shaking her head.

Fifteen more minutes and she was done. She hurried back. "Tom—Tom, are you ready?"

He punched a key and watched the display change and his chess pieces realign themselves. "Just one more move . . ."

"To-o-om . . ." Caledonia's rumble was as ominous as distant thunder. "Come on! Do you want them to be right outside the door, on their way in, as we make our exit? How would you like to explain that? Besides, I need you to put this ledger away where it belongs, so he won't know anyone's had it out!"

Brighton sighed. "Oh, all right, Mrs. Wingate." He turned the switch off and watched the bright eye of light on the screen contract itself swiftly to nothing. He shifted his weight and gasped. "Oh-boy, oh-boy, oh-boy! I shouldn't have sat still so long. That hip . . ." He hoisted himself painfully upward and took the black ledger from her outstretched hand.

"Can we tell anything worth knowing from what little we have? There are only a few papers you haven't seen . . . I've got 'em here in the file . . ." Caledonia waved her hand. She had appropriated a brown manila envelope from the room where the copy machine stood and it now held about fifty pages of copied material. "It isn't much . . ."

"Can't be sure," Brighton said in tight, pinched tones as he limped across to the desk. "Here . . . the ledger goes in right behind the first file folder . . . There! Neat as a pin!" He slid the drawer shut again and limped back toward her. "I think I'll be able to tell you something tomorrow. I'll want to see whatever you found, and put it together with my stuff, of course. Just for what it's worth, I haven't found a thing out of line. Except . . ."

"Here, let me close the door behind you," Caledonia said, standing aside so he could start down the stairs, leaning heavily on the banister. "I'll be sure it locks this time . . . Now, except what?"

"Oh," Brighton said, and his voice was tenser than ever, his voice coming in staccato bursts as he tried to control any sign that he was in pain. "Well, he doesn't seem to have any books on anybody but Edna Ferrier. And for a going accounting office, that's a bit peculiar."

"I'd say so. I'd say . . ."

"*Agh . . . oooh*, wait a second and let me catch my breath!" He paused on a step midway down the flight of stairs. "The joints are giving me a fit . . ."

"I'm sorry about the stairs, Tom. You were a real sport to agree to come up here at all!"

He was breathing deeply through his nose, and Caledonia thought there were tears standing in his eyes, but it was too shadowy in the stairwell to say for sure. "Now," he said abruptly, starting off again, still one step at a time, holding tightly to the rail on one side and Caledonia on the other.

"You sure you're going to make it okay?" He nodded wordlessly. Caledonia held one arm to help support his weight. One thing she'd learned over the years was that pain is more bearable if you can forget about it. So she primed the conversational pump. "I was impressed with you learning to run a computer so fast. I thought you said you'd never used one before?"

"I hadn't. But I didn't really learn to—*ooooh*"—he drew a sharp breath inward. Then he regained control and went on. "I mean, there's nothing to it, apparently. I told you how I did it. I turned the switch on, I pushed the buttons it said to push . . ."

"How did it tell you what to do?"

"It had little notes printed on the screen . . . like 'Enter data and press RETURN' and even the little parakeet in our lobby could have learned to do that, eventually! There was no real mystery to it that I could see."

"It sounds simple enough." Caledonia let her skepticism

show. Anything to keep him talking while he worked his way down the stairs.

"I tell you, Mrs. Wingate, if that's all there is to running a computer, I might just have to consider getting one. I've got to the age where I hate to see the bank statement come in each month because it means I've got to add and subtract and compare . . . and numbers just aren't as easy for me to handle as they once were. I used to be able to run figures in my head that I need a calculator for now. I used to get a kick out of the relationships I'd find in groups of numbers . . . now I just think of my bank statement as a chore. And sometimes I even let it go a whole month. Then it's harder to do than ever! But with this wonderful little machine . . ."

"You're not serious! You'd actually get a computer for yourself? I don't believe you!"

"Now, Mrs. Wingate, I didn't quite say that. I said I'd consider . . . I'd have to be sure that I could really figure out how to use it, not just slap at it hit-or-miss the way I did today. I'd also have to be sure my eyes could stand it! It's hard to read words and numbers on that screen . . ."

"Our eyes are getting old, I suppose . . ."

"Well, and maybe it's habit. I'm used to reading things that are lying flat, not things that are standing vertical! I'm used to handling the paper and turning the pages, rather than just pushing a button! But whatever the reason, I'd have to be sure I could read those beady little letters and numbers. Besides, it'd be different learning how to handle complex information and . . . Ooooh. What a relief!"

They had reached the bottom of the stairs, and Brighton sagged against the wall and closed his eyes for a moment.

"Are you all right?"

"Yes, Mrs. Wingate. It's just the effort . . ."

"Well, if you're all right, we'd better get moving again. No telling when the forbidding Miss Stoner will appear. I suppose we could say we were just thinking of going up to the office, if we see her, but . . ."

"I'm ready," Brighton said, levering himself away from the wall and once more upright. And they moved off, down the street.

They reached the shelter of the bookstore doorway, when Mr. Brighton asked to stop again. "Just to catch my breath," he assured Caledonia. "I'm not really hurting so badly. Nothing would seem painful, after those stairs . . ."

They thumbed through the sale books once more and the clerk, recognizing them from their first visit, smiled professionally and moved over within easy hailing distance, hopeful that they had been drawn back by the bargains. They had not been pretending to look at the books for long, however, when Angela sailed into view, still talking and punctuating her words with lively gestures, still attached by an invisible string to Miss Stoner, who was looking faintly dazed.

"Yes, I'm sure," Miss Stoner was saying, as the two passed within earshot of the bookstore. "All terribly interesting, of course. Though I don't see that it will influence your finances in the least . . . You really are going to have to excuse me. It's all been fascinating, of course . . . a pleasure to have your company, naturally . . . and on any other day than a workday . . . but I do have to return . . ." She waved her hand vaguely upward, indicating either the second-floor offices or her eventual home in heaven. "Another time perhaps . . ." and Miss Stoner took to her heels, disappearing—as Caledonia saw when she popped her head around the bookstore's corner—up the office stairway.

Angela's grin, as she turned and retraced her steps to join Caledonia and Tom Brighton, was almost fiendish with glee. "Bored her to death with a discussion of the influence of astrological signs on one's personal fortunes and the stock market . . . She couldn't wait to get rid of me, and she really didn't think to ask me a single question . . ."

"You don't know anything about astrology! You don't even believe in it!"

"Of course not, Cal, but I read the columns in the daily

papers—everybody does. So I certainly can talk about the stuff—sun signs and what's in the ascendant and so on . . . Well, any luck?"

"Yes and no." Caledonia took her by the arm, nodded Brighton to come along with them, and started out onto the sidewalk where nobody could overhear. "Yes, we got in, yes, we think we found the accounts, no, we didn't find the evidence of any funny business going on. I have some papers here from the files . . ."

"You didn't steal the files!"

"Of course not, Angela. I copied them on the office machine . . ."

"Can they tell it's been used?"

"I thought of that, too. It doesn't have a usage-counter on it or anything, so it should be okay. Anyhow, we can look at those at our leisure. But—well, you tell her, Tom."

Brighton beamed. "I played chess on his computer . . ."

"Computer!" Angela was clearly surprised. "I didn't know either of you could work one of those monsters . . ."

"Monster isn't the right word," Brighton protested mildly. "I found this one to be a friendly little pet of a machine. Actually, I've been thinking about getting . . ."

"Tom, when I said 'Tell her,' I didn't mean tell her about your game-playing and your new toy. I meant tell her about the accounts and Edna's business interests."

"Oh, yes. Well, I did find a ledger with some accounts, and everything seems perfectly open and aboveboard. A statement from a cash management account that was tucked inside tallies perfectly with the entries in the ledger, and she's got sound investments—nothing questionable there— and she seems to be making money, rather than spending principal . . ."

"Oh, dear!" Angela was clearly disappointed. "But that would mean the Unmitigated Wallace is perfectly honest! What a terrible disappointment! I had really hoped . . . Drat! Double drat!"

Her face settled into a pout that put her lower lip up over

her upper and drew her brows down in the center. She looked as though she were puckering up to cry, and at the sight of her obvious disappointment, both Caledonia and Tom Brighton burst out laughing.

Chapter 7

"WELL, AND where does that get us, after all? All that effort and so little to show for it," Caledonia said in a discouraged tone, when the three of them finally arrived back at Camden.

Tom Brighton shook his head. "I, at least, have acquired something—a bad ache! If you'll excuse me, I'm heading for some aspirin, a heating pad, and a rest before supper." Bowing slightly at the waist in a gesture of farewell, Brighton began to limp painfully off toward his own rooms.

Caledonia hated to stop him, he was moving with such obvious effort, but she had to call out, "Tom . . . Tom Brighton . . . wait a minute . . ." She lumbered across the lobby to hand him the manila envelope full of copies she had made at Clayton's office. "They're probably not worth looking over," she said apologetically. "But if you have the time?"

He nodded and tried to smile, though his mouth was pinched tight. Then he turned and continued his excruciating progress across the lobby toward his first-floor hallway.

Angela looked after him and shook her head. "Poor man," she said. "Cal, I'm afraid we shouldn't have imposed on him. It was such a strain!"

"The mind was willing, but the hips and knees were weak! I agree. I just didn't realize the stairs would be that hard on him. Going up wasn't so bad, you know. It was going down. I thought he was going to die right there halfway down the steps, it hurt him so bad. At one point, I thought I'd have to give him a push and let him fall the rest of the way, to get him down. I don't think bumping down head over heels would have hurt him one bit worse than he was hurting inching down a step at a time. And it would have been over with a lot quicker!"

"I do wish," Angela said primly, "that he'd consider that joint-replacement operation. At least for that bad hip. You know Hazel Hanson had it—and now, a year later, you wouldn't guess it, she moves so easily. I think I'll just talk to him about it . . ."

"Leave him alone, Angela. He's a big boy now. He can make up his own mind."

"But Cal—"

"But nothing! Just let him be. He knows about the operation—he knows Hazel's had it—and he knows which room she lives in, if he wants to ask her about it. If he starts hurting bad enough, he'll probably have the operation. But you—you just skip the whole subject and let him make his own decisions. We—uh-oh—What time is it?" Caledonia held up her ample wrist to show she was not wearing a watch.

"Let's see . . ." It took a bit of squinting for Angela to focus on the hands of her wafer-thin gold watch . . . about the size of a dime, though made larger by the diamonds set around it "Oh . . . it's two o'clock already."

"Oh, *peanut butter*!" Caledonia's booming voice woke the parakeet, dozing on its perch across the lobby. It started and gave a few feeble *"Chirrk-chirrk"* noises, looking nervously about to see the source of the thunder. "I've missed lunch!" the thunder roared on.

"What was that you said?"

"I said I missed lunch, and . . ."

"No, before that. Peanut butter?"

"Oh! That! Peanut butter? Surely you've heard me say that before?" Caledonia barked, as the parakeet seemed to tremble in response to the blasts of sound.

"I don't recall—"

"That was my Grandmother Parkhurst's swearword. She had a violent temper, but women of her generation couldn't express themselves freely with the words men used. And women's words like 'heavens to Betsy' or 'botheration' didn't seem nearly strong enough to her. So she always said 'peanut butter' . . . and, believe me, it's a good word. Lots better than 'Oh fudge.' Nice plosives, and you can bite off the *t*'s . . . we even had a rhyme she made us memorize. Let's see . . .

> When a swearword you would utter,
> Pause, then just say 'Peanut butter!' "

Caledonia walked over to the bird's cage, looked him in his beady eye, and said firmly, "Peanut butter!" She popped the *p* and the *b* loudly, and the bird shuddered and turned its head away.

Caledonia beamed. "You see? Even this little blue nuisance recognizes that as a high order of cussing! You must start using it yourself. Very satisfying. Well," she went on, her good humor obviously restored despite her hunger, "come on down to the cottage with me while I see what's in the refrigerator. I must have something to snack on that will hold me till dinner. And you—you must be famished . . ."

"Well, not exactly," Angela said a little sheepishly. "I had my lunch. With Miss Stoner. That's how I got her to come away from the office, you see . . ."

"Oh. I was going to ask you that," Caledonia said, moving through the lobby with her purple caftan swirling behind her, creating a kind of lavender-tinted breeze as she walked along. "I wondered what on earth you'd said to get her out and keep her out of the way for a full hour. I should have guessed it was lunch."

"I wondered how long it would take you to ask," Angela said in a slightly annoyed voice. There was little that pleased her quite so much as being given the chance to boast of her own cleverness, but one had to make at least a show of modesty. It was very helpful to have a friend who would ask the right questions. Usually Caledonia obliged. This time she hadn't. It had been, Angela felt, rather thoughtless of Caledonia.

"Well, I meant to ask, of course." Caledonia was perfectly well aware of Angela's need to show off. She was gracious enough to apologize as she sailed out of the lobby. "I'm really sorry. But first we were busy getting away from the vicinity of Clayton's office, calling from that pay phone in the drugstore to get the van to come back for us—and then we couldn't talk in front of the driver. And of course he stopped and got those others who'd been to the craft show in the mall, so we couldn't even whisper in the backseat, because they could overhear. This is the first time we've been out of earshot of someone else, since we left downtown!"

"Well," Angela pouted, "it's just—I thought you'd be more curious. I thought you'd ask at once."

"Angela!" Caledonia said, marching through the sunlit September afternoon garden, oblivious to the rosy hydrangea and the pale blue agapanthus as she concentrated on her steps. She tossed her words back over her shoulder to Angela, pattering along in her wake. "Angela, this *is* 'at once.' This is as 'at once' as I could manage. I really do want to know about it. I'm trying to tell you . . . here . . ."

She had reached her front door and held it open for the two of them. "Come on in and stop pouting. It doesn't become you. Sit down . . ." she waved a hand at Angela's favorite little velvet chair, ". . . and while I go and fish around in the fridge, you can tell me everything. Absolutely everything."

Angela sat, and in spite of herself, her eyes began to shine. She could stage a pretty convincing case of hurt feelings, but this was not the time. She was anxious for applause. "Well, to begin with, I had to explain to Miss

Stoner what I was doing there in the first place. Because she knew me, you see. So I made up a story . . ."

Caledonia, head down in the refrigerator, knew a cue when she heard one. "What story?" she prompted, lofting her voice slightly to get it out of the meat-keeper drawer.

"I told her something had come up and I had to change our appointment with Mr. Clayton to some other time," Angela called, raising her own volume slightly to reach Caledonia, now burrowing through the lettuce-crisper. "And then I realized I could just have phoned to tell her that. That didn't really explain why I was doing it in person. So I thought of another story." She could hardly keep the pride out of her voice.

"And? For goodness' sake, go on . . ." Caledonia was equal to the task of playing straight man, and didn't mind in the least.

"I told her," Angela's delighted inflections would have warned anyone that she was beaming with self-congratulation, "I told her I was downtown shopping anyhow, and when I walked past the office door, it jogged my memory about the appointment. So since I was there anyhow, I just came on in. She didn't think that was unusual in the least!"

"Well done," Caledonia boomed, her voice still partially muffled by the enameled walls of the refrigerator. "Ah-ha! Found something edible here. Not much, but . . . well, what next? Go on . . ."

Angela heard the refrigerator door close.

"Thank you for the compliment. It was pretty good thinking, if I do say so. Well, anyhow, then she wrote down a new appointment time . . . and I wrote it, too, in my little weekly diary that I carry. And then I had to think of something else to keep the conversation going. So I asked if maybe she was taking the afternoon off herself. I mean, that would have been so helpful—it would have solved the entire difficulty!" From the kitchen Caledonia gave a half snort of agreement, nudging Angela's story along.

"So anyhow, to try to find out if she was going out, I said, 'Oh, you have on such a nice dress, you must be going to lunch with someone special, dressed up that way . . .' And she said she wasn't, and the dress was old—something she wore all the time to the office—but you could tell she was pleased, all the same. So then I said that as long as she wasn't going out to lunch, why not join me? I had to get something to eat because it was nearly lunchtime anyhow, and why didn't she join me at Camden Corners. She jumped at the chance to have some company."

"Caang-ungh Cow-nguhf? Huft hat? Ngew flafe?" Caledonia's mouth was obviously full of something that kept her from closing lips and touching tongue in the accustomed way. One had to guess her intent.

"Yes, it's a new place," Angela said, after a moment—the time it took her to translate. "It opened sometime last month or so. It isn't exactly the Ritz, but they don't poison you, either. They served a nice enough Monte Cristo. That's what I had, and the salad looked—"

"I hong hare!" Caledonia said firmly, her head appearing around the corner, her jaws working while she talked. "Hut-ut fee fay?"

"You don't care and what'd she say?" Angela asked for confirmation and Caledonia nodded briskly. "Cal, I wish you'd swallow whatever that is. I can hardly understand you."

Caledonia's hand came around the corner holding a large carton of soda crackers. "Eeoo wang fum?"

"No, I don't want some, thank you. It'll spoil my appetite for supper."

"Ng-ilk?" Caledonia reached the other hand into view with a glass of milk.

"No, thank you. No milk. Cal, I told you I already ate. You better not stuff in much of the crackers and milk, or you won't want any supper. Come on . . . give up on the munching and come in here where I can see you while I talk to you."

Caledonia came, quite meekly, perching on the love seat opposite Angela and swallowing busily to clear her mouth. "Ngu-hing in 'e refri . . ." She swallowed again hugely, and that did the trick. "Nothing in the refrigerator except crackers and milk, I'm afraid. I don't cook at home here much . . . why should I, when Mrs. Schmitt does so well for us? Oh, and some fruit . . . and all those photographs . . ."

"Photographs! In the refrigerator?"

"Color pictures that got all stuck together with damp. I read someplace that if you chill them thoroughly, they'll peel apart. I'm trying to save them."

"Cal, how long have they been in your refrigerator?" Angela said suspiciously.

"About a month," Caledonia admitted sheepishly.

"Don't you think they're about done, now?"

"Well, they won't come apart yet. I think I better leave them . . . Anyhow . . . I'm here now . . . so go on with your story."

"Wait . . . what happened to all the cake and corn curls left over from that plateful you served Lieutenant Martinez and me? Surely—"

"I ate them!" Caledonia confessed. "Well, I was a bit hungry the other evening, and . . . Never mind! Just tell me—did you learn anything important at lunch?"

"Not a thing," Angela admitted sadly.

"Ha! Did you talk all the time so she couldn't get a word in?"

"I did not!" Angela was slightly miffed. "Well, that is, I had to talk a little just to get things going, of course. But she talked very freely. I learned all about her education. She studied to be a teacher, but had to drop out of school because her mother was ill. So she got a job as a secretary and she did very well. Then after a few years her mother died, and Miss Stoner thought, why should she stick it out in those awful winters in the Midwest? So she moved to California. First she worked for an electronics firm, and later . . ."

"You really got the whole life history, didn't you? Okay, I retract my suggestion that you talked all the way through lunch! Apparently, you did listen more than you talked. But did you hear anything worthwhile? Did she tell you all about her present boss, for instance?"

"No," Angela said regretfully. "She seems to be a very loyal employee. But I got the impression, just an impression because she never actually said . . . Cal, I think she's worried about him. Or about the business and her job, or both. She was just a little overeager to please me . . . a bit too glad I was coming aboard as a client, a bit too delighted to leave her desk and have lunch just to keep me company . . . I tell you, it made me wonder if they maybe don't have a lot of other business?"

Caledonia snorted. "Angela, you do have the most incredible nose!"

"Nose?"

"Nose for smelling out a problem that somebody only hints at. Because that's kind of what we thought from what we found in the files! They don't seem to have many clients, at least as far as we can tell."

"Okay, but I don't see how that connects with the reason we went there in the first place. The question is, does there seem to be anything phony about Wallace Clayton's accounting for Edna?"

"Don't be so hopeful. Of course, Tom Brighton may be able to tell us more when he goes over the paper files. But from what he gathered from a quick look at the books, the whole thing was perfectly open and aboveboard. Clayton took good care of his sister-in-law and her money."

"Oh, dear. I was hoping . . ."

"You were hoping, my dear Angela, that he was a big-time embezzler and we'd uncover the evidence just by glancing through a few casual papers he'd strewn across his desk. Girl, if he were a big-time crook, you'd surely never find a record of it lying around on his desk in an unlocked office."

"Unlocked?"

"Yes, the inner office had no lock at all. If that isn't the mark of a clear conscience . . ."

"Oh, that reminds me! Wasn't I clever to jam open the lock on the outer door?" Angela seldom asked for applause quite so directly. But since she couldn't have the joy of un-covering an evildoer, she wanted recognition as a plotter.

"Frightfully clever, dear girl. You're a natural-born bur-glar! Well," Caledonia sighed, "I suppose we should report to Martinez that we've come up with nothing . . ."

"Not yet. I mean, don't report yet. We haven't nearly fin-ished looking around here. We need to talk to poor Edna again—she may be calmer, now. We might actually learn something. And there are other people the man got ac-quainted with, after all . . ."

"That's right!" Caledonia smote her head with a broad palm! "I forgot! Dr. Grainger and his wife! Didn't you say . . ."

". . . that Edna told me they'd got to be quite friendly! Well—what are we waiting for?" And Angela was on her feet and heading toward the door. "They only live down there . . ." She waved her hand out toward the garden and to her left . . .

"Wait-wait-wait . . . What are we going to say?"

"Why, we're going to tell them we want to know about . . . Oh. I see what you mean."

"We have no real reason to ask about Lightfoot . . . not without letting on we're gathering information for Lieuten-ant Martinez. And I don't think we should do that. I mean, people will talk easier to us if it's just us, you know . . . If they think we're passing the information on to the police, they won't talk at all. Maybe."

Angela nodded. "You're right, of course. Well, maybe we could just ask for information on our own! Just because we want to satisfy our curiosity," she said blithely, and started out the door. "If I can't think of any better reason, I'll just tell the truth! Well, are you with me?"

"All right, all right—hold it—I'm coming . . ." and Caledonia lumbered out into the late afternoon sunshine, hard on Angela's heels.

Mrs. Grainger answered their knock almost at once, as though she had expected company. In fact, that was what popped out of Angela's mouth . . . "Oh, dear, you weren't expecting someone? Someone else, I mean?"

For the hundredth time since the Graingers had come to Camden, Angela noted mentally "Gray Lady" when she looked at Mrs. Grainger. "Even her height is gray," Angela said later to Caledonia. And then she explained, "I mean, the woman is so incredibly average! Gray hair, no makeup, gray plastic frames on her glasses—she even wore a gray dress and shoes. Pleasant face—no special features like, say, a big nose—not fat, not thin, not tall, not short . . . She's just . . . like I said, gray! All over!"

Now, the pleasantly smiling Mrs. Grainger answered, "No, goodness, I wasn't expecting a soul. I just saw you coming down the walk, and I . . . Please come in. You two don't often come calling, I hear—I'm flattered."

Angela said hastily, "Oh, this isn't really a call." To the present generation "paying a call" has mainly business connotations, if any, but to a woman of Angela's age, it meant something more formal. "Making a call" meant planning in advance—not exactly the impression she'd hoped to create. She had hoped to seem more spontaneous.

"Oh?" Mrs. Grainger said. "You're not coming to call?"

Angela felt trapped. The conversation had got beyond her control already, and she'd only just arrived. "Well, of course it is a call, in one sense. I mean, I suppose I should have called on you formally long before now to make you welcome. Because you've been here several weeks now . . ."

"Six months," Thelma Grainger corrected, and sounded amused.

"Well, goodness! Has it really been so long!" Angela

was only slightly fussed. "Well, then, this call is long over-due. You're right about that."

Actually, Angela never bothered to make the kind of duty call other residents made—to welcome newcomers and ask them a few questions, invite them to join various activities, and perhaps to bring a little bunch of flowers or a bright potholder so they knew they were accepted as "part of the family" now. Angela had always scorned such niceties, saying she'd wait till she knew whether or not she was going to be able even to tolerate the newcomers. Nor did she enjoy merely casual social encounters. So she left the welcoming visits to other people.

But it was hard to explain that politely when you were put on the spot. Angela bit her lip and wrestled with some tart remark about the empty courtesy of such duty calls . . . and finally decided it wasn't worth the effort.

Caledonia didn't help Angela's sense of guilt by saying rather smugly, "Well, I called on you. The second week you were here."

"Yes, I remember," Mrs. Grainger said. "Well, it really doesn't matter—it's nice to see you both now, whatever the reason. Do come in, the two of you . . ." and she directed them into her tiny living room.

"Won't you sit down and join me? I was just about to have a cup of tea," Mrs. Grainger said. "Oh, Fred . . . look who's here to visit," she added hastily. "It's Mrs. Benbow and Mrs. Wingate, dear. You remember . . ."

Dr. Frederick Grainger was coming from the bedroom area and looked up abruptly at his wife's comment. "Oh! Oh, I'm so sorry. Yes, of course, I remember—I do. Or rather, I think I do. I—But I don't want to interrupt . . ." He was lean and tall—or rather, he had been tall, for he was slightly stooped, a man with a deeply lined face and large, bony, capable-looking hands. His thin, straight hair lay close to his scalp, his rimless glasses slid slightly forward on his nose so that he looked faintly anxious.

"We weren't doing or saying anything private, Dr.

Grainger," Caledonia assured him. "In fact we were hoping you'd be in so we could have a nice chat with both of you!"

"Oh, no. I'm not very good at that sort of thing," Grainger said, backing a step or two toward the bedroom. His eyes sought out his wife's. "Thelma'll tell you . . . I leave the small talk to her, don't I, Thell?"

"Indeed he does. He says my tongue wags at both ends, don't you, darling?"

They smiled at each other and Frederick Grainger took that as his cue to move to the outside door. "Say, I just think I'll go for a stroll in the garden . . . maybe look at the ocean. I'll be right back . . ."

"Oh, Dr. Grainger," Angela spoke up. "Please don't go. We really do want to see you, too . . ."

He shook his head a little vaguely. "Oh, I'm not really good at all that social stuff," he said again. "You and Thell do the talking. 'Bye . . ." and he was out the door before anyone could protest again.

Thelma Grainger smiled apologetically. "I suppose it's because he was always involved with children, but Fred doesn't handle casual conversation with strangers very well. At least, not with strange adults. He's fine with children. He just never got used to talking easily with adults. But do let me pour you some tea . . ." She busied her hands with the cups and silverware and with pouring coral beige tea from a lovely silver luster pot.

"Tea?" Mrs. Grainger passed along a cup so brimming full it required all of Caledonia's concentration to avoid spilling it into its saucer. "That's to go along to Mrs. Benbow . . ."

"Angela. Just call me Angela," she said, because it was obviously expected of her.

Mrs. Grainger smiled and nodded and busied herself preparing a second cup.

"And I'm Caledonia to everyone here," Caledonia added carefully, her customary animation somewhat damped down lest she set up a tannic tidal wave in the delicate porcelain and slosh tea over the rim.

Mrs. Grainger nodded again and offered the sugar. "Unless you're dieting?"

"Perpetually," Caledonia said with real regret. "But Angela takes sugar."

"Not with this tea," Angela protested, with a little nod to her hostess, who seemed pleased. Caledonia shrugged, puzzled by the exchange and waited for her own cup.

At last the ritual was completed, and the first few sips emptied the cups to a line of safety, so that spilling became less likely. Everyone seemed to relax a bit. There was a moment of silence as Angela and Caledonia racked their brains for something to say. Then Angela caught sight of a painting over the Graingers' bookcase. "Oh," Angela said, delighted. She had found an opening. "It's an Edna Ferrier."

"Yes, isn't it lovely?" Thelma Grainger turned her head sideways to catch a glimpse of the picture. "She was just working on it—had only started it, when I first saw it. But there was something about it . . ."

The subject was a squat, distorted tree, preening itself in the Pacific sunshine of Edna's painting, alone and ancient, and rather as though it were aware of its craggy loveliness, perched on a rocky outcropping and backed by an aquamarine ocean.

"You know, I think I know that tree!" Angela said, surprised. "It's . . . It's . . ."

"It's every artist's favorite subject," Caledonia said. "The famous cypress on Seventeen Mile Drive up at Monterey."

"Oh, of course!" Angela nodded with satisfaction, smiling not only because she had recognized the subject, but also because she had her conversational wedge to start her investigation.

"Edna really is a marvelous artist, isn't she?" Angela began with a small wave toward the painting. "You're a friend of hers, Mrs. Grainger, so perhaps you can tell me . . . I'd thought that I'd like to have one of her paintings myself, but she's had this personal tragedy and I didn't want to disturb her by asking her about something so trivial. Or rather . . . not trivial, but at least something that could afford to wait."

Caledonia was looking fixedly at her saucer, as though counting the lines in the pattern. Angela might keep a straight face through the recitation of one of her inventions, but Caledonia had a difficult time.

"Of course," Angela was going on cheerfully, "we don't know Edna as well as you do, so I simply can't guess how long she's going to remain prostrate with grief. I mean, do you have any idea how she's doing? How long she'll be incommunicado in her room?" Angela hoped that Edna had not mentioned that Angela had already visited her once. And that seemed to be exactly the case. At any rate, Thelma Grainger did not seem to suspect that Angela had an ulterior motive in her inquiry.

"I really can't say. Mourning is such an individual matter," Mrs. Grainger said. "I'm sure it will be a while at least. Such a shock," and she subsided into silence. Angela waited, but Mrs. Grainger didn't seem disposed to discuss Edna and the accident. At least not without help. So Angela tried again.

"Well, what was their relationship? Edna and Lightfoot, I mean. We've heard they were planning to be married!"

Thelma Grainger's mouth opened slightly and she seemed genuinely distressed. "Oh, dear, I hope not! Why, that would make it even worse . . ."

Caledonia felt safe to join the conversation, now that it had turned away from Angela's bright-colored fibbing. "Oh, hadn't you heard the rumors?" she asked.

"I knew they were friendly, of course," Thelma Grainger said.

"Well, of course. I understand you and your husband entertained them—even went with them on a trip to the zoo or something? I seem to remember something of the sort . . ." Angela was suitably vague as though she had not got the story of the trip from Edna herself.

"Yes, yes . . ." Thelma bit her lip. "But that was before Fred . . . Well, anyway, that was a little while back. We certainly haven't seen anything of him recently. Of that Lightfoot man, I mean."

"But he was here at Camden almost every day," Angela protested, apparently oblivious to her breach of good manners in arguing the point. "Surely you saw him when he came to call on Edna?"

"If he was here recently, I'm sure I wasn't aware of it," Thelma said reluctantly. "We—Fred and I—were not really taken with the man, you see. The occasions you refer to were after we'd just met him."

"But Edna thinks that you liked him!" Angela bit her tongue. She certainly hadn't meant to reveal that she'd already talked with Edna. But Thelma didn't seem to notice the discrepancy. Instead, Mrs. Grainger rose from her chair and took up the teapot.

"I'm fond of Edna," she protested, "but I don't really care what she says! The truth is we didn't know the man at all well."

"Oh!" Angela tried to think of a way to object without calling Mrs. Grainger a liar. "But didn't your husband know him rather well? Have him over as a guest and perhaps play golf . . ."

"No! Neither of us did! Believe me! We truly weren't together very much at all. And Fred scarcely knew the man! Honestly! As for having him as a guest, why that would have been out of the question with a relative stranger, wouldn't it? Now, I'll just get some hot water from the kitchen." She turned on her heel and moved rather rapidly out of the room.

Caledonia looked at Angela and made a face that said, "Well! What was that all about?" and Angela raised her shoulders and her eyebrows proportionally to respond, in silence, "Who knows? I certainly don't . . ." But neither

woman uttered a sound. The apartment was far too small—
even a whisper would have carried to the kitchen. Thelma
Grainger might not have been able to pick up the words,
but she'd certainly have realized they were whispering, and
all three women came from a time when it was bad manners to whisper and thus exclude someone, or arouse the
suspicion you were talking about the excluded party.

So they sat in silence; Caledonia picked at a chocolate
cookie, Angela nibbled a cheese-snap. From the kitchen
there came the sound of kettle bottom against stove top,
kettle spout against china pot, kettle bottom against stove
top, china lid against china pot . . . and after a brief pause,
Thelma Grainger appeared again carrying the pot, from the
spout of which a faint thread of steam was rising.

"It won't be quite as fresh this time," she said. "I like to
warm the pot first, put in fresh tea leaves and boiling water
fresh each time—but I seem to be short of this Lapsang
souchong . . . and I dearly love this flavor."

Caledonia, whose palate was not attuned to fine differ-
ences in tea had not caught anything unusual. Now she noticed a distinctly smoky scent as the fresh cup was poured.
"Oh. Oh! I see . . . this is a little different. I'm afraid that
I'm not the world's most discriminating tea drinker. Orange
pekoe from Tommy Lipton is usually good enough for me.
But this is . . . kind of special."

"Very special," Angela said, with a dreamy smile on her
face, "I tasted it first in the fifties when Douglas and I were
stationed in London at the embassy. It was a cold, damp
October evening, and an English couple we'd met invited
us in for tea. We drank Lapsang souchong in front of a fire
. . . and for me the taste of this tea and the smell of wood
smoke always go together." She closed her eyes.

Thelma Grainger smiled. "Yes, it takes me back to New
England, where Fred and I lived most of our married life.
He was in practice there, till he retired. And this flavor
means autumn to me, too—a nip in the air, colored leaves,

a fire in the fireplace . . . That's why I brought out the tea. It's autumn, after all."

"I wonder why Californians call this 'autumn'!" Angela said. "This isn't my idea of how September should look!" All three women turned their heads to gaze out of the view window to sunny sea and the garden, lush and warm and decked with flowers.

"All right," Caledonia said briskly. "Let's be practical. Who'd change Southern California for forty below zero, shovel a path to the garage, car won't start, wear your over-shoes and mittens, scarf-over-the-nose bloody winters, even in exchange for a lovely autumn?"

Angela sighed again. "Not at my time of life, I know. But all the same, I miss having a change of seasons."

For a moment the three women sat in silence, gazing out across the flower-strewn gardens, sipping their tea and recalling autumns when they were young enough to brave the winter cold that followed.

"Well." Caledonia was the first to shake herself into the present. "Look, this is all very pleasant, and all, but we have to dress for dinner almost immediately. It's . . . what time is it, Angela?"

Angela, who had also risen, checked her wrist. "Just after four."

"There. Time indeed. It's been pleasant, Mrs. Grainger—uh, Thelma—and we certainly thank you. I haven't tasted this tea before and I think it's very nice. What was the name again?"

"Lapsang souchong."

"I'll remind you," Angela said. "In fact, I think I have a small tin myself, hidden away back at my apartment . . . something I saved to cheer up a gloomy day. Well, Mrs.—uh—Thelma. Thank you so much for a lovely visit." And then, with the impulse of some half-forgotten remnant of her childhood training, she added the words that mark the end of every Southerner's visit, "Let's do this again real soon, now."

Caledonia grinned. "Pay our respects to your husband, won't you?" she said, rolling majestically out the door onto the porch and thence into the garden. "We're sorry to have missed him. Perhaps he'll be in next time? Or you two could come to see me ... my cottage is just over ..."

Mrs. Grainger, standing at the screen door to watch them on their way, like a good hostess, stiffened visibly. "Oh, I don't think so," she said hastily. "I warned you, he's not relaxed with strangers and he might not ... of course, we'll see," she added rather more brightly. "He might surprise me. Sometimes he feels better than other days ... Well, we'll just have to wait and see. Thank you again for coming." And she waved brightly at them as they moved off, away from her front door. "Goodbye, goodbye ..."

"I feel as though she's giving me the bum's rush!" Angela muttered. Caledonia, stumping straight ahead, did not seem to have heard.

Chapter 8

"WELL, DIDN'T you think she was determined to keep us away from him? I felt as though she'd decided that the moon would turn blue before she got us all together, if she could stand in the way to keep it from happening!"

"You've mixed your metaphors, Angela. Or whatever!" Caledonia said. "Pass the rolls, please. And take one yourself as they go by?"

"No, thank you. I don't think I'll have any. I had a cookie at the Graingers'. I don't see how you can eat anything more yourself, Cal. You had milk and crackers at two, tea between three and three-thirty or so, and now it's only five, and you're already . . . You're changing the subject. What is she protecting him from?"

"Who?"

"Thelma Grainger. Why is she protecting her husband? She practically hustled him out the door, to begin with . . ."

"Oh, Angela, you're exaggerating. It was his idea to go for a walk. I think she was telling the truth when she said he was shy with strangers. He surely looked startled to see us. He was pleasant enough, and she seemed the same. So I don't think . . ."

"But how about when we asked about Lightfoot? And she got so funny and nervous. How about that? Then she started covering for her husband. Oh, here, Cal . . ." Caledonia had swept her sleeve back so it wouldn't drag in the salad and stretched her arm toward the butter plate. Angela moved the butter dish across the table, closer to her huge friend. "What about the way she covered up for the good doctor? How about that?"

"Angela, I still say you're imagining things. I admit she got terribly flustered when we said that she and her Fred had spent time with—had actually entertained Alexander Lightfoot. She went to the kitchen so fast she looked like she'd left something on the stove! How about another roll?"

"I said I didn't want any," Angela snapped.

"Not for you. For me! I meant 'please pass the rolls,' not 'will you have a roll'! There's no need to get cross," Caledonia went on rather smugly, "just because you've chosen to deny yourself and I haven't."

"Well, here." Angela slid the little covered basket closer to Caledonia's side of the table. "Go ahead. Stuff your face. See if I care."

Caledonia grinned. "Thanks. Anyhow, back to the Graingers . . . I admit I thought that was odd. I mean, that she denied they had entertained Lightfoot, when you knew for a fact they had. Isn't that what you told me?"

"Yes. Edna told me so! That's why I didn't believe Thelma."

"What exactly did Edna tell you?"

The women turned to see Lieutenant Martinez standing beside their table.

"Oh, Lieutenant! How marvelous. Do bring up a chair and join us," Caledonia beamed.

"Chita! Oh, Chita," Angela trilled. "Bring something for the lieutenant to eat!"

"Nothing to eat, thank you," Martinez said quickly, pulling a chair for himself from an unoccupied table. To sit squarely at the third side of their small table for two would have put his chair half blocking an aisle, since there wasn't room for him to tuck his legs underneath. So instead he angled the chair slightly and ended up sitting across a corner from and close to Angela, and half-turned facing Caledonia.

"I grabbed a bite at a fast-food place between stops

earlier this . . ." He shot a cuff and glanced at his watch. "Oh, Lord. That was four hours ago! I certainly don't keep good track of my mealtimes!"

"Here, Lieutenant," Conchita Cassidy said, swinging by to slide silverware down and to center a small green salad directly in front of him. "How're you doing? We don't see much of you around here these days."

"Be grateful, Chita-mia, be grateful. When I arrive, it usually means there's been trouble. Serious trouble. Though I could stand to see friends more often. You look well . . ."

She smiled slightly as she poured a glass of ice water and added that to his setting, returning the pitcher to the tray she balanced so deftly while she talked. "I feel marvelous. I always do! But it's been more than a week since . . . Lieutenant, is Swan-sohn in the car? Did he drive you over?"

Lieutenant Martinez nodded. "I left him parking in front, Chita. I told him he could come in and see you."

"I'm not sure he'll want to, Lieutenant. We—we had words about a week ago. Didn't he tell you?"

Angela and Caledonia both straightened visibly and inclined their heads in her direction. Here was news indeed! The lieutenant looked taken aback. "Chita, I don't push my men about personal business. Swanson didn't tell me a thing, and I didn't ask. Of course, I'm sorry to hear you've quarreled. I hope it's nothing serious."

Just then the dining room door opened and Officer "Shorty" Swanson entered a few steps, caught sight of his lieutenant and Chita in conversation, hesitated in midstep, half-turned as though to leave, and then at last thought better of it and came toward the table. Young Charles Swanson was, like so many men nicknamed "Shorty," tall and thin. His skinny Adam's apple and gawky gait made him seem extremely boyish, as did his habitual expression of delight and wonder with the world around him. He did not look quite so young and vulnerable at the moment, however, for his brows were drawn down into a formidable scowl as he advanced across the room.

"I had to park across the street. Some delivery van's stopped right in front of the main door, and all the other parking places are full, Lieutenant. Hello, Mrs. Benbow, Mrs. Wingate . . ." He paused a moment, and then, looking straight down at his feet muttered, "Hi, Chee."

Not daunted in the slightest, Chita moved close to him so that, short as she was, she stood directly below his downturned face. "You going to talk to me today or what, Swansohn?"

"I'm talking. I said hello, didn't I?" he muttered, still looking down.

Chita edged closer and bent her knees so that she put her face directly under his. To do this she had to swing her heavy tray to one side, and it barely missed Caledonia's head, but Caledonia was too fascinated with the progress of the scene to do more than duck and keep watching.

"Look at me, Swan-sohn. Don't look at the floor. Are you gonna stay mad all month? What about our date for Friday? Are you gonna come by and pick me up the way you said or is that off? You got to talk to me some time. You might as well talk now."

"Chee!" The young policeman's golden tan was gradually turning the color of tomato soup and he hissed in a half-whisper as he talked. "Chee, this isn't the time to talk about personal things."

"No?" she challenged. "Then when is? You walked out mad, you wouldn't answer my telephone call, you didn't come by all week . . . when do I get to talk to you about personal things?"

"Lieutenant," Shorty said desperately, "will you excuse me a moment? I'll be right back."

He grabbed Chita's free hand and headed, full tilt, for the door that led through a butler's pantry area to the big kitchen behind. Chita, encumbered by the big silvery metal tray, was literally towed along. But as Shorty hit the swinging door with the heel of his hand and disappeared through it, she managed to turn her head and flash a broad grin, with a delighted wink, at the group they'd just left.

"Lieutenant, do you mean to say you have no idea what that's all about?" Angela asked.

"No idea at all. Oh, I knew they'd quarreled. Or rather, I guessed it, because for the first time since they met last year, Shorty hasn't been asking me if he could come along when I had to come anywhere near here. Not only that— something even affected his appetite. And that would have to be something as serious as a quarrel with Chita."

"His appetite!" Caledonia was incredulous. "Why, he's the only living human I know who can eat more than I can!"

"Ah," the lieutenant said with mock sadness, "you should see him now! Only one super-deluxe burger with just a regular order of fries, not the giant. One medium soft drink and the midsized hot fudge sundae for dessert. Not like the old days. He's wasting away!"

"Are you sure you can't even guess what's wrong between them, Lieutenant?" Angela coaxed, tilting her head to one side in that half-flirtatious, half-absentminded imitation of the Southern belle talking with her beau at the garden party. "We're really concerned. Not that we'd interfere, of course. We're just two harmless little old ladies who worry about their friends."

"Hah!" Martinez's laugh was both rueful and sarcastic. "The reason I won't speculate about their quarrel is because you're anything but harmless. I've never seen two intelligent adults who could make more out of a scrap of information than the pair of you seem to. And not tentatively or hedged with 'If-then's' either. You take a single fact and run it to its logical extension and beyond—and you're absolutely sure. But all that aside, I'm always suspicious when you emphasize your innocence. Your pure motives. That's generally a smoke screen."

"It is?" Angela was blank.

"Absolutely. You only do that when you have been up to something you think I wouldn't approve."

"Do what?" Angela said archly. Caledonia just grinned.

"You ask me about some unrelated question to get me off the dangerous subject. I think you'd better tell me what you've been doing since I asked you to look over the residents for me. I came here for a report, and I shouldn't let you turn me aside so easily!"

"Lieutenant," Caledonia said, lowering her customary rumble to a whisper, "I'm not sure you want to talk about this here in the dining room. We're perfectly delighted to oblige you with a full rundown, but elderly pitchers have big ears."

"What?"

"Just a variant on 'Little pitchers have big ears.' "

"And what does it mean?" Martinez asked.

"It's just a saying. Figuratively, it means that kids hear more than you think they do—or than you want them to. Literally—well, I haven't the faintest idea! Why one would say a pitcher had ears, or call a child a pitcher . . . All I know is that you're diverting me from the point. Everybody in this place is agog to know what you're doing here."

Martinez had been at Camden many times, and he was used to the staring eyes, but it still amused him that so little escaped the residents. Now he looked around the dining room in what he meant to be a casual glance and encountered one pair of eyes after another, fixed unwaveringly upon him. The expressions ranged from Mary Moffet's transparently eager curiosity to Grogan's menacing though unfocused glower.

"You're probably right, Mrs. Wingate," he conceded. "Perhaps you'll allow me to join you at your cottage after you finish your meal?" He made a gesture as though to rise from the table.

"Sit down, Lieutenant. By all means join us now for the meal, and come to the cottage afterward! As my guest, of course," Caledonia added.

"Our guest," Angela corrected sweetly.

When Martinez had been at Camden on previous occasions in the course of a murder investigation, Torgeson had made it a point to invite the officers to eat in the dining room with the guests, hoping to speed the investigation along by saving the policemen time, and simultaneously to influence them to be sympathetic to Camden's residents—to handle things gently and discreetly. Torgeson wanted the murder solved quietly, of course, and quickly—but *quickly*—before Camden lost its reputation for secure living for the elderly.

Of course, Torgeson's rigid sense of what constituted good business would not have moved him to extend the same invitation for free meals now, even though the death of Lightfoot was vaguely connected to one of his residents. But that didn't stop Angela and Caledonia from inviting a guest. And Martinez accepted with pleasure. The main course was one of Mrs. Schmitt's special treats—veal in a velvety brown mushroom sauce with little new peas and baby carrots, all seasoned with bay leaves and cloves to a spiciness near sweetness. There was a small helping of wild rice, homemade rolls, and to the lieutenant's delight, a slice of Mrs. Schmitt's incomparable lemon pie. He hardly spoke at all as he ate, but once or twice he sighed audibly and marveled that he, who cared so little about food ordinarily, should be so enslaved by the magic of a heavy-bodied Swiss woman with a red face and flat feet!

He noticed but did not mention, nor did the two ladies, that their meal was served by Beverly, one of the longtime waitresses who ordinarily tended another part of the dining room. Chita had not appeared again, nor had Swanson. But the fact did not enter their conversation. They did not even discuss the death of Alex Lightfoot. Mindful of the eager ears around them, all three talked companionably of only trivial things: the weather, outrageous teen fashions, the new television season, who would take the baseball pennants, and how the Chargers were doing this year (the latter two topics much to Angela's annoyance, since she was not a sports fan).

At last the meal was over and Lieutenant Martinez accompanied the ladies down the garden path to the first cottage, still talking casually of the garden and the incredible scent of evening flowers like the nicotiana, and how the sunset looked at sea—until they were safe within Caledonia's place with the doors firmly shut against eavesdroppers.

"I'll offer you a liqueur, Lieutenant . . ."

"No, thank you, Mrs. Wingate. I have work yet to do tonight, so technically speaking, I'm on duty. Not on duty enough to turn down one of Mrs. Schmitt's meals, but enough to avoid drinking."

"Even a teeny thimbleful?" Angela coaxed.

"Even so," he smiled. "Sorry. Now . . . to business . . ."

Angela had settled herself in the rose velvet chair, Caledonia on a love seat nearby, which she filled exactly the way Angela filled the little chair. Martinez pulled up a small wing chair to sit equidistant from the two ladies, and he began.

"You were going to report everything Mrs. Ferrier told you," he began, taking the offensive. "But it's been two days . . ."

"We didn't have anything to say," Angela protested. "I mean, I went there to see Edna, but she hardly talked at all. She just told me about how happy she'd been with their engagement and how devastated she was by her fiancé's death. She told me they'd both been married before, though neither of them much liked to talk about the previous marriage. Her husband drowned in a storm . . . did you know that?"

Martinez shook his head but did not interrupt.

"She told me Lightfoot was never ill and didn't seem suicidal. She thinks he was killed, because she said she can't imagine him falling accidentally—he was apparently very hale for his age, which incidentally was younger than she is. And he wasn't depressed about anything. On the contrary, he seemed to be happy about the coming marriage, too."

Martinez smiled. "And you say you had nothing to report! That's all very important background detail—and not something I could have gathered by myself." He waited a moment. "Well? Was there anything else? If she thinks he must have been pushed in front of that train, who does she think did it?"

Caledonia snorted. "Angela tells me that Edna can't imagine who would do it, because according to Edna, the only thing he should have died of was falling off his pedestal!"

"That's right. She said he was the perfect man—charming, witty, handsome, and loving—and she says everybody else thought so, too. She says he was popular with people he met around here . . . the Graingers, for instance . . . She told us about a trip they all took together to San Diego to the zoo . . ."

"That must have been what you were talking about when I came up," Martinez said. "There were a lot of 'she said's' being tossed across the table, as I recall. You were saying that 'she' had denied something-or-other . . ."

"Denied entertaining Lightfoot," Caledonia filled in the gap. "We went to call on the Graingers today to confirm the information we got from Edna and maybe to fill in a little more detail about Lightfoot, because Edna said they'd hit it off so well. We thought the Graingers would have some valuable impressions of him. But we came away completely bewildered by the whole—"

"Thelma Grainger practically denied they knew Lightfoot at all," Angela blurted out. "Though when we pressed her on it, she admitted they had gone to the zoo together. But she said they hadn't entertained him otherwise. Edna said they had. But Mrs. Grainger says . . ." She shook her head and shrugged. "It's confusing. Or at least, I'm confused about it."

"Interesting," Martinez said. "Well, that's one path for me to follow along, at least a step or two. I'll sniff around a little and see if I pick up the delicate odor of something rotten in Denmark . . . as it were. Is there anything else?"

"Yes," Caledonia said.

"No," Angela said.

Then there was a pause while they looked at each other.

"Well, no, not really," Caledonia said.

"Well, there sort of is," Angela admitted, talking at the same time.

Again there was a pause, a look, another patch of silence . . .

"Well, I'll break the impasse for you," Martinez said. "It's as I said before back in the dining room. You two ladies—you've done something you don't really want me to know about, haven't you? You've got hold of some kind of information. Perhaps you're not really sure it's worth much. You think you should tell me, but you're afraid I'll scold you about it for some reason. Probably about the method you used to acquire your information." He paused and peered at their guilty faces. "Well? Am I getting warm?"

"Burning up," Caledonia conceded.

"Oh, dear," Angela said. "We were hoping to get something valuable to tell you because then you'd forgive us. But we don't know . . ."

"The truth is, we did a little breaking and entering," Caledonia rumbled sheepishly.

"Why," Martinez said to the ceiling, "do I find that I'm not surprised?"

"We wanted to discover what the Unmitigated Wallace had to do with this," Angela said. "You see, I knew that, as an accountant who handled the estate—"

"Hold it!" The lieutenant's hand went up in a traffic policeman's "Stop" gesture. "Hold it! Start at the beginning. Who or what is the Unmitigated Wallace?"

"Wallace Fairleigh Clayton, Junior," Caledonia said. " 'Unmitigated' means, as you know, not softened, shortened, or diminished. Our Wallace has no nickname. Nor, in our opinion, ever could!"

"Mrs. Ferrier's brother-in-law," Angela said.

"He's an accountant," Caledonia added.

"He handles all Edna's business—all her investments," Angela went on. "He's not her husband's brother, you understand. His wife, the late Mrs. Clayton, was Edna Ferrier's sister. Apparently they were all four quite close, when they lived back in Wichita, and the two brothers-in-law arranged that whichever one should die first, the other would assume responsibility for being executor and manager of the estate on the widow's behalf. And we thought . . ."

"Angela thought," Caledonia put in hastily. "I just went along with it."

"All right, *I* thought, if you insist," Angela said arching her eyebrows to show scorn for weasling. "I thought Wallace might be dipping into her funds for his own use. I thought maybe he was afraid his embezzlement would be discovered when Edna married Lightfoot, because then Lightfoot would take over the managing of her funds. And if that were so, then maybe it was Wallace who pushed Lightfoot in front of the train, and . . ."

"What gave you that idea?" Martinez said curiously. "It's the plot of a movie I saw on late night television last week, but other than that . . ."

Angela beamed. "Yes. I saw the same movie, Lieutenant. An old Charlie Chan?"

He nodded, and the corner of his mouth twitched slightly.

"The guardian kills the fiancé, so he can keep control of the girl's fortune? Well, we thought maybe Wallace was like that actor, that H.B. Warner . . . He usually played villains, so I knew it was he before Charlie Chan did. But of course Wallace Clayton doesn't look as menacing as H.B. Warner always did! He's as skinny, but not as tall, and . . ."

"Angela!" Caledonia impatiently cut her little friend off. "Enough!"

"So what did you do about your idea?" Martinez asked,

and put a hand over his mouth, hiding his lips by smoothing his moustache, first one side, then the other. If he was smiling behind his hand, neither of them could see.

"We went to his office and looked at his accounts," Angela said rather stiffly, and closed her mouth into a prim line.

"That's it? You just walked into his office and looked at his books?"

"Well, no, but you two don't seem to want to hear the details of the story. And that's the heart of it . . ." She sniffed daintily. "I could use a glass of that liqueur you offered, Caledonia. The Chambord, I think. . . ."

"Of course." Caledonia flowed off the couch. "Anything to get you out of a snit! Angela, there's embroidery and there's embroidery. You were putting in so many squiggles and little details we couldn't see the main threads of your story. The lieutenant wants to hear the details and if you don't tell him, I will—just so we don't go off into the movies you've seen, while we're talking about it. Sure you won't join us, Lieutenant?" she said, as she poured two tiny glasses of the ruby liqueur.

He shook his head and turned to Angela. "I'm sorry you feel offended, Mrs. Benbow. Perhaps I was too abrupt in expressing my interest—my eagerness to hear about your adventure—and you mistook that for a request to cut to the end. Please forgive me. You must know I'm hanging on every word!"

She beamed at him and accepted the glass of Chambord from Caledonia's large hand with a gracious nod to the lieutenant. A tiny sip, a deep breath, and she began again with great satisfaction. "Well . . ." Five minutes later she had progressed through her initial reconnaissance, her cleverness in decoying Miss Stoner, her taping the door open for Caledonia, and their return to Camden with the envelope containing the copied documents—and she paused for breath and for another sip of her drink. She had carefully left out all mention of Tom Brighton. No need to get him involved any more than he had been, she was thinking.

Martinez shook his head. "You were right to think that I couldn't approve of your methods, not even in a good cause. On the other hand, I have no scruples about profiting from your evil deeds after the fact. What have the papers shown about the accounts? Because," he smiled at the delighted Angela, "that's really not a bad idea at all, you know. It would be a good motive for murder, if Mrs. Ferrier is really well off."

"We think she is, Lieutenant," Angela said eagerly, glowing at his apparent forgiveness and at his interest. "And I'm glad you think it's a good idea, because I told Caledonia at the time we ought . . ."

"Angela!" Caledonia interrupted. "I think the lieutenant wants to know what we found out, not how happy you are that you're not going to be scolded!"

"Well, that's the thing." Angela was a little crestfallen. "Apparently there's really nothing suspicious. At least, nothing that we know about yet. I mean, he seems to be perfectly legitimate."

"The papers we took are just duplicates, by the way," Caledonia interrupted. "The originals are right back in the files because there really is a limit to our crookedness!"

"I'm glad to hear that, Mrs. Wingate. But I'm sorry to hear the raid was for nothing."

"Well, like Angela said, we don't know that for sure. Not till Tom Brighton reports . . . uh-oh."

"Tom Brighton?" Martinez was quick to pick up on Caledonia's slip.

"Oh, dear! I shouldn't have mentioned him. And I was just applauding you," she said mournfully to Angela, "for having had the wit to leave him out of your story entirely! You may not remember him, Lieutenant—"

"Isn't Brighton that nice fellow with lots of white hair that won't seem to lie down flat, and the bad limp in one leg?" Martinez tried to recall.

"That's the fellow. Except the limp is in both legs . . . it's just worse in one than the other, sometimes. He used to be an actuary, so we figured he could look the books over . . ."

"You wanted an accountant, Mrs. Wingate. Not an actuary."

"Sure. But we didn't have one. And any old mathematician in a storm! Half an accountant is better than none! An actuary in the hand is worth . . ."

"All right! So, you involved Mr. Brighton to the extent of giving him stolen information to analyze, and . . ."

"We did worse than that," Caledonia confessed. "We brought him with us when we went to look in Clayton's office. Angela left that out of her story because we didn't want to get him into trouble. But the truth is, we dragooned the poor man into going snooping with us."

"But he wanted to come!" Angela protested. "He was as excited about it as I was!"

Martinez shook his finger at them. "It's not enough that the two of you have become addicted to a life of spying and petty crime—now you have to turn your fellow retirees on to the thrill of evildoing! Shame! Unless . . . Has Mr. Brighton found anything out I should know?"

"Well, that we were about to find out. Shall we phone him now?"

"Why not go directly to his rooms? Anything that has to do with books and figures might need a firsthand examination to be understood. Of course, I'll accompany you," Martinez said smoothly.

"But why? We can just as easily . . ."

"I want to go. If I left it to you, you might or might not share with me what you found!"

"If you don't trust us," Angela said in annoyance, "why don't you go alone, then?"

Martinez smiled. "I want you to be my guides to show me where he lives, I want you to be my guarantee of legitimacy so he'll admit to having the papers and tell me everything he's found. And of course you two are simply dying to hear what he has to say. Confess it now—" Again he shook a finger at them, but they were both smiling apologetically.

"And I have no objection, incidentally, to your hearing what Brighton says. Having come this far, you might as well go that much farther. It can't do any harm. Besides, I know you two—you'd find out for yourselves, if I didn't invite you to come with me and find out firsthand! So ladies, drink up and come along."

Chapter 9

"I'M AFRAID you're going to be disappointed, ladies." Tom Brighton ran a hand from back to front through his white mane so that it stood up a little like the crest on an angry cockatoo. "I've looked over everything, and unless there's something I missed . . ."

"He really is innocent, then? He isn't embezzling Edna's funds?" Angela seemed genuinely distressed. "Oh, dear! I really thought that when you looked closer you'd find something! I was so sure!"

"You're always sure! About every theory you come up with. At least for a few minutes—till somebody points out the holes in it," Caledonia said. "Tom, don't worry about not finding anything suspicious. We wanted to know if he was honest or a crook, and now we know. We're sure he's honest."

"Well, not entirely sure," Martinez said. "May I?" He stretched his hand out. "If you were to ask me to look these over for you, without telling me how you came by them, Mr. Brighton, I would feel free to have them examined by my accounting expert."

Brighton handed the envelope across cheerfully. "Well, then, by all means . . ."

"Of course I couldn't do that with illegally acquired documents, so . . ." Martinez held up a warning finger, "don't say another thing about them, please."

Brighton looked amused and nodded with understanding,

but Angela was puzzled. "But I told you where he got them . . . he and Cal."

Martinez smiled pleasantly. "Now, now—that's mere heresay. It's secondhand knowledge. No competent attorney would allow it to be entered as evidence without protesting. And if nether Mrs. Wingate nor Mr. Brighton cares to confess personally to breaking and entering . . ."

"Heaven forbid!" Caledonia said hastily. "But suppose someone asks you where you got these papers? Would your superiors really believe that you didn't think they were stolen, mainly because you hadn't heard it firsthand?"

"I doubt it," he said, still smiling. "Of course, they're used to me at headquarters. They know I'd never out-and-out break the rules, but they also realize I allow the rules to stretch and bend from time to time. So they might have their suspicions. But they'd never be sure how I acquired these unless you told them."

Brighton beamed. "Mrs. Wingate and Mrs. Benbow said you were clever. I love a good equivocation! When I was in college, I used to be on the debating team, and hairsplitting is a great technique!"

"It has its limitations," Martinez said. "For instance, even supposing these papers gave me information with which to bring a case, I'd never be able to use what I got as evidence in court. I'd have to find legally admissible evidence elsewhere."

"How could you do that?" Brighton wondered.

"Oh, I might subpoena his records, for instance, and then I'd be in possession of the originals, which I could use in court. But getting a subpoena has its own problems. To do that I'd need some reason to give the judge who issues the papers—something more than just a suspicion to account for my need to dig into private documents. Do you see?"

Angela frowned. "But if you're not going to be able to use what you find out reading these papers, why bother to read them at all?"

"Because knowledge gained by whatever means is valuable. If Clayton is innocent, knowing so will save me time. I'll know better than to chase after what my grandmother used to call 'wild herrings.' "

Caledonia snorted. "Sounds like something you'd say, Angela!"

Angela ignored her, with all the dignity she could muster. "Well, I still am not sure what you hope to find in these papers, Lieutenant. Tom couldn't see anything in them."

"I probably couldn't see a thing either, on my own. But I have experts who might be able to find something you've overlooked, Mr. Brighton. For instance, even if he's playing absolutely square with his sister-in-law, Clayton might be cheating another client. I don't say he is," he hastened, as Angela seemed to brighten up and look hopeful. "But it's possible. Anyhow we'll have a look."

"Now, Lieutenant, that's the thing," Tom Brighton said. "Clayton doesn't seem to have any other clients."

"No other clients! What makes you think that?"

"Because we found no files with any other clients' names in the cabinets," Caledonia boomed. "And there were no other files in his desk drawers . . ."

"His secretary, Miss Stoner," Angela said eagerly, "was really worried about him. She was a little vague, but I got the impression the business wasn't doing well. I said so to Cal, didn't I? Before Cal told me what they'd found as they searched the office. Or rather, what they hadn't found."

"Furthermore," Brighton said, warming to the subject, "he had a personal computer in his inner office—a kind of neat rig, from what I was able to see. But all the programs we found for it were games."

"Games!"

"Yes. Chess; and a computer pinball game; and a disk labeled 'Shooting Gallery' and one labeled 'Guess the Secret Number' or something like that—I really can't remember them all. There was a storage box for disks sitting beside the computer, and all that was in there was these games!"

"Games!" Martinez said it again softly, and it was obvious he was puzzled. "That's all? No accounts? No files? No form letters?"

Brighton shrugged. "Well, I didn't check all the disks because there wasn't time. But that's what the labels said."

Martinez stood up. "Well, you know, I really think it's time—it's past time—that I had a little talk with Wallace Clayton."

"Why? Because he plays chess against a computer?" Angela said, genuinely puzzled.

"No. Because that seems to be all he does. At least, all he does when he's at the office," Martinez responded. "It really sounds as though he has a lot of time to kill every day, doesn't it?"

"Only in the morning," Caledonia said. "He keeps the office open all day, Miss Stoner said, but he only comes down there in the morning."

"Or when he has an appointment," Angela put in.

"I see. So he sits there all morning playing chess—and apparently the only other thing he does is take care of his sister-in-law's business! Now, why do you suppose he bothers to keep that office open at all?" Martinez said.

"Well, maybe he keeps hoping to get other accounts," Caledonia said. "Miss Stoner certainly seemed eager when she thought we were potential new clients."

"Pride?" Tom Brighton said. "Could it be pride? So he could pretend he is successful here in California the way he'd been back home in Kansas City?"

"Wichita," Angela corrected gently. "Assuming, of course, that you call anything a success if it's located in"—her tiny nose wrinkled with distaste—"in Wichita! What I thought was, maybe he's fooling himself more than other people. It seems to me that when it's time to retire, men have trouble letting go of their old lives. Career women seem to retire more gracefully than men do; the men seem to want to cling to the past. Maybe he's trying to feel as though he's still important—still active in a business, if you follow me."

"Well," Martinez said, "whatever the case, I think you

can see why I at least need to have a talk with Mr. Clayton. It's an interesting picture. He's there, apparently busy, but actually doing nothing more than playing a continual chess game."

He moved toward the door, carrying the envelope full of copied documents in his hand. "I think I'll take a leaf out of your book, ladies. I'll take the chance tomorrow to go to Clayton's office on some casual business: a few questions about his sister-in-law, perhaps—something I'd be asking him anyway. And while I'm there, I'm going to 'discover' his game-playing for myself. I'll walk casually over and just glance at his computer, and I'll be so surprised to read the names on those disks in the storage box! Then perhaps I'll end up finding out whether he really has clients or not."

"Other than his sister-in-law," Caledonia corrected.

Martinez smiled acknowledgment. "Even so."

"That sounds like something I'd do," Angela said. "Good for you! But you won't tell him we were looking around there too, will you?"

Martinez paused at the door. "That's the nice part of my little scheme. I can take the blame myself. I won't have to tell him that you've been peeking into his file cabinets! Well, ladies—Mr. Brighton—I thank you all for your help . . ." and he whirled out the door, walking rapidly down the hall.

"He moves as fast as you do, Mrs. Benbow," Brighton said.

"Tom, you really must call us 'Angela' and 'Caledonia' now. I should think that having conspired to spy on an apparently respectable businessman puts us on a first-name basis. Don't you agree?"

He smiled and bowed. "May I offer you ladies a liqueur? This is a small room, but not too small for a small stock of crème de menthe and crème de cacao . . ."

"No, thank you," Caledonia rumbled. "Angela can if she likes. But I am about ready for bed. I don't think you two realize how much walking tires me out. I have to carry such a load. You two are relatively small. But my bulk . . ." She heaved herself upward from the chair she'd taken and rolled toward the door. "I'm really bushed!"

"I'll decline tonight, Tom." Angela smiled sweetly. "I usually go to bed early and rise early myself. Cal's a night owl who sleeps late every morning, but my eyes are about to close . . . Do ask us again, another time."

The women walked the length of the hall together wordlessly. The excuse had been no fabrication—they were dead tired after a full day. It was times like these, when they'd been active all day and after the adrenaline of excitement had been completely absorbed into the system, when the evening had reached or passed their usual bedtime and years of conditioning took over . . . it was times like these that they felt their age. They walked slowly and their shoulders were ever so slightly rounded forward.

" 'Night, Cal. See you tomorrow," Angela said as she peeled off at her own apartment.

" 'Night, Angela."

In the quiet of her apartment, Angela undressed, meticulously hanging up her suit and blouse, depositing her undergarments in a little satin laundry bag, and carefully sudsing out her hosiery, which she spread to dry on the heated towel rack. She had not been exaggerating her fatigue, and as she creamed her face lavishly, and wiped off every vestige of makeup and the day's accumulation of grime, all she was thinking was whether it would feel better to take a quick shower and go straight to bed, or to relax for fifteen minutes or so in a hot tub with blue bath salts to oil her skin and with the gentle warmth of water to ease her stiff muscles.

"There probably isn't enough hot water for a deep tub," she reasoned. "Not after everyone else in the building has had an evening bath. I'd hate to sit in tepid water. There'd be enough for a quick shower, even if it would feel better to tub . . . Shower it is." She discarded the last facial tissue, snapped on her shower cap, and started the water. Mercifully it was piping hot still; the undersized, elderly central reservoir had either reheated after the usual nighttime tubs were over for the evening, or a few other residents had put off customary evening baths till morning. Whatever the reason, she felt a moment of gratitude as the steam rolled upward in the room, obscuring the ceiling above her.

The water felt wonderful. It was odd though, she told herself, how it had a kind of metallic sound—it pinged against the tub in a way that would make you think you were hearing bells, if you didn't know better! She scrubbed a little more and listened to the faint, bell-like sound . . . and then she realized, it *was* a bell. It was the bell of her phone, out in the bedroom.

She stumbled from the tub, turning off the taps. She nearly slipped on the tiled floor and caught herself by clinging to the towel rack on one side, the sink on the other. As she scurried past, she grabbed the huge white terry cloth robe that hung from a hook behind the bathroom door. It enveloped her and toweled her off at the same time, and it dragged on the floor around her feet, making her stumble again as she flung the door open and lurched out of the bathroom toward the phone.

"Hello . . . hello . . .?"

"Mrs. Benbow? Sorry to disturb you. Were you asleep?"

"No. No, I was in the shower," she snapped. Her ear was covered by her shower cap and with her bad hearing, the telephone voice was muffled. She impatiently pulled the cap off and tossed it back toward the bathroom. "Who is this, anyway?"

"It's Lieutenant Martinez."

"Oh! Oh, Lieutenant!" Her voice changed to an agreeable purr.

"Well, I'm terribly sorry to interrupt your shower, Mrs. Benbow. But I'm going to have to ask you to get dressed again and come downtown."

"Sorry I was so—but, I'm not sure . . . Downtown? Are you calling from San Diego?"

"No-no-no ... In Camden. Look, I'll send Shorty to fetch you and Mrs. Wingate and Mr. Brighton. I just wanted to warn you so you'd have time to pull yourself together."

"Lieutenant, I've told the others ... I'm dreadfully tired. It's past my ordinary bedtime, and I did more than I usually do today. I ache between my shoulder blades, and my eyelids are heavy ... Can't this wait till tomorrow?"

"Well, I suppose it could. But you were the last to see the deceased alive—that we know of. And I felt that the sooner ..."

"The deceased?"

"Yes. Miss Stoner has been killed."

"Ding-dong, the witch is dead!" Angela gasped, without thinking.

"What?"

"Oh, you know—the song the Munchkins sang. Because she looked so much like Margaret Hamilton, we thought, that ... I'm sorry. It's really awful! I shouldn't ... how did it happen?"

"We think she was hit by something. And before you suggest it, not by a house! By a more traditional blunt instrument. Here at Clayton's office. Now, you saw her alive at ... what time was your lunch over with?"

"Well, let me think. Cal and I were back here at home at almost two o'clock. We had to wait fifteen minutes for the van to come and pick us up ... I'd say Miss Stoner and I parted at the street-level office door sometime between one-thirty and one-forty-five. Closer to the latter."

"Doc here says she died sometime between three-thirty and five-thirty ... approximately. He's bound to get a more accurate idea from the autopsy. Especially if you can pinpoint the time you were served your lunch ..."

"Oh, dear!"

"Sorry, but it's necessary. Because except for Miss Stoner—and whoever it was who murdered her, of course—you three may have been the most recent visitors to the office. You will come?"

Angela's head was up and her eyes were shining. As she had been talking, she had pulled the phone cord to its limited length so she could rummage with her free hand through a dresser drawer, pulling out a slip and garter belt . . . a pair of stockings . . .

"Oh, yes. Of course. It won't take me fifteen minutes!"

"Good. Oh, by the way, wear your raincoat. Surprisingly enough, we've had a light shower this evening and it might surprise us again."

"All right. But, Lieutenant . . . wait . . ."

"Yes?"

"Need Mr. Brighton come along? Those steps are very steep and you've seen how much it hurts him to walk. He'd say yes, if you insisted, but I'm sure it would be only because he felt it was his duty. He . . . Lieutenant, did you laugh?"

"Sorry. I realize it's not funny. But I phoned Brighton first of the three of you, and I think you'll find he's in the lobby already waiting for Shorty to bring the car around! The steps may hurt him . . . but not as much as being left out of what he referred to as 'the fun.' "

Martinez was right. Brighton was already in the lobby, seated by the front door, peering eagerly out toward the dark street when Angela arrived, struggling into her raincoat as she came. He hauled himself to his feet. "You look, if I may say so, like a college girl in that skirt and sweater and those little flat-heeled moccasins."

"Thank you, Tom. You know, you're going to have to learn not to jump up that way when a lady enters. You have a fine excuse to stay seated."

"I try, but my legs are too well trained in manners." Brighton beamed at her. "Ah, Mrs. Wingate!"

"Caledonia," she corrected him. "I thought we settled that it was first names from now on." She had pulled a man's navy blue trench coat—probably her late husband's uniform raincoat—over her usual flowing caftan, out of deference to the weather.

"Isn't this—" Brighton sought for a word. "It's ... well, of course it's terrible. And very sad. But it's also ..."

"Exciting?" Caledonia supplied, amused. "Exhilarating?"

"Fascinating?" Angela said. "Absorbing? Novel?"

"All of that," he agreed. "I never in my life felt so ... Oh, here's the car." Headlights swept the glass door as Shorty turned into the circular driveway in front of the entrance. "Ladies?"

Settling himself into the car and getting his legs under the dash made Brighton wince and gasp. (The ladies had decided the backseat provided too little room for him to stretch out arthritic knees and hips.) But the car demanded nothing, as forbearance went, to what the stairs required of him.

"Say, if you don't object," Shorty said with deep concern after they'd laboriously achieved only about a quarter of the steps. "If you don't object, I think we can save you a lot of trouble. Wait right here." He lunged upward, taking two steps at a time, and returned with a beefy uniformed policeman. "We're going to make a seat from our hands—you know, holding each others' wrists, like we did when we were kids—and we're just going to carry you up that way."

Brighton argued politely but feebly. "It's too much trouble for you ... please ..."

"Not half the trouble it is for you to walk it alone," Shorty said calmly. "Here we go ... we're right under you now, so sit yourself down ... that's right ... and hold onto our shoulders ... Ready, Malloy? Then one, two, three—LIFT!"

As though Brighton weighed almost nothing, he was borne upward on their human chair, just high enough that his feet did not drag the stairs, and the two men brought him to the top, setting him gently down so that he felt hardly a twinge as his legs gradually took his full weight. "Thank you, gentlemen," he said, a bit embarrassed.

"Don't blush about it, Tom," Calendonia called, lumbering and gasping her way up, one hand on the rail to help hoist her bulk, the other sweeping aside the full-length skirt of her caftan, so it wouldn't trip her up. "I wish they'd offered to carry *me*! But no! You got a hundred percent of the sympathy that time around. We'll see if we can't arrange it a little more equitably next time . . . but for this time, enjoy! Ah! At last. You doing okay, Angela?"

"Right here." Angela had climbed lightly and steadily behind her large friend, but she too was winded by the exertion. "I think it's the humid air after that rain," she puffed as she made the top step. But of course she was deceived. Bending slightly forward to help her breathing as she leaned against the wall gasping, Angela finally confessed. "Marlene Dietrich is supposed to have said, 'You can lie about your age, but you can't fool a good flight of stairs!' How right she was!"

"I'm going back down and get my notebook," Shorty said, easing around them as they entered Clayton's outer office. "I left it in the car. You go right in."

They heard his feet pounding down the stairs, two at a time, as they looked around them, and for a moment all three registered nothing but confusion. There seemed to be men everywhere—most of them in civilian clothes, one or two in uniform. They carried cameras, lighting equipment, brushes, tweezers, stretchers, plastic bags, measuring tapes and chalk, papers, medical bags, notebooks and pencils . . . they talked constantly to each other in staccato, business-like, short-tempered utterances like:

"Got it?"

"Yeah. Next?"

"Yeah. All set. Done."

"Watch it—"

"Right. Now move. There."

"Okay."

The three stood close to the door and tried to make themselves small and tried to keep out of the way.

In a straight chair on the far side of the room sat a plump, roundish woman of about forty or so, snuffling into a handkerchief and occasionally letting a small sob or a moan escape. She wore battered tennis shoes, an old Army shirt, and patched jeans that strained painfully at every seam. Beside her there were a bucket and mop, a duster, and several grimy cloth squares. Activity in the room swirled around her, but she kept her head buried in her hands, determinedly wielding the handkerchief, which was rapidly becoming sodden with tears.

The door to the inner office was open and through the door the three could see more men moving about, they could hear the crisp monosyllables of professionals doing their job rapidly, and they could see stretched out on the floor a pair of legs that terminated in a pair of women's shoes, the body itself hidden by the wall. Miss Stoner's shoes, Angela knew. She had noticed them at lunch because of the unusual buckle on the alligator-finished leather. She turned her head away and carefully watched only the bustle going on around them in the outer room.

The men with the stretcher had entered the inner office and for a few moments the door was swung shut. Then it opened again, and they came out bearing a lumpy burden swathed in black zip-closed plastic. The three visitors moved nervously aside as the men carried out and toward the stairs what looked like nothing so much as someone's garment bag that had fallen and left the garments knotted and tumbled inside it. Angela thought to herself that someone should tidy it up a bit, smooth it—and she shivered.

All three white heads swiveled back toward the inner office, and six eyes were not too elderly to see the chalk outlines where the body had lain and the quick wink of blinding light that meant flash photography.

"Does the lieutenant know you've arrived?" It was Shorty, coming into the office behind them.

"I don't think so," Angela said, in an awed whisper. "They're all so busy. We didn't want to interrupt . . ."

"Actually, what it is—we didn't really want to see Miss Stoner's body, if you want the truth," Caledonia amended. "I'm sure I speak for all three of us when I say we're not strong on staring at murder victims. And especially not when it's someone we met even briefly."

Swanson edged around them. "Let me tell the lieutenant . . ."

Just at that moment Martinez came through the door. "Oh, there you are. Good. Come into the inner office, will you? All three of you? It's a madhouse out here, with all these people running around. But they've just finished here in the inner office, so . . . Swanson?"

Shorty guided them in and the lieutenant sat down at Clayton's desk. Swanson helped the ladies into the two rather uncomfortable visitors' chairs across the desk, while Mr. Brighton took the secretary's swivel chair that stood before the computer. Shorty seated himself on the couch, using the coffee table in front of it to hold his notebook as he scribbled.

"You were right about the computer disks, Mr. Brighton," Martinez said, gesturing to the small file box on the computer table. "They really are games. I wondered if the labels might be false—there might be something else recorded on the disks—but that's not the case. One of my men knew enough about a computer to check them out. To 'boot them up,' he said . . . It's no wonder I can't understand a word these computer people talk! It sounds like English, but the words don't appear to refer to the same things we mean when we say them. At any rate . . ."

"What actually happened to Miss Stoner, Lieutenant? Was she murdered?" Angela interrupted, her eyes shining. She wriggled her tiny frame uncomfortably in the large, leatherette chair. Short as she was, her feet dangled a couple of inches away from touching the ground.

"There wasn't a lot of blood . . ." He gestured at the chalked outline on the carpet; only a few muddy-looking smears marked the spot where Miss Stoner's head had lain.

"But there was an obvious impact wound. We think she was hit with one of the bookends . . ."

Martinez gestured to the marble figurine of Michelangelo's *David* standing on the table by the couch. Lying beside the statuette were the books it had helped to hold. Its mate, *Venus*, was nowhere to be seen. "We've got the other statue at the lab. And unless she found a way to hit herself over the head, then to replace the bookend on the table and tidy the books before she dropped dead, I'd say she was murdered. Yes."

Brighton and Caledonia nodded solemnly and waited without comment. But Angela was galvanized into excited participation. "Well, why are we here? What can we tell you?"

Martinez leaned back in his chair. "Mrs. Wingate—Mr. Brighton—if you'd glance around this room and try to think how it was when you left it . . . Take your time and tell me anything at all that occurs to you."

"How about me?" Angela said.

"You didn't see this room yourself, did you?" Martinez asked.

"Well, no, but . . ."

"Then we'll wait till the men are through out there. That's when you can make yourself useful for me. Till then, you and I can just chat while the others work."

Angela was slightly mollified. "That woman out there . . . the cleaning woman . . . She found the body, didn't she?" Angela asked, as Brighton and Caledonia rose and obediently began a slow circuit of the room, each viewing it from a number of angles, their brows furrowed as they tried to reconstruct their memories.

"She did indeed . . . but how did you know? I suppose she told you so while you waited out there?"

"No, she didn't say a word. I even guessed at who she is. But that part was easy, because she's got the tools of her trade right there with her. As for her discovering the body—well, she's very upset. More than if she merely found out about Miss Stoner's death secondhand. I mean, I know what emotional people you Latins are, but there must be some limits even to Latin self-dramatizaion."

Shorty caught Martinez's eye and grinned. They had agreed long ago that there wasn't much one could do about Mrs. Benbow's built-in prejudgments. Now Martinez said nothing, and if he pinched his lips a bit more tightly, Angela didn't seem to notice as she rattled on. "The way the woman's carrying on, I thought it was more than likely that she had stumbled on the body personally. Of course, you wouldn't have to be Latin to be upset by that. Finding a dead body would upset anybody!"

At last Martinez shrugged. He had perfect command of himself and even seemed a bit amused. "You've worked it all out very well. Mrs. Ruiz has a contract to clean in several buildings including this office. She starts her night's work here and goes on to the next building on her list and the next . . . Tonight, she may not get any further than this."

Angela made a vague noise that she hoped was sympathetic and turned her eyes around her. "You know, when I was here before, the door to this room wasn't open, and I couldn't think of an excuse . . ."

"I'm sure you'd have looked in here if you'd had a chance," Martinez said soothingly, and Swanson ducked his head to hide a grin.

"It's a drab room, isn't it?" Angela did not see any hidden meaning in the remark. "Look. No decoration . . . just that picture and the fern . . . and that umbrella stand . . . and the magazines on the coffee table by the couch—and nothing has much color! The magazines are mostly black and white, and even the painting"—she peered at it—"is of a foggy day! Black umbrella, white bookends, grayish-green fern, and all the wood and metal everywhere else. Everything is so—so office-colored!" She shivered. "It reminds me of Wallace Clayton. Of course that makes sense; I mean, it's his office, isn't it?"

"Do you suppose it was Clayton who killed Miss

Stoner?" Caledonia had joined them after her circuit of the office and this was her contribution.

"Killed his secretary? Well, it's possible, of course. But what for?" Martinez said. "Why would he do that?"

"Well, my husband used to say that nobody knows a man as well as his wife does—except for his secretary," Angela interjected. "Of course *his* secretary—Douglas's secretary—was a man—a yeoman. Because he was in the Navy in the days before they had a lot of women in service, you see. But the point is, in civilian life, I suppose a female secretary would know a lot more about her boss than a male secretary would. You see?"

"No, not really," Martinez said. "Why would that be? Wouldn't any secretary be in on the private correspondence and the decisions that . . ."

"Douglas used to say that men—civilian men, of course—see another man as a potential threat! I mean, if a male secretary learned everything you know about the business, he might some day move up and take your place. Douglas said that's why men prefer women as their secretaries—because they assume women will not be trying to take advantage of their knowledge to supplant the boss!"

"I'm not sure I see how that ties in . . ."

"Well, in my day, women were always the secretaries and men were always the bosses, you see. And so because even bosses need someone to talk to and confide in—and because men can't imagine a woman being a rival—they tend to let their secretaries in on a lot of business secrets!" She paused as though she expected applause for her reasoning.

Martinez was doubtful. "I believe times have changed somewhat, Mrs. Benbow. Nowadays—"

"Ah," she said triumphantly, "but you forget . . . Wallace Clayton is from our era; he's a rather old-fashioned man!"

"*Rather* old-fashioned!" Caledonia snorted. "His dialogue is a Victorian throwback! His mind probably works that way, too! I'd say he was a good bet to see a female secretary as no threat at all and to open up to her and trust her. So Miss Stoner might very well have been in a position where she could blackmail him . . . And if she did, then maybe he *did* kill her! Good thinking, Angela."

"Oh, no-no-no, Cal, you misunderstood me!" Angela was earnest in her denial. "What I was getting at was that Clayton *wouldn't* be likely to kill her. You see, one kills people who are in the way somehow, or who represent a threat. Isn't that right, Lieutenant? And my point was that it would never occur to Clayton that a mere woman—a secretary—could ever get in his way or be a danger to him! He'd trust her with his secrets, but he wouldn't kill her!"

Martinez held up a hand. "All very interesting—but business before speculation. Mrs. Wingate, did you find anything out-of-the-way around here?"

She shrugged. "Nothing that I could see. Except maybe the magazines—they aren't arranged as carefully as they were. And of course the books," she pointed to the side table by the couch, "have fallen over."

Martinez nodded. "My men glanced at the magazines, and probably didn't replace them as they had been. It didn't seem important. And of course because we think somebody used one of the marble bookends as a weapon, it's gone to the lab. The books fell over when we moved the bookend somebody had so carefully replaced. The bookend was stained, I think I told you . . ."

"You did. Sorry I asked," Angela said. "You don't need to tell me any other details."

"Did you notice anything else, Mrs. Wingate?"

"Well, the umbrella stand looks a little odd to me. I think it's been moved a little, or something."

"I'll make a note to ask if one of my men shifted it around. Anything more?"

"Sorry." Caledonia shrugged. "I wish I could help you. But except for the things I mentioned . . ."

"Mr. Brighton . . ." Brighton had seated himself at the computer, turned it on, and was busy playing chess against the machine. "Mr. Brighton!" The lieutenant's voice was not loud, but it was insistent.

"Oh, sorry!" Brighton swung his chair around to face the others. "I was trying to work out a move here ... This wonderful little machine ..." he patted the computer on its metal head, "... this dear little chap is a marvelous player! They give you a choice of your level of competition, so this time I pushed all the buttons to make it into a beginner, instead of an expert. But it still beats me every time! Incredible!" He became aware that the four others in the room were silent. "Oh. I beg your pardon. You wanted something?"

"Mr. Brighton," Martinez said patiently, "in your circuit of the room before you started the chess game, did you see anything out of place? Anything different—missing—added—changed?"

Brighton shook his head. "Nothing. I really wish I could help."

"Well, then, I'm going to have to ask you to abandon your game ..."

Brighton sheepishly reached behind the machine and turned the power switch off.

"... and come into the outer office and do the same examination out there. My men will have gone by now and we need to look it over, as well as this room."

Brighton pulled himself upright, using the computer table as a prop, and stumped toward the outer room, still looking rather apologetic. Caledonia and Angela joined him. "Don't feel bad, Tom," Angela whispered. "I'm always being scolded for getting off the point and being interested in side issues ... things that other people think are a diversion. They're interesting to me, or I wouldn't get involved ... just like that computer is to you. So you just pay no attention to them. At our age, we've earned the right!"

Brighton grinned, and then hastily wiped the smile off his face. "It's just that this is such a serious business!" he whispered. "Murder! And of someone we knew! Or at least, you did, Angela. And Caledonia had met her. I only saw her briefly as she walked past."

"Now," Martinez, leading the way, crossed the office and turned back to them, "take your time and look at everything." He crossed the room and spoke quietly a few moments with the uniformed man who stood there, ignoring his witnesses and letting them move at their own pace.

Brighton walked back and forth between the outer door and the door to the inner office, then shrugged and sat down in a chair at one side. "Sorry, Lieutenant," he said. "Again—I see nothing. But remember, I was only in here once, and then I went straight through to the inner office and spent my time there."

Caledonia went from the file cabinet, which she opened and surveyed carefully, to the workroom where the duplicating machine stood. Angela went behind the desk.

"Here's where maybe I can be of some help. I looked over Miss Stoner's shoulder to see her appointment book while I was here yesterday," she explained to Martinez. "I wanted to see when there'd be nobody here. You know, so we could look the place over. She said Wallace only came in mornings, unless he had an appointment, and I noticed that the page for the next day—that's today—was blank all day ... Yes, it still is. She didn't write down anything new ... That entry over there" she pointed at the next week's page—"that's us. The appointment we made. We didn't mean to actually keep it, of course. Making the appointment was our excuse to come up here and reconnoiter."

Martinez had moved forward and glanced down at the book. "Winsledge and Bingball?" he asked, amused. "Your aliases, perhaps?"

"Of course," Angela said triumphantly.

"Not a bad idea, really, Lieutenant," Caledonia put in, emerging from the storeroom door. "Angela pretended to have a cough, so she could muffle her voice with her handkerchief. It could have been anything she was saying, when she gave Miss Stoner our names. And so if the Unmitigated Wallace found out it was supposed to be us, we could always claim that was Miss Stoner's misunderstanding, you see."

"I thought it was quite brilliant, actually," Angela said loftily.

"Nothing I can see in the storeroom looks different from when I was there before, Lieutenant. The copy machine's been refilled with paper. But there's nothing that would be suspicious . . . just office work kind of things."

"You don't see anything either, Mrs. Benbow?"

Angela shook her head mutely.

"Well, I'm sorry to have brought you down here for nothing. I was hoping something might just jump out at you . . . that there'd be a new name in the appointment book"—Angela shook her head—"or something odd about the computer—" Mr. Brighton shrugged. "Or even perhaps a delivery of supplies to the storeroom?" Caledonia spread her hands. "Look, I'll get Shorty to take you home again. Thank you all for coming."

"You're not going home yet, Lieutenant?" Angela asked eagerly. "I mean, we could stay a while, too . . ."

He smiled. "We have a lot of routine work ahead of us. Nothing you could help with or that you'd even find very interesting. For instance, we must talk to Mrs. Ruiz. The cleaning woman, remember? My officer says one of my men took her to the diner down the street, where she's being fed coffee and donuts till she settles down and till I'm ready to talk to her."

"Ah, now, that I understand," Caledonia said. "There's nothing so soothing as a glazed donut in times of stress!"

Martinez grinned. "And of course we must talk to Wallace Clayton. I'll phone him as soon as you're gone. I've waited far too long to notify him and get him down here, but I didn't want you to run into him. He'd wonder why you three were here at all!"

"Oh, dear! That would have given away that we were looking around earlier," Angela said alarmed.

"Thank you, Lieutenant. How very thoughtful." Caledonia smiled.

"Detective Swanson," Mr. Brighton said as he stood up. "Do you suppose you and that uniformed man by the door could give me the same elevator service going down the stairs you did coming up?"

Shorty jumped forward, casting a glance sideways at Martinez, who merely nodded. "Yes, sir. Certainly. I was only afraid you might think we were being too helpful."

"Not at all, son. It was very thoughtful. I admit it embarrasses me to be fussed over, but I'd a whole lot rather be embarrassed than walk down those stairs without help!"

So Brighton was chairlifted down the stairs by Swanson and the uniformed officer, though much more slowly than when they brought him up, since carrying a large burden requires bending forward, to take up the extra strain on shoulders and back. And going downstairs while leaning forward and carrying a weight is difficult, not to say downright dangerous. Not to mention that the stairs were narrow, and three men abreast, two of them fighting their balance, made for several very clumsy moments.

Once safely in the car and started on the short ride home with Swanson at the wheel, Angela could contain herself no longer. "Detective Swanson," she began, "I know you're going to think it's just idle curiosity. But I simply must ask. Did I understand that you and our dear Conchita have had a quarrel?"

"Angela!" Caledonia cautioned. "Don't pry."

"Well, he doesn't have to tell me if he doesn't want to. Did you, Detective Swanson?"

"Ma'am, we—yes, we've—uh—we have disagreed. I—I wish you'd ask her if you want to know about it. It's . . . well, we've been going together a long time now, and her family is asking her when we're getting married, and . . .

No, I better not talk about it. She'll tell you, if she wants anyone to know."

"But, we just thought, if you told us, maybe we could—"

"*Angela! NO!!*" Caledonia said sharply. "You just mind your manners now!"

"Oh, very well." Angela sulked into her corner of the backseat and held her peace as they drew into the semicircular driveway before Camden's main doors. Caledonia noted that the back of Detective Swanson's neck was as red as though his collar had chafed him all day long, and although he opened the car doors politely for them and said a deferential "Evening, ma'am. Evening, sir. Evening, ma'am . . . ," he almost ran back to the car and wheeled rapidly off, back to duty—away from being questioned and back to the comfortable position of being the one who asks questions.

"I don't know how we can ever find out anything if you won't let me make the simplest inquiry, Caledonia," Angela snapped with obvious annoyance.

"Oh, Angela, not tonight," Caledonia protested. "I'm so tired I could crawl back to my apartment."

"I feel the same," Brighton sighed. "Good night, ladies," and he turned without another word and trudged toward his rooms.

"Believe me, I'll fight with you tomorrow, if you insist," Caledonia went on. "Just not tonight. Excitement and late hours are hard on an old doll like me. And don't wake me for breakfast!"

"As if I could!" Angela said pertly. "Honestly, I don't know how you can even think about sleeping. I'm going to be wide-awake for hours!"

But Angela's prediction was wrong. Even with a bright array of thoughts and questions scrambling and whirling inside her brain, she was blissfully asleep within seconds after her head touched the pillow.

Chapter 10

WHEN ANGELA went in to breakfast the next morning, she was a little surprised—considering the lady's condition when last they met—to see Edna Ferrier already dining on country ham and scrambled eggs. When she realized Angela was looking at her, Edna had the grace to look a bit embarrassed about the size of her appetite.

Angela routed her passage between the tables to bring her near to Edna's place, and she took a moment to stop and touch Edna on the shoulder and whisper, "Don't worry about it, dear. We all get over mourning some time or other. The appetite comes back, things start to seem interesting again. And one day, when you're not being careful to be sad, you suddenly find yourself enjoying something—a book, a joke, a flower . . . It surprises you when it happens, but it always will happen."

"It seems so soon, though," Edna protested, pushing a bit of the ham around her plate with the tip of her fork and finally hiding it under the toast, as though to deny its existence. "He was a very special person and he deserves more than this from me . . ."

Angela patted Edna's shoulder. "That's just guilt talking. Remember how you felt after your husband died? The first time you did something even halfway normal, you felt guilty about it! The first time you laughed out loud you felt like you'd insulted his memory. Well, it's the very same thing now. But you know that's foolishness. It's natural, but

151

it's foolish. Your life is going on, and there's nothing to feel guilty about."

"But he's dead. And here I am eating—even enjoying the taste of food, and . . ."

"And he'd do the same, if he were here. You just can't mourn forever and I'm glad to see you starting to move back to a normal life again. Keep up the good work, my dear." Angela moved on quickly, to avoid further discussion. If mourning was depressing in itself, talking about it with someone was just as depressing, in her view.

Chita came to the table, wordlessly set down a glass of orange juice—Angela's customary first course at breakfast—along with a thermos of coffee, and then waited with pad and pencil ready to take an order.

"I'll take one poached egg, one little sausage, a slice of wheat toast and some jelly," Angela said. "Any kind but that bitter marmalade. I really don't like . . ." But Chita, having scribbled on her notepad, simply turned and walked toward the kitchen without waiting for Angela to finish her explanation. She had not smiled once nor spoken, only nodded her head.

"Well!" Angela gasped, thoroughly annoyed.

"She made only a minimal concession to being pleasant," Angela told Caledonia later the same morning down at Caledonia's apartment, all the details of her encounter. "You talk about someone who doesn't look good. Her eyes were red and puffy—I think the child had been crying already, and it wasn't even seven-thirty! I said to myself, 'What can that Detective Swanson be thinking of to make her so miserable? Imagine him refusing to marry a lovely girl like that,' I said to myself—because even though she was a little abrupt at breakfast, she is a lovely girl, don't you agree?"

"I thought about that yesterday," Caledonia said. "When he told us the little he did say about it, I wondered if he was being snobbish about her job?"

"I thought of that. But it isn't as though she'd chosen to

be a waitress at the local all-night truck stop. Or a cocktail lounge. The women who work here are all either working at more than one job—doing this one for a little extra money—or it's a part-time job for a young girl while she finishes school—or . . ."

"Or it's a kind of community service and Christian duty!" Caledonia agreed. "I know. Some of the ladies think they'll go to heaven if they come here and put on a program for us at Christmas—or read to the sick—or take the waitressing job. It's better than doing volunteer work at the county hospital, because your help is needed just as much but you get paid a little bit for your trouble!"

Angela nodded. "Chita does it because she likes us, she can use the extra money, even living at home with her family for nothing, and of course she's been here longer than some of those little high-school girls—I'd say she actually makes a fair salary by now. She's not a professional waitress, even though she's an awfully good one. Of course, being a waitress is a perfectly respectable profession . . ."

"Don't tell me!" Caledonia protested. "Tell that Swanson kid! But he doesn't really seem to me like he'd be a snob."

"Well, I couldn't think what other reason it might be. 'What reasons are there, after all, why a young man won't talk marriage?' I asked myself."

"The reason's simple: Swanson's an idiot!" Caledonia snapped. "Wants to stay a happy bachelor all his life, forgetting that he'll not be young forever, and someday he'll want to settle down in a home of his own. Of course—" she pinched her lower lip, "you know, in my day, a young man didn't ask a girl to marry him until he had the money saved for a house and some furniture . . . I wonder if that's his problem? If he's old-fashioned enough to want to be able to offer her . . ."

"Young people don't think of things that way now, I'm told," Angela said. She furrowed her brow to show she was thinking deeply. "Swanson doesn't seem like the perpetual bachelor, so what can it be? I just can't work it out myself.

But you see, that's why I was simply dying to hear about it. So, to make the story short . . ."

"Yes, Please!"

"What I did was—I asked Chita right out."

"Angela! You didn't!"

"Oh, but I did!"

Chita had returned to the dining room shortly after taking Angela's order, and she carried a tray from which she set down an English muffin and two sausages with a fried egg.

"Here," Angela called before Chita could leave them. "Child, this isn't my order."

"Oh. Oh, dear . . ." Chita was blank for a moment. "I think I've picked up someone else's order!" She hesitated a moment, then pulled her notebook from her apron pocket. "Oh, this goes to Mrs. Stainsbury across there. I'm sorry, Mrs. Benbow. I know you don't take anything fried . . . I don't know what I was thinking of." She took the offending plate up and whisked off to deliver it to Trinita Stainsbury, sitting across the room, drinking coffee and reading the morning paper. After a very few minutes, Chita came back, slightly out of breath, with Angela's correct order.

"Sorry about this," Chita said. "It's just—I'm a little addled today," she confessed, and sighed deeply as she turned to go.

"Chita." Angela could contain her curiosity no longer, and her tiny hand darted out to grasp the girl's wrist firmly and keep her from leaving. "What's the problem? Is there anything at all we can do?"

Chita snuffled, but controlled herself so that no tears came. "No, thank you for being concerned. But there's nothing anybody can do. It's just that—that darned, stubborn Swanson . . ."

"I really can't figure it out, Chita," Angela said eagerly. There was no Caledonia present to restrain her, so Angela simply barged ahead and asked what was on her mind. "You two are a perfect couple! Everyone says so . . . and you're so very fond of each other . . .?" She finished the sentence with a slight question mark and waited, but Chita merely nodded.

"Well, you're fond of him, of course . . . and I'm sure he's very fond of you . . .?" Angela finished the sentence with another question mark, and watched Chita's face closely. The girl's chin quivered, but her mouth set tight and she merely nodded.

"I know you'd be well suited in every way. So the question is, why won't he marry you?"

To Angela's dismay, Chita's tears, so well restrained before, now squirted out and she pulled a handkerchief, already damp, from her apron pocket.

"Oh, my stars!" Angela gasped, appalled. "I never meant to upset you that much. Won't you let us know what the problem is and if we can help? We're so fond of you, my dear. And we'd like to help out . . ."

Chita wiped her eyes and tucked the handkerchief away, controlling her sniffles with difficulty. "Thank you, but there's nothing anyone can do. But—" She hesitated, half-turned to leave. "You've got it all wrong, you know. Swanson wants to get married! He's asked me over and over, four maybe five times. More, maybe."

"Then what on earth . . .?"

"It's me that doesn't want to get married! He wants us to—my family wants us to—and they all get mad at me because I say no, and . . . Oh, what's the use? If he can't understand, nobody can . . ." and she moved hastily away, banging her tray against the swinging doors to the kitchen, her tears starting up again as with her free hand she pressed the soggy little handkerchief to her eyes. And Angela was left to speculate—and to report to Caledonia.

"I don't understand!" Caledonia was genuinely bewildered, as she listened later. "He does want to get married? And *she* doesn't?"

"So it would seem! Which makes even less sense than all the things I was thinking about him. It's as I said—

they're a perfect couple! What ever do you suppose is her problem?"

"Well, do you suppose *she* wants to wait till they have money to buy a house?" Caledonia yawned with a mighty, shuddering gasp. "Sorry . . . it's so early for me . . ."

"One thing I feel confident of is that it isn't money. Everybody marries on credit these days! You don't need to have money in the bank, now, the way you did when we were young, Cal. Besides, he must make quite a decent salary on the police, you know."

"Well," Caledonia said, "it doesn't make sense, to me! 'Scuse me . . ." She yawned again. "It's just because it's morning. You know how I feel about mornings . . ."

"I don't know what to think, really. But you can bet I'm going to make it a point to find out! There must be some way we can help them," Angela said firmly.

"Don't you have a murder to solve to keep you busy?" Caledonia asked sternly. "Angela, making a game—a kind of intellectual puzzle—out of a murder may sound callous, but we've come to terms with it because it's stimulating. It's a challenge. And if we stay out of the way of the police, we can have the excitement without hurting anybody. But it's a different kettle of fish when you start messing around with the lives of young people like . . ."

"Well, yes, but it's a matter of priorities," Angela said primly. "First things first, you know. Mr. Lightfoot and Miss Stoner aren't going anywhere. They can wait till I see if there's not something I can do about Chita and Detective Swanson."

"Angela! I just can't approve of your interfering!"

"Oh, I wouldn't really interfere. All I ever wanted to do was to find out what's going on. And then, if there was something we could help with . . . I mean, what's the use of letting nice people suffer, if there's something you can do to help them out?"

Caledonia smiled fondly at her. "You really are a nosy old Parker, girl! Look—Chita is as much a favorite of mine as she is of yours, and so is Swanson. I feel the same concern you do. And, I may add, I have exactly the same amount of curiosity. I just want to be sure you don't barge in offering free advice where it's not wanted—trying to fix things up behind the scenes and ending up making them worse!"

"Oh, Cal! Trust me. Anyhow, assuming I find out something that we can do to help, suppose I promise you to talk it over with you first, before I actually go ahead with any plan? Would that make you happier?"

"Yup. That would help, all right. Well, then, since I assume you're going ahead with your Cupid project, what's the first step?"

Angela shook her head. "Oh, I don't know that. I hadn't got that far in my thinking. I was just starting out to take a walk—to get my morning exercise and kind of mull things over—and as I passed your place I saw you come out to get your morning paper, and I wanted to tell you about Chita, of course, so I never did take my walk. And so I hadn't had time to think yet what I was going to actually do about it all! I mean, I could have thought on the walk. I can't think and talk to you at the same time. Or—no—I didn't mean that, exactly . . ."

"Yes, you did. You almost never think when you're talking, Angela. I believe talking shuts off the oxygen to your brain! But I'll tell you what," Caledonia said, and interrupted herself with another gigantic yawn, so cavernous her huge hand could barely cover it. "I'm going to roll on up to the dining room for coffee—because I really don't care whether school keeps or not, till I've waked up a bit more. And you—you just go for your little walk. And think your little thinks. Then, after you get back—oh, say between ten and eleven—about time for morning coffee and some cookies—you just come on to my place and we'll go over it all again. Together. How about that?" And she yawned again, so wide Angela wondered if she had perhaps dislocated her jaw! But Caledonia's mouth did finally close, and she heaved herself out of her chair to flow toward the doorway.

"Come along, Angela," she said. "Walk for you, breakfast for me . . ."

They left the apartment together, Caledonia turning eastward toward the main building and the faint scent of coffee and bacon that drifted from the open dining room doors, Angela turning westward toward the sea and her morning constitutional.

But as Angela passed the halfway point in the garden—near the giant eucalyptus tree that overhung the little stone fountain (empty at the moment so the gardener could clean out the pool)—she became aware of steady footsteps on the walk behind her.

"Why, Dr. Grainger!" she exclaimed, as she turned around and recognized who it was striding along. "How lovely to see you! Are you taking a little exercise before breakfast? Or working off calories after breakfast, like me? I didn't see you in the dining room, though . . ."

Dr. Grainger looked a little taken aback as she pounced on him. "Oh! Mrs. Benbow! Well, yes, I always walk in the morning. Thelma says it's good for my circulation. If you'll excuse me . . ."

"Oh, do let me walk with you, Dr. Grainger," Angela said, delighted. Chita and her problems slid neatly into a drawer in Angela's mind marked PENDING, and the drawer marked MURDER slid open wide. "I'd be grateful for the company. Exercising—is such a bore without someone to talk to."

Grainger hesitated noticeably. "Well, I'm not sure . . . I walk quite fast."

"I'll keep up," Angela said with a bravado she did not feel at all. "Trust me . . . Now, which way do you usually turn as you leave the garden?"

"South along Beach Lane," Dr. Grainger said with obvious reluctance. "Are you sure it isn't just a little early for you to be taking a walk?"

"Not at all. It's Caledonia who can't get up before eight or nine. I'm an early riser myself."

"Well," he tried again. "I mean, most people here walk about midmorning. They say it's good for the digestion. If you try to walk too early . . ."

"But I always walk early like this, right after breakfast." He only looked more miserable, so Angela barged right ahead. "It's really sweet of you to let me join you . . ."

The steamroller had its way. Dr. Grainger ducked his head in meek submission, and with Angela scuttling a bit to keep up with his long stride, they moved out of the garden and down Beach Lane, Grainger using his cane now and then, Angela panting to catch up when she lagged too far behind.

They walked for nearly a full block in silence, till Angela could stand it no longer. If he wouldn't make the first move, she would! "I love the cool mornings and warm afternoons here in Southern California," she began. "Don't you?"

"Mmmph," Grainger said, keeping his head down. Like many elderly people, he watched his feet much of the time as he walked. Angela, by contrast, looked up and around her nearly all the time, trusting her instincts—and her luck—to guide her feet correctly.

"We were saying to your wife how we missed having a true autumn, though. There should be colored leaves about now, back in the East and the Midwest. I love the autumn, don't you?"

"Mmmph," said Grainger again.

"You come from the East, don't you?" Angela said.

"Mmmm-hmmm."

"You had a private practice there?" Angela pursued. "With children, I understand?"

"Yes." He smiled for the first time. "I loved working with the children. I didn't want to retire and move out here. Oh, I don't miss the winters . . . but I miss the children."

"Do you have a family of your own?" Angela went on.

"No. Thell and I had a daughter, but she died very young." He did not go on, but kept walking, looking earnestly at his feet.

"Douglas and I had no children," Angela said. "It made it easier when we had to move around. He was in the Navy, so we changed stations frequently. But now I wonder if I made a mistake . . . Except I'm not sure I could have survived losing a child as you did."

"It was a long time ago." He shrugged. He said nothing for a while and then he said in a soft voice, "Dorothy wasn't quite six years old when she died . . . meningitis. I thought, because I was a doctor, I should have been able . . . well . . . you know . . ." His voice trailed away and he caught himself with his cane as he stumbled slightly.

"I hope you don't blame yourself. Meningitis is a terrible disease, and years ago it was almost always fatal!" Angela said, soothingly.

"I know. I don't feel I'm to blame. Not anymore. I did for a while. But I turned to the church. It was—it was a great comfort, you know. I used to blame myself. But they taught me to be patient with God's will. Besides, it's been so long ago now . . ." He sighed.

Angela was starting to puff slightly at the pace they had kept as they walked. Talking and walking made it worse, and she was beginning to feel a slight stitch in her side. "Can we slow up a little?" she begged. "I didn't mean to be a nuisance, but I find that you walk a little too fast for me . . ."

"Oh. I'm sorry." Clearly, she thought, he had originally meant to outwalk her—but Grainger was a kind man and a polite one, and he stopped in midstride, waiting to let her catch her breath. Wearing her out and tricking her into having to turn back might have been his original goal, but he had apparently relented. "Mrs. Benbow, perhaps we should turn and go toward home now."

"Yes . . . yes, if you don't mind. And could we go a bit more slowly?"

He sighed as they turned. "I will take shorter steps. I forget . . . Thelma has to remind me whenever she walks with me."

"Let's change the subject. I don't want to make you sad," Angela began, as they started back. They had only come three blocks from the grounds of Camden-sur-Mer, and it occurred to Angela that she really hadn't much time left in which to press her inquiry. So she took her usual route to truth—the direct one. "About these murders . . ."

"Murders?"

"Well," she said, "I'm sure you heard about the death of Miss Stoner—she was secretary to Wallace Clayton, you know, and he's the brother-in-law of our Edna Ferrier."

"But more than one murder?"

"Well, of course I'm assuming that Edna's fiancé, Alex Lightfoot, was pushed in front of that train deliberately. It was always a possibility. And Edna swears that was what happened. She says he was hale and hearty, so he didn't faint or have a stroke. She says he was well coordinated, so he couldn't have stumbled. She says he wasn't in the least depressed, so he couldn't have committed suicide . . ."

"It would have made things simpler if he had," Grainger said.

"Oh, I agree. Infinitely. Then there'd have been a note, and everyone would have known for sure! Edna says it just had to be murder, but she says that doesn't make sense, because everybody who met him liked him, and—"

"Hmph!" Grainger snorted, and ducked his head to stare fixedly at his feet as he stepped off a curb to cross a side street.

Angela scurried to catch up to him again. "What do you mean? Do you mean that you disagree?"

"Yes!" Grainger said. But he didn't continue. He only strode ahead a little more doggedly.

"That it was murder?"

"No."

"You mean, you don't agree that everyone liked him instantly?"

"Yes."

"Now, that's very interesting, Dr. Grainger. Why?"

"Why what?"

"Why do you disagree? Did you dislike him?"

"Yes. Very much."

"But your wife said you only just met him. What did he do or say . . .?"

"Nothing. Here."

"Then why . . ."

"That man was trash, and somebody knew it and killed him. But I don't want to talk about it. I don't want to think about it."

"Oh dear! B-but Edna says he was a wonderful person, and—"

"She was a silly woman, getting herself involved with a man like that. She's lucky he did get himself killed."

"But I don't see . . . what was so awful about him? You say he didn't do anything bad . . ."

"Here."

"All right, here. Where, then?"

"Home. Back home. He came from back our way. Mrs. Benbow . . ." They had reached the open gateway that arched across the entrance to the hotel gardens, and Dr. Grainger hesitated just under the arch. Angela thought how dramatic he looked, as she glanced back and saw him framed there—tall, gaunt, the wind stirring his thin white hair, his cane partly raised in his clenched fist—with the gray sea beyond the cliff's edge forming a backdrop and the wooden posts of the gate on either side of him to set the picture off. He looked, as she told Caledonia later, like an Old Testament prophet.

"Mrs. Benbow, I told you that man was trash. Just trash. He doesn't deserve your sympathy. Alex Lightfoot is where he belongs, in Hell! I'm only sorry I didn't put him there myself!"

And while Angela watched, stunned out of anything she might have tried to say, Dr. Grainger strode off past her and up the garden path toward his cottage.

Chapter 11

THAT AFTERNOON Lieutenant Martinez came to Camden in answer to Caledonia's urgent request, relayed by phone to wherever he had been working throughout the morning. Angela had skittered back up the path, calling only a quick goodbye over her shoulder to Grainger, and she had gone straight to Caledonia's without waiting for their agreed-upon appointment at milk-and-cookies time. She reported her encounter fully, and they agreed they should tell Martinez as soon as possible. Unfortunately, when they called the police number listed in the phone book, they had simply been put on hold for a wait that stretched out for five minutes or more, till Angela, pacing up and down the center of Caledonia's living room, had begun to chew the quick around her fingernails.

"Stop that!" Caledonia hissed.

"But it's taking so long for him to come to the phone! It's driving me crazy! The waiting is so awful that ..."

"Chewing your nails won't help!"

"I'm not chewing my nails! I'm chewing on the little bits of dead skin around ..."

"Angela! That's repulsive!"

Angela crimped her mouth tight shut and continued to walk. After a few more minutes, Caledonia began talking to the phone, and it was obvious that all she would be able to do was leave the message asking the lieutenant to get in touch as soon as he could.

She hung up with disappointment. "They say it'll be after one o'clock before he can possibly get back to us." Then she brightened. "But they do say he's here in town, so perhaps instead of calling, he'll come over."

"Oh, dear. I can't wait that long," Angela moaned. But of course she could—and she did, though both she and Caledonia, struggling with repressed excitement, ate less than usual at lunch.

After the meal, Angela and Caledonia jittered together at Caledonia's apartment for what seemed hours, but it was only about two-thirty when there was a knock at the screen door, and Martinez appeared in person.

"Now ladies," the lieutenant said, settling himself comfortably after the usual greetings had been passed around the room at least twice. "You had something you urgently wanted to talk to me about?"

"Absolutely. We think we've discovered something of unusual interest," Caledonia began.

"*I* discovered! *I*, not we!" Angela protested. "*I'm* the one who went for a walk after breakfast and *I'm* the one who talked to Dr. Grainger, after all . . ."

Caledonia waved a huge hand. "It really doesn't matter, girl. Just tell the lieutenant what you found out. This is really interesting, Lieutenant . . . I couldn't even imagine a reason why . . ."

"Caledonia! It's my story!"

"Oh, all right, go ahead. I was only . . ."

"I met Dr. Grainger in the garden quite by accident." Angela began her story in tones louder than her usual little-girl voice would sustain. She wanted to drown out Caledonia's thunderous mutterings, which were, at least in Angela's opinion, hardly to the point. "I wanted to ask him about his association with Alexander Lightfoot."

"We were curious, you see," Caledonia put in, not to be denied entirely her rights to at least a little of the tale. "Edna told Angela the Graingers had entertained her and her fiancé on more than one occasion, but . . ."

"But Mrs. Grainger denied having any more than a nodding acquaintance with him," Angela squeaked excitedly. "It didn't fit at all, you see . . . so today I took the chance to go for a walk with Dr. Grainger, and we got talking about Lightfoot . . ."

"Not by accident, I'd wager." Martinez smiled.

"Of course not," Angela admitted. "I steered him to it. And he exploded. He stood there with his hair blowing in the wind and the gray sea behind him . . . he looked . . ."

"Never mind how he looked. Tell the lieutenant what he said!" Caledonia implored. "Get on with it!"

"He said Lightfoot was trash! He said Lightfoot deserved to be killed. And furthermore, he said he wished he'd done it himself! Because of something that happened back East . . . the Graingers are from Connecticut, you know. Well, obviously, there's something in Lightfoot's background that . . ."

Martinez nodded and held his hands up, palms forward, gesturing in a soothing, gentle push that she should calm down and hush up. "I know about that."

"You know! You know what Dr. Grainger said about . . ."

"Well, I know about Lightfoot, at any rate. I wasn't aware Grainger knew about it . . . but I do know Lightfoot's background. After all, that's my job! What do you imagine police do, anyhow?"

Angela looked bewildered. "I don't know—grill suspects, pick up fingerprints, arrest speeders . . . what do you mean?"

"He means," Caledonia said, grinning, "that they look into the background of everybody involved in a suspicious death—including the background of the corpse, I suppose. Isn't that it, Lieutenant?"

Martinez nodded. "Of course. We put his fingerprints into our computer, and we knew within hours all about Mr. Lightfoot's unsavory past."

"Unsavory?" Angela sounded more eager than displeased. "Grainger was right?"

"Oh, yes," Martinez sighed. "Oh, indeed he was. Lightfoot served time for arson and insurance fraud."

"Arson? Insurance fraud?" Angela's obvious disappointment made her voice even squeakier. "But—but—"

"Angela doesn't mean to sound rude, Lieutenant, but I'm sure she means she thought—she hoped it was something a little more . . . a little more awful, Lieutenant. Something—oh, I don't know—something juicier."

"Yes. I thought at the very least he'd have been an ax-murderer. Or a serial strangler. Or . . ."

Martinez sighed. "That's one of your troubles, ladies. Not that I mean to criticize, but your imaginations tend to run to the—the colorful. There's nothing charming and cute about insurance fraud, you know."

"Skip the lecture," Angela said impatiently. "I know it's a crime. But what was there about it that got Dr. Grainger so upset? That's the point. I mean, he carried on like Moses bringing the Ten Commandments down from the mount—"

"You probably mean," Martinez said gently, "like Charlton Heston playing Moses."

"Well, of course," Angela said, surprised. "I didn't actually see Moses, naturally, but for anybody who saw Charlton Heston in the movie, it was every bit as good as seeing the real thing. Oh, do you remember that scene where he discovers that—"

"Angela!" Caledonia was abrupt. "You're off the point again."

"No, I'm not off the point." Angela's defense was, as usual, to attack someone else. "The lieutenant is. You mustn't pay attention to me, Lieutenant Martinez. You must tell us all about this—this insurance fraud thing."

"It happened back in Bridgeport, where Lightfoot comes from. He was a businessman—real estate, I believe. Police suspected that he burned a number of properties his company owned—properties that weren't selling. They could never prove it, but they finally caught him torching his own home, and . . ."

"I never understood how anybody could do that," Angela said. "Burn their own home and their precious possessions . . . Douglas and I collected so many beautiful things. I'd have been devastated to lose my family silverware and my collection of little antique boxes . . ."

"Well, actually, that's one of the things that make the authorities suspect arson. If the most prized possessions are discovered somehow not to have burned with the house, for instance. And if none of the family are endangered by the fire—not even the family pets," Martinez said.

"Well, what about Lightfoot's case, Lieutenant?" Caledonia asked.

"Oh, it fit the pattern. It surely did. Lightfoot and his wife were at the local shopping mall when the house burned. The family dog was being boarded at the vet's, ostensibly for its yearly shots and deworming. But the biggest signpost of all: two weeks earlier Lightfoot had finally rented a safe-deposit box at the bank that was big enough to hold both his wife's diamond earrings and his grandmother's silver tea set. He joked with the teller about there having been robberies in the neighborhood, although as the prosecuting attorney pointed out, there'd been no evidence of any in the vicinity of the Lightfoots' rather elegant home."

"And what about the financial side, Lieutenant?" Caledonia asked.

"Ah, yes. Well, Lightfoot had just been sent a notice that his house—and a number of others in their development— were built on what used to be a landfill, and there might be a problem with toxic waste permeating the soil. The house had a hefty mortgage, and the drop in its value would have been financially disastrous for him, of course."

"And for all his neighbors. But they didn't burn their places, did they?" Caledonia said.

"No. None of them had criminal leanings, apparently. Only Lightfoot."

"I wonder why Dr. Grainger was so violent about him,

though," Angela said. "That still doesn't make a whole lot of sense to me. It's not as though the fire killed anybody. You said it didn't."

Caledonia put her two cents worth in. "I suppose the Graingers recognized him. There can't be too many Lightfoots in Bridgeport, Connecticut, after all. It's a distinctive name."

"Oh, the name wouldn't help. He used to be Thomas Alexis Headington. He dropped the 'Thomas' part, expanded the second name, and made a kind of reverse pun on the third name: 'head' became 'foot,' and a ton is heavy so it became 'light'—you see? Then he grew a beard and he moved as far away from Bridgeport as he could get without falling into the Pacific Ocean."

"What about that wife you said he had? Edna thought he was a widower."

"Lightfoot's wife left him—and rather conspicuously, too. He was out on bail during the trial, and of course they were living together then. She supported him a hundred percent through most of the trial," Martinez said.

"Well, she probably thought he was innocent," Caledonia said. "You would stand by your husband, no matter what he was accused of, as long as you really believed he didn't do it."

"But she finally left?" Angela asked.

"That's right, Mrs. Benbow. The trial had been going on for a week and the prosecution witnesses had finished testimony. Then came a lengthy parade of witnesses put on by Lightfoot's lawyers, all saying what a fine man he was, what a pillar of the community, and that he was somewhere else when the alleged arson allegedly happened . . ."

"Where?"

"I told you, he and his wife had gone to a local mall. It was late in the year and they were buying some Christmas presents. He came along to carry packages, she said. She made a good witness . . . earnest, loving, concerned, and obviously telling what she believed to be the truth.

"Then, at the last, Lightfoot got on the stand himself, and the trouble started. In telling about the shopping trip, he mentioned that one of their errands had been to get his wife's hair styled. I don't know if you've ever noticed, but liars often embroider too much—fill in too many details to get you to believe them. When Lightfoot said all that about his wife's beauty parlor appointment, the prosecution jumped on it and asked a lot of hard questions."

"Well, where was he while she was getting her hair done?" Angela demanded.

"That's one of the things the prosecution asked. Naturally. He was on a bench right outside the shop juggling their packages, reading the morning paper, and sipping a container of coffee from the Orange Julius stand across the way, or so Lightfoot claimed. And so his wife testified. But in cross-examination, the prosecution got the wife to admit she really wasn't in a position to see him every single minute, with her head being rinsed or toweled, or while she was sitting under the dryer.

"Then the defense called the beauty operator and the shop manager, and they too said he was right outside the whole time. Under cross-examination, they admitted they'd got pretty busy and hadn't been where they could see the bench every second. But they did see him greet his wife when she came out with her hair done . . . he was on the bench then, all right, his arms full of awkward bundles, looking as though he'd never left. They both said with great sincerity that they believed he had never moved from that spot, and sincerity is convincing. So it looked for a while as though he'd be acquitted."

Angela's forehead was knit in a frown. "Well, maybe he *was* right there in the mall the whole time."

"No. You see, two women showed up for the next day of the trial, apologizing for being so slow to realize what they'd seen. After some objections by the defense, the judge let them testify, even though the prosecution was technically through calling witnesses."

"Oh, gosh," Caledonia said. "Mightn't that be grounds for an appeal?"

"A second judge didn't think so when an appeal was attempted later. Anyway, that late-arriving testimony was devastating to the defense."

"Well, what was it the women had seen?"

"On the day in question, they'd gone to the mall and happened to get a space for their car next to Lightfoot's. They were maneuvering into it when he came out, and they remembered him clearly because they noticed he was having such a hard time juggling his parcels and unlocking the car at the same time that they thought he was going to drop his packages onto the ground. And they remembered because they thought he was so good-looking. They commented on it and giggled about it."

"But he could really have gone to the car just to leave the packages, couldn't he?"

"No. He got into his car and drove away while those women watched. They remember that in particular because his car was crowding their line, and his leaving gave them plenty of room to get out their door on that side. And one of them even remembered the time, because her watch was fast and she reset it by the big mall clock as they left their car. Don't worry, the defense thought to ask about times. Most damning of all, when his wife joined him later, after her beauty parlor appointment was over, Lightfoot was carrying his armload of packages again. A man on an innocent errand would have come back empty-handed from the car . . . would have left those hard-to-juggle bundles locked in the trunk.

"So what the prosecution argued and the jury believed was that Lightfoot got into his car, drove to his home, set fire to the house, and then drove back to the mall. And that he took his parcels back into the mall with him to make it look as though he'd never been anywhere but right there on the bench, waiting for his wife the whole time."

"And it nearly worked, didn't it?" Caledonia said. "Well,

when did his wife finally leave him? When he was found guilty?"

"No. She left the same night the new witnesses appeared. I suppose she had believed in him, even though the prosecution's questions made her realize how long it took to get her hair styled—how long he'd been out of her sight, when she really couldn't know where he was. But the last straw was when the two women from the parking lot testified. About that time, the wife must have realized that he had deliberately set her up as an alibi. That night she apparently just packed her bags and walked out. Lightfoot was in court the next day by himself. She'd gone and nobody knew where she was."

"Maybe he killed her!" Angela said suddenly. "Maybe he believed her testimony would damage him and he . . ."

"The police thought of that. They did a search and found nothing. A few weeks later she turned up, living under her maiden name and working as a secretary in Denver. They found her when she filed for a divorce. No, he didn't add murder to his sins that anybody knows of. But it doesn't matter." Martinez sighed. "His sins were big enough to send him to prison for ten years. And for my money, it should have been a lot longer. I have as little patience with white-collar fraud as with armed robbery."

"How come you know all these details, Lieutenant?" Caledonia asked. "I'm sure the computer records weren't this full."

"I phoned Bridgeport and spent more than an hour talking to the detective in charge of the case. He remembered every detail."

"Do you suppose Edna knows about all this?" Caledonia asked.

"I doubt it," Angela said. "She was perfectly sincere when she told me how wonderful he was. I wonder . . . is it true that you can get rehabilitated in prison? Maybe he really had changed . . ."

Martinez shrugged. "She may not have known about his past. But the Graingers knew, if what you tell me is correct. Please, tell me in detail about your conversation with the doctor."

"I already told you." Angela was pouting slightly. "Didn't you listen?" But she went back through the whole morning's conversations.

When she finished, Martinez rose to his feet. "I'm going to have to talk to the Graingers, of course, and I might as well do it right away. The sooner—Whoa! Where do you two think you're going?"

"With you, of course," Angela said. She and Caledonia had risen and moved toward the apartment door.

"Under no circumstances!" he said. "Absolutely not. This is now official police business, and you have no place in it."

"But, Lieutenant, we discovered the evidence in the first place," Caledonia protested.

"Lieutenant, it isn't fair. You promised . . ." Angela, obviously distressed at their exclusion, didn't even try to correct Caledonia, to insist on full credit for the discovery.

"I promised you information and a chance to help. I did not promise you that you could take part in formal investigation. If something came out of this that we could use in court, I'd have to explain your presence on the scene to a judge—and what's worse, to my boss—and I'm not sure I could do either one."

"But . . ."

"No! You aren't a pair of actors, playing deputy sheriffs backing Bat Masterson in some TV western. This is real life. If either of the Graingers should be guilty of the murder . . ."

Angela's mouth set into a thin, stubborn line. "I did think of that, but—"

"Well, so did I, my dear lady. Now, your front office tells me that Dr. Grainger is suffering from early symptoms of arteriosclerosis. Slight confusion from time to time, some forgetting . . . I don't know how far it's gone or what form it's taken. If he sees himself as some sort of holy avenger . . ."

"All right. I follow the argument," Caledonia said resignedly.

"Well, I don't! Why would he be any more dangerous now than he was this morning? I was alone with him then, and he didn't harm me!" Angela's chin was thrust forward and her lips were pressed into what her late husband called her "mule mouth."

"It isn't that he might be dangerous, Mrs. Benbow. Although that's always possible. It's keeping the evidence useable . . . making sure nobody asks something in a way that a lawyer could discredit . . ."

"Go ahead, Lieutenant," Caledonia said. "I'll explain it to Angela when you're gone. But does the promise still hold that you're going to tell us about whatever you find out? Whatever you can tell without compromising the case, of course."

"Yes, it still stands. And I'm sorry if you feel I'm being ungrateful by shutting you out at this point. But it has to be. Official evidence must be gathered carefully, and I just don't dare take a chance." He bowed slightly in that courtly way of his and headed out the door and down the walk toward the Graingers' apartment, across the garden.

"Cal, you gave up too soon," Angela protested. "He'd have let us come, I'm sure of it!"

Caledonia sighed. "I bet when you were a child you used to get everything you wanted by lying on the floor and drumming your heels and holding your breath till your face turned blue! I bet if you just held out long enough, people gave in to you!"

"Cal! What a dreadful thing to say. I am not spoiled . . ." but Angela, who knew that was exactly how she had got her way through her childhood and into her teens, smiled in spite of herself. "Oh well, I guess there's nothing to do now but wait until the lieutenant comes back and fills us in on what he's found out."

Chapter 12

ANGELA WAS awash with curiosity, but the lieutenant did not return, and as the September shadows lengthened through the garden, residents from the other cottages began drifting past in ones and twos on their way to supper. At last, reluctantly, she had to concede that perhaps Martinez would not return at all that day.

By mutual consent, she and Caledonia made their way to the lobby, wandering among the groups of waiting residents, and though they didn't see the Graingers or the lieutenant or Edna Ferrier, they did spot Tom Brighton standing by the parakeet's cage with the Jackson twins and Mary Moffet. Little Mary was standing tiptoe to peer into the cage that was hung at what would be head height for the average resident. The Jackson twins fluttered around, seeming slightly blurred to Angela's eyes, as they rippled constantly, their plump bodies racked with giggles (generally at each other's wit), strapped tightly into identically ruffled pink and flouncy cotton dresses that were two sizes too tight for them.

"Highly irregular! Highly irregular," the bird was saying, as Angela and Caledonia got near enough to hear. *"Highly irregular!"* He seemed to be looking unhappily from one twin to the other. Brighton chuckled, and Mary Moffet, blushing, stood mute, looking fixedly away from the Jacksons.

"Chirrk—highly irregular!"

The inflections the bird was using seemed vaguely familiar to Caledonia—but it was a moment before she made any connection. Then she guffawed loudly enough to make the bird hop nervously on its perch. "That little feathered mimic is taking off our beloved administrator!" she crowed. "He sounds just exactly like Torgeson!"

"Oh! Oh, my!" Mary gasped. "So that's what he reminded me of!" She was transparently relieved to have someone to look at and something to think about that did not direct her gaze at the Jacksons' ruffles.

"I don't catch it myself," Angela said. "I like birds a whole lot better than you do, Cal, but they sound pretty much alike to me."

"*Highly irregular!*" the bird said again. "*Same to your cat!*"

"There. Don't you hear it? The lilt of the irascible Scandinavian is unmistakable!"

"Tom." Angela ignored her friend, as she usually did when she simply didn't get the point of what Caledonia was saying. "We do have something to discuss with you, so perhaps after dinner . . .?"

"Oh. Oh, to be sure, ladies." Brighton cast a wise eye from one to the other, clearly signaling his willingness to be conspiratorial. "I'll wait for you in the lobby."

Donna Dee Jackson—or was it Dora Lee?—looked slightly annoyed. "Why, Sister," she addressed her twin, "I do believe these mean ol' people are leavin' us out of their fun!"

"What fun? What are you talking about?" Mary Moffet begged. "Is there something I missed?"

"No, no, Mary dear," Caledonia soothed. "The Jackson twins have misunderstood entirely. Donna Dee . . ."

"Dora Lee," came the quick correction.

"Oh, yes, of course. Dora Dee . . ."

"Donna Dee!"

"That's what I said the first time! But you told me . . . Oh, I see. So, it's Donna Lee . . . Ooof!"

Angela had put a firm elbow into her large friend's ribs. "Cal can't tell the difference . . . isn't that surprising? But what she's trying to say, my dears, is that you're more than welcome to come along, if taxes interest you. Tom was going to talk about tax strategies for the coming year . . . and . . ."

She had judged her audience accurately. The Jackson twins' wrinkled faces folded themselves into even deeper lines. "Oh, dearie me, no! Lordy, anything to do with taxes gives us both such a headache . . ."

"Or money," the other one chimed in. "My daddy used to say we girls didn't have the head for money. 'Course he took care of the family finances in those days. But goodness, I don't see how you two can even stay awake when somebody talks about taxes!"

Mary Moffet was looking from one to the other earnestly, trying to keep up with the conversation. At last, just as the light was breaking over her clouded brows, the sound of the Westminster Chimes (on tape) sounded over the loudspeakers, and the crowd surged toward the dining room's double doors. "I think I understand . . . it's just advice about taxes?" Mary asked hopefully, as she trotted along with the group.

"That's right, dear," Caledonia soothed. "Don't trouble your head about it. The Jackson girls are right . . ." They simpered and cocked their heads in modest acknowledgements of what they took to be a compliment. "Everyone finds such things as account books and ledgers and receipts boring beyond belief."

"And confusing," Angela added. "I wish I didn't have to think about them, either. Alas . . ." and she sighed with exaggerated regret, "to my everlasting sorrow, it's necessary once or twice a year to look into my own accounts, and . . ."

But the Jackson twins, their smiles growing somewhat rigid and artificial with boredom, walked just a little faster and entered the dining room ahead of her, peeling off from the group toward their table on the far end of the room. Mary Moffet, trotting behind, turned to her right and called, "Count me out. I'm not interested in anything like taxes or finances! Sorry to desert you!"

Brighton hesitated a moment before he went on to his own table, making sure Mary and the Jacksons were out of earshot before he spoke quietly. "Very smartly done, ladies! I was at a complete loss there, and for a moment, I feared we'd end up with the whole bunch sitting down to a conference together. Your invention was quick and effective. If I had a hat, I'd doff it. Now, do I take it that you want a private conversation because you have some news for me about our investigations?"

"Sort of," Caledonia said. "Sort of. At least, well— you've earned a share of everything we've learned, and we mean to give you what we've gleaned so far. Your room or mine?"

Brighton grinned and ran a hand through his white mane, so that the hair stood on end like the parakeet's crest did when the bird was nervous. "I haven't had an invitation like that in years, my dear lady. Mine, if it's all right with you . . . not as far for me to walk on these painful joints of mine. See you both down there after dessert's finished?"

"Right." And the two women turned off toward their small table by the window, while Brighton went beyond to his own.

Chita Cassidy came out with a tray full of sherbet glasses that held a cranberry whip appetizer. Angela perked up immediately. "Oh, good," she said. "I can't wait till she gets here!"

"For the appetizer? Or to ask her some more questions?"

"Both."

"Well, forget it. Oh, I'll let you eat your appetizer. But you leave Chita alone, Angela. Let her have some space to settle her own problems! Your curiosity leads you into crowding people, and . . . Ah, hello, Chita. A lovely evening . . . is this cranberry whip tonight?"

"Yes'm . . ." Chita set their dishes down and scuttled away to the next table, before Angela could open a conversation.

"You see?" Caledonia insisted. "She doesn't want to talk about it. Now just let her be."

Angela sulked through most of the meal. But it was hard to stay angry for long at her best friend. Loud and blustering and entirely dominant, Caledonia was so obviously warmhearted and well-meaning that almost no one ever took real offense at her manner. So by the time they walked down the corridor past Angela's apartment toward Tom Brighton's place, they were chatting amiably and giggling like schoolgirls over the sight of the Jackson twins' flouncy rears bouncing down the corridor about fifteen feet ahead.

"Come in, ladies. Sorry you have to be bored so soon after dinner by all this talk of taxes," Brighton said loudly in greeting, just in case, as he explained as soon as the door was closed, anyone like the Jacksons might have been listening. "Now," he went on, "I do have one bit of news myself. It isn't much, but I should get it out of the way first. The auditors hired by the police—"

"I think they have their own. I mean, auditors who are policemen," Angela said.

"Oh, I don't think that can be so," Caledonia objected.

"In either case," Brighton went on, overriding the interruption, "the auditors found nothing unusual in the papers. Martinez came by here to tell me so earlier this afternoon—on his way to your place, he said. I thought then that, if you'd summoned him, you must have found out something or other. I wondered if you'd care to share it . . ."

"Why, Tom! You're part of the team," Angela said. "Of course we'd tell you."

"I take it that when you say the auditors found nothing unusual, you mean they reported no embezzlements, no thefts . . ."

"Mrs. Wingate," Brighton said, "I had it absolutely right

when I told you Edna's investments were doing well under her brother-in-law's management. He made sound use of her money—all for her benefit. Her assets have grown enormously. I'm rather proud of myself, by the way, that a professional accountant reached the same conclusion I did."

Angela sighed. "Then there's nothing in my theory at all," she said. "I'd have sworn it was a good idea."

"It was," Caledonia soothed. "Just not for this situation, that's all. Now, our news, Tom. And I think you'll find it a bit more suspicion-arousing."

And they spent a happy half-hour going over Angela's meeting with Grainger, and Martinez's revelations about Alexander Lightfoot's criminal past.

"Well, my stars," Brighton said, for the twentieth time, as he saw them to the door. "It's more than I can really take in! An arsonist, and a fraud—but he looked so ordinary. So respectable. So—I don't know—so perfectly clean and decent!"

"Well, that's what they say about a lot of criminals," Angela said primly. "I guess it's true that you can't judge a book by its cover, you know. Cal and I have certainly learned that not all criminals have unshaven faces and wild, bloodshot eyes ... though it would be nice if they did. You'd know who to watch out for, then."

"Well, what happens next?" Brighton paused with his hand on the knob, not opening the door to the hall lest someone be walking near enough to hear their parting words. "Are we out of the investigation now?"

"Of course not!" Angela protested. "Why, this just makes me more anxious than ever to find out what is going on! You worry sometimes about hurting the feelings of nice people. But I wouldn't care if that man's feelings were hurt!"

"Angela, do you mean Lightfoot's feelings? Aren't you a little confused?" Caledonia asked. "The man is dead."

"Well, I know that, but I meant—"

"Well, you aren't going to hurt Lightfoot's feelings

whether he's guilty or innocent! But you might do damage anyhow—the person who's likely to be hurt is Edna."

"She knows about his past?" Brighton asked.

"Apparently not."

"Oh, dear! You surely aren't planning to tell her, are you, my dear ladies?"

But that is exactly what Angela was planning to do, and as soon as possible. "Well, I'd want to know if I were in her shoes," she argued to Caledonia as they walked the length of the hall toward her room, talking in hissing whispers so as not to be overheard by the residents whose rooms they were passing.

"I wonder if Edna would thank you? Sometimes it's better to be left in ignorance," Caledonia cautioned. "Think about it a while, at any rate, won't you?"

It was a warning written in water, for within a restless fifteen minutes after returning to her rooms, Angela was starting up the side staircase, headed for Edna's apartment on the second floor.

Angela was simply unable to let the matter drop. She had tried—oh, she had really tried. She had turned on television for an after-dinner, pre-prime-time quiz show and hadn't heard a single question. She had stared vacantly at the screen as a husky private eye on the next show fired a .45 at a fleeing criminal, and as cars followed cars through barriers and around corners and down alleys in the obligatory chase scenes that end most spy and detective shows on TV. Angela saw neither bleeding gunshot victim nor careening vehicles; she saw only Edna and Lightfoot and the gray-haired prophet of doom standing under the garden arch waving his cane in defiance at the wind . . .

At last she gave up all pretense of watching television and turned it off, but the silence was less restful than the clamor of shouts and sirens and shots and screams. And that was when she headed for Edna's room.

Edna admitted her without the delay she'd created on the occasion of Angela's first visit, but with obvious reluctance.

"Oh, Angela, can't it wait? I'm just so exhausted. I've been going to meals all day for the first time, talking to people, fighting to keep on an even keel and not to leak tears all the time . . . It's just got too much for me. I thought I'd go to bed early, and . . ."

"Well, something's come up, my dear. I won't stay long, but there's something I think you should know. Sit down here beside me . . ." Angela took one end of the chintz love seat ". . . and let me hold your hand. This is difficult—"

Edna sat down without a word, but stayed at the opposite end of the love seat. Despite this, Angela reached out and took her hand.

"My dear, how much did you actually know about your fiancé's life before he came to California?"

"A lot . . . and very little. He told me about the death of his wife, for instance . . ."

"Well, just for starters, she isn't dead. She divorced him."

"Oh, I know she divorced him," Edna said. "They weren't married anymore by the time she died."

Privately Angela thought, "I'll check that out. That wasn't the impression Martinez gave me," but she didn't say that aloud.

Instead she merely nodded, "I see" and went on. "Do you know where he spent the past few years?"

"Back in Connecticut," Edna said. "Angela, I really don't understand what you—" She tried in vain to pull her hand from Angela's grasp, but Angela clung tighter.

"Did he tell you he'd been to prison?"

"Prison? Angela, no. Of course he didn't. Because he hadn't. Been to prison, I mean."

"I'm afraid he had, Edna. Lieutenant Martinez found out from the police computer."

"Alexander in prison? Whatever for?"

Instead of answering immediately, Angela said, "Oh, by the way, did you know that wasn't his real name? That he'd changed it?"

"No. No." Edna was clearly bewildered. "I didn't. I don't believe—"

"He was Thomas Alexis Headington, according to the computer. He changed it to Alexander Lightfoot after . . ."

"Well, I'm glad of that," Edna said. "Headington sounds a little clumsy, doesn't it? Three syllables are—Well, I like the name 'Lightfoot' better, anyway. And I never cared for the name 'Thomas' for some reason. I suppose that's because when I was a child, I had a little boy living next door who used to tease me, and his name was Thomas . . . what is it, Angela?" Angela had been staring so fixedly and with such apparent concern at Edna while she rattled on about the name that Edna was forced to notice in spite of herself.

"He changed his name because he went to prison. And he didn't want people to know who he was, after he got out."

"That isn't possible, Angela. None of what you say is possible! What could that dear, sweet man possibly have done that would be so bad he'd go to prison?"

"At that point," Angela said to Caledonia, "things started to happen so fast, I can't remember all the details." She had trotted straight from Edna's room to Caledonia's apartment. In spite of the hour—well past Angela's usual bedtime— Caledonia had been wide-awake, laughing at a rerun of "The Dick Van Dyke Show," and she had answered Angela's knock almost at once.

"Oh, Cal, let me in! Do you have any—well, of course you do, you always do. Give me something to drink, won't you? A little sherry perhaps . . . I could use . . . Oh, Cal, I've had the most awful evening!"

Once Caledonia—alarmed because the usually well-groomed Angela looked positively frazzled—had brought her friend in, seated her, sherried her, and calmed her, she seated herself as well. "Okay, do you feel up to telling me what this is all about now? I thought you were always in bed by nine o'clock, so you could be up with the birds and trotting in to breakfast with our idiots who jog each morning!"

"Well, I thought Edna ought to know what kind of man her fiancé was, so . . ."

"Oh, Angela! My God! You didn't!"

"Yes," Angela confessed sheepishly. "I went upstairs to talk to her." She brought Caledonia through the first moments of her meeting with Edna rapidly, and then got to the climactic point of her revelation of Lightfoot's crime.

"To begin with," Angela said, "she didn't believe me. Oh, she was shocked, of course—I think the word 'criminal' is always a little shocking, you know? But then she got up and walked across to the window and stood looking out a minute . . . I thought she would cry, you see, so that didn't surprise me. But I was shocked when she turned around, because she was laughing! She laughed right out loud! She told me I was mistaken . . . it had to be I'd heard about the wrong man—I'd got the wrong name, or something! There was simply no way her Alex could have done something like that. Period."

"Doesn't surprise me. I'd never have believed it if somebody'd come barging in and told me something nasty like that about Herman! You wouldn't have believed it of Douglas!"

"Well, of course not!"

"So why does it surprise you?"

"Well, because—I don't know, but it was just so—so out of place! You don't expect anyone to laugh at an accusation of fraud and arson! You might not believe the person accused was guilty—but to laugh?"

"Well, you're right about that! Wasn't she outraged that you should think such a thing? That's what I would have been . . ."

"Oh, I'm getting to that part. That came second. At first, when she laughed, I said I didn't find it amusing. On the contrary, it was a very unhappy situation. He'd spent ten years in prison, I said, and there seemed little doubt of his guilt. And that's when she started throwing things."

"Angela! She threw something at you?"

"Not at me. You see, she kept saying it wasn't true and I kept telling her he was the man, all right, and that, whatever she thought, he was a convicted criminal . . . and suddenly she picked up a book and threw it against the wall!"

"But not at you?"

"Well, no. But she wasn't finished. She took up a cushion and threw it, too! She started shouting 'No-No-No' and crying and throwing whatever she could reach. She threw a little box of paper clips and they flew all over . . . and she threw the newspaper . . . she dumped a holder full of magazines and picked them up and threw them again . . ."

"Well, what happened? Did any of that stuff hit you?"

"She wasn't aiming anything. Finally she collapsed onto the love seat in tears. And that's when I made my mistake."

"Oh, no!" Caledonia snorted. "You made your mistake going up there and telling her in the first place! Didn't I warn you—"

"Cal, she had a right to know!"

"So you said! So you said! But why was it your job to tell her?"

"Why, because—because—"

"Because your curiosity bump was so big you just had to find out how much she already knew, right? And you wanted to see her face, to gauge by her expression how she felt about it, right? And you were afraid Martinez would go up there and rob you of your fun, and—"

"Oh, Cal, that's not fair! It wasn't fun! Anyway, at the very end, she did throw something right at me!"

"No kidding! Tell me—"

"She picked up a box of paper . . . she said, 'His letters . . . his letters . . .' and something I didn't quite hear, and then she just threw the whole box. Sort of at me, and sort of up in the air . . ."

"She lobbed it at you underhand, you mean?"

"Well, yes, I guess so ... and she shrieked, 'Get out of here ... get out,' and banged over to the door and flung it open. I didn't wait to be told again, of course ... I simply ran. And she—she pushed me out and slammed the door behind my back!" Angela's voice quivered with outrage. "She pushed me out!"

"Well, tell you the truth, I'm not surprised. Girl, sometimes you haven't got the brains you were born with! In olden days they always killed the messenger who brought the bad news!"

"But I didn't do anything ..."

"Don't I remember your saying you're the big Shakespeare expert? Majored in English lit. in college? Didn't you ever read *Macbeth*? One of the scenes I always remember myself was the one where Macbeth tried to beat up on the poor son of a gun who told him Birnam Wood was moving toward Dunsinane?"

Angela was still quivering with disbelief, so Caledonia tried another tack. "Here, girl—let me get you another drink. I'll get myself one, and we'll talk about something else till you're calm enough to go to bed and get some sleep. Believe me, with the mischief you've got into tonight, you should really sleep well. You must be exhausted!"

Chapter 13

THE NEXT morning, to Angela's surprise, was shrouded in a fine sea mist. "It's all the wrong season for this," she grumbled to herself as she walked to the dining room for breakfast. "I really don't expect fog till winter." As surprising to her as the fog was her own prickly sense of malaise. The nearly empty dining room that greeted her didn't help much to ease her vague sense of something wrong or something missing.

"This must be the way dogs and cats feel just before an earthquake," she muttered to herself as she hesitated at the juice bar, poured herself a glass of orange juice, and carried it to her customary table by the garden window.

Of course Caledonia did not come in to breakfast, nor did Angela expect her. Angela didn't expect to see Tom Brighton either, for the weather would affect his arthritis severely, she was sure. And she was grateful not to see Edna Ferrier anywhere among the few diners who had already arrived. The Graingers were usually up early, but they customarily ate in their own cottage, so she could not find a way to insinuate herself into their company and perhaps ask a few questions. Conchita Cassidy was on duty, but running from one task to another, and as more residents arrived, she obviously became much too busy to stop and talk about personal affairs.

It was going to be, Angela told herself disgustedly, a wasted morning. Then she felt a light tap on her arm, heard a diffident clearing of the throat . . . and turned to see the rabbity face of Wallace Clayton.

"Ah, Mrs. Ah—Mrs. Benbow? I wonder if I might . . . that is, would it be an imposition if I joined you for breakfast?"

"For breakfast?" Angela said blankly. "With me?"

"Oh, I'd pay for my own," Wallace said hastily. "I am not asking you to be my hostess *de facto*. But I would like the chance to talk to you and I would like to have some breakfast, and this seems the perfect way to combine the two objectives. If you do not mind?"

"Oh. I see. No, certainly not. Please sit down."

"Mrs. Ah—the other lady . . . Mrs. Ah—She's not coming to breakfast?"

Angela smiled wryly. "Not unless today is judgment day and only those at breakfast can expect to be saved. I can think of very few things for which Caledonia would voluntarily get out of bed and come to breakfast before at least nine o'clock."

Clayton looked skittishly at his watch. "Oh. I see. And it's only—well, just after seven, isn't it?"

"Please do sit down. I don't mind a little company in the least. I'm finding the weather a bit more depressing than I usually do. Ordinarily I'm not a weather person."

"Weather person?"

"You know. One of those people who are so affected by the weather that they can't control their moods. They're only smiling when the sun's out and they feel like grim death when it's raining. I never seem to mind what the weather's like—it's just another fact of life. Something outside me. At least it usually is. Today, though . . ." She shrugged and gestured to the chair across the table.

Wallace pulled it out and took his largish umbrella off his arm, to lay it carefully under his chair. "Fog is like rain," he said apologetically. "And this linen suit seems to wrinkle easily . . ."

"Aren't you out a bit early yourself?"

"Well, perhaps. But I wanted to be here when Edna rose . . . and I certainly wanted a chance to talk to you first. You see . . . Oh, thank you!" He had both arms on the table, leaning across to talk earnestly, but in an undertone, and he moved his elbow aside sharply as Chita Cassidy slid a cup of coffee in near his place. "Toast and jam and some fruit juice, please, miss, while I'm waiting. And for my meal— two fried eggs and some bacon . . ."

"Two slices?"

"Certainly!" He looked annoyed.

"They ordinarily only serve one, unless you ask," Angela explained. "Too much sodium for our diets. But guests sometimes ignore that and ask for extra."

"Oh. I see. Well, two slices, yes. And perhaps an English muffin. With marmalade."

"The juice is over on the bar," Chita said. "But I'll be happy to pour you some. What kind do your prefer? We have most of the usual . . ."

"Oh, prune juice, by all means," he said. "Thank you. Yes, a generous glass of prune juice, please, Now, Mrs. Benbow . . ."

Angela had been gazing over his shoulder, watching in awe the entrance of the Jackson twins, arm in arm, wearing hair ribbons of pink chiffon tied into large, floppy bows and identical pink "model coats" with large, floppy, puffed sleeves and huge, floppy flowers appliqued on the pockets. Angela turned her attention with gratitude back to Wallace.

"Edna phoned me last night after your visit to her, Mrs. Benbow."

"Oh, dear . . ."

"Yes. In my view, she was nearly hysterical. She told me of your accusations against . . . against her late fiancé. I phoned your resident doctor—Dr. Ah—I forget his name . . ."

"Carter. Dr. Carter."

"Yes. Carter. Ah—I asked him to come and give her a sedative. She was weeping and ranting . . ."

"Oh, dear!" Angela said. "That's all my fault, I'm afraid. Did Dr. Carter get her calmed down?"

Wallace nodded. "He phoned me some time later to assure me she was sleeping soundly at last and would till this morning. So I didn't feel it necessary to come over here last night."

"Did she tell you what it was all about? I mean, what Lightfoot is supposed to have done? Who he is supposed to be?"

"Some man who'd gone to prison for arson. And for defrauding an insurance company. Yes. Thoroughly reprehensible crimes, both of them. Mrs. Benbow, is it all true? Oh, thank you . . ." Chita had set down his coffee and the prune juice, which Wallace seized and gulped eagerly. "Delicious!"

"Mr. Clayton." Angela was delighted that he had not renewed his request to be on a first-name basis. "Mr. Clayton, it's true. I'm sorry to say that Alexander Lightfoot was not a nice man."

Clayton sighed and finished his prune juice in one more enormous gulp that set his Adam's apple wobbling. "Ahhhh . . . nothing like prune juice to start the morning right." Then he sighed and shook his head. "I didn't like the man. I've told you that. I thought Edna was mistaken about him. But I never—never in a million years—would have guessed what kind of villain he truly was! Please pass the cream . . ."

Angela obliged. "None of us would have guessed. He seemed so ordinary and . . . and nice. At least, I thought . . . oh, here's your toast and jam."

"Thank you, miss," Wallace said, grabbing hungrily at the toast and slathering a piece with the pineapple-apricot preserves Chita had set down beside his plate. "Delicious. I must find out where they get this jam! Now—you were saying?"

"Yes. I was saying that he didn't look like a criminal. But then I don't suppose most criminals look anything other than normal. Murderers, I'm told, look very ordinary. At least, the ones I've met have. Like you and me. It's hard to tell . . ."

Clayton ladled jam onto a second piece of toast and crammed it greedily into his mouth.

["You'd have thought he had been told that a cloud of locusts was approaching," Angela told Caledonia later. "My stars, but that man can pack food away, and the richer the better! It's really a star turn in gluttony, when he eats!"]

"Mrs. Benbow," Wallace went on, moving the now empty toast plate aside as Chita came into the room with the main course of eggs and bacon—two of everything and a buttered muffin for him, one egg and a small sausage for Angela. "Mrs. Benbow, I really came this morning partly to see how Edna is doing after her emotional upset of last night and partly to thank you for telling her about Lightfoot."

"To thank me?"

"Yes, it seems to me it will in the long run help her to erase that unfortunate episode in her life—to wash her mind clear of it so she will stop behaving as though the world were going to end because that dreadful man is gone! And she will start acting like herself again!

"Mrs. Benbow, I have taken great pleasure in my sister-in-law's company, over the recent years. And I have missed her, while she was gradually more and more involved with this Lightfoot fellow. And when she announced she was going to marry him—well, it seemed she had no more time for *me* at all. I don't believe I saw her, except in the line of business, more than three times in as many months. That was not a situation I enjoyed. I am a lonely man, Mrs. Benbow. Since my own dear wife, Edna's sister, died, I have depended on my few friends and my only relatives to fill my life. And Edna has been a real part of my existence."

"This period of mourning, when she confined herself to her room and wouldn't talk to people—this must have been very hard on you, Mr. Clayton."

"Ah," he said beaming proudly. "But she saw *me*, you see. She didn't shut *me* out. Edna and I have enjoyed a very special relationship in the past, and I had hopes it would be restored, now that Lightfoot was gone. All the same, the mourning was going on entirely too long. It was time she came back to the real world, as I told her repeatedly.

"Before this Lightfoot came into her life, she and I used to take an excursion almost every week. Delightful times. An afternoon on Cabrillo Point watching naval ships coming and going—a boat trip to watch migrating whales—a luncheon up at the marina in Oceanside—an evening seeing the living masterpieces tableau at the Laguna art festival . . . I really looked forward to doing those things again. But she just wasn't quite ready, she said, for that sort of joyful experience. She felt too sad. So I waited . . . but it was drawing out too long. Too long."

It was amazing, Angela thought, that he could keep right on talking and eating at the same time, without seeming to pause in either activity.

"I had become, I admit it, impatient. And now—now that she knows that her mourning is wasted—that Lightfoot was a thoroughly unworthy person altogether . . . now perhaps she will come to her senses and perhaps a normal life is not out of the question for her. Soon. And I am really most grateful to you, Mrs. Benbow. For your news may have shown the way for dear Edna to return to the world . . ."

Angela found herself feeling quite sorry for the little man, although the way he was packing away the food, she privately thought that one day soon he'd be a big fat man, instead of a little skinny one.

"And now," he said, wiping away the butter that had dripped from his English muffin onto his chin, "I really must go to see how dear Edna is getting on. I know this will be a difficult time for her—in a way, much more difficult than the man's actual death! But like the surgeon who cuts and causes pain in order to bring health, sometimes one must cause mental anguish in order to promote healing. And I feel, my dear lady, that is what you have done for Edna. She's going to be better off in the long run.

"In a way," he went on, "this is a relief. I feel my assessment of the man has been vindicated. One is uncomfortable, going on blind instinct alone. To dislike him was a powerful and overwhelming response, but I could never have proved to anyone—that is, I could never have justified my attitude. Your revelation, on the other hand, shows that I was right all along! Ah . . . look there. The sun is coming out!"

Angela glanced into the garden. The fog was indeed lifting and faint, watery sunshine was painting the leaves with silver that would, within an hour, turn to midmorning gold.

"That goes right along with my mood, my dear lady. Mrs. Ah—Mrs. Benbow . . . thank you again . . ." He took her hand with his and to her dismay, she realized that despite his pat-pat-patting his mouth over and over again with his napkin, his fingers were still slippery with butter. "I am most grateful to you, and I wanted you to know that. And thank you for letting me be your breakfast companion . . ."

"Oh, before you go, Mr. Clayton, let me extend my condolences about your secretary."

"My secretary?" Clayton looked absolutely blank.

"About her horrid death. What a shock it must have been to you."

"Oh, yes, of course," Clayton said. "A real shock. But life goes on. The worst thing to me personally is the inconvenience."

"The inconvenience?"

"Yes. They've closed and locked the office. They won't let me back in till they've finished whatever it is they do at the scene of a crime. They came to my house to tell me Miss Stoner had died, they brought me down to the office to see if there was anything missing, and then—can you believe it—they wouldn't let me take anything home with me. Not even my little computer . . . not a one of my files. Well, naturally, I protested. But it was really no use. Ah well . . . at least it's not income tax time, is it? I can wait to get at my records. And now to pleasanter things. Good day, dear lady." And with that he turned and walked almost jauntily away, whistling softly. Angela recognized the tune, a song of celebration from an old musical called *Hit the Deck!* He was whistling "Hallelujah"!

"Callous little beast! So he ran off to be with Edna, did he?" Caledonia asked after Angela had come to her cottage to report on the encounter. "To comfort her, I have no doubt."

"To ask her to go on a picnic, probably," Angela said sourly. Her own idea of purgatory would be a picnic—sitting on the ground, fighting off ants and mosquitoes, getting cramps in the legs and chill on the bottom while eating tuna salad or cold fried chicken and discovering someone had forgotten to pack the salt . . .

"Well, what do you care if they go on a picnic?" Caledonia said. "As long as he doesn't expect you to go along!"

"Cal, he seemed so happy! It was downright strange. I felt awful about upsetting Edna like that, but he was really pleased. Too pleased to even spend a minute mourning poor Miss Stoner. You know something? I think Unmitigated Wallace was jealous of Alexander! I think he had designs on Edna himself!"

"Well, maybe he did, and maybe . . ."

Just at that point, there was a knock at Caledonia's screen door and Lieutenant Martinez was there, bowing lightly and smiling in greeting. "Ladies, may I come in?"

"Oh, wonderful, Lieutenant," Caledonia trumpeted.

"We've been hoping for an update," Angela said. "We thought you might come back here yesterday after you'd been to see the Graingers . . ."

Martinez eased gracefully into the room and sat down on

the edge of one of Caledonia's antique chairs—gently, as
though he feared he might break it. "That was a session I
wouldn't like to repeat. I'm used to people in distress. It's
part of my job. But I really don't take any pleasure in it.
Especially when nice people like the Graingers are upset."

"What happened?" Angela pressed him. "Come on, you
promised to tell us . . ."

"I will. In a minute," he agreed. "But I have another reason for this visit . . . I'm looking into one more loose end
while my men are starting back over the ground we've already covered. Mrs. Wingate, you're something of a friend
of Sam Dunlop's, aren't you?"

Caledonia was puzzled. "You know I am. I know you remember that he came to me hoping I'd ask you to go easy
on his secretary at the lumberyard. What is this, anyway?
Has something happened to Sam?"

"No, ma'am . . . not that I know of. But . . . Mrs.
Wingate, did you know his wife Felicia?"

She nodded. "A real tramp. Ran off with a salesman who
used to call at the lumberyard. In those days Felicia did
Sam's office work, and she saw this fellow every time he
came through. Made goo-goo eyes at him, and eventually
she got what she wanted. They took off together. I thought
it would kill old Sam at the time. But he seems to have recovered nicely, though he's never married again."

"Would you say he really loved his former wife?"

"At the time, yes. But he got very bitter . . . Why? Has
Felicia come to the surface again?"

"Well, in a manner of speaking. But Felicia Taggart—as
she was before she married Sam Dunlop—was from Connecticut and worked in a beauty parlor there. In a shopping
mall."

Angela could stay out of the conversation no longer.
"Lieutenant, you're not going to tell us she was one of the
witnesses in Lightfoot's trial, are you? That would be a coincidence of the wildest sort, and not the kind you believe
in!"

"Believe in it or not, Felicia Taggart certainly was manager at the shop where Mrs. Headington had her appointment on the day of the crime. And Felicia's was the testimony that almost got Headington-Lightfoot acquitted, till the two women from the parking lot showed up."

"Oh, peanut butter!"

"I beg your pardon?"

"Just a substitute for real profanity, Lieutenant," Caledonia growled. "This is going to upset Sam horribly and I'm very fond of him. How in blue blazes did you find out about Felicia though? It was so long ago . . ."

"I have now read everything there was in newspapers and official files about that trial, Mrs. Wingate. And of course I made some effort to trace the main actors in the drama. It occurred to me that someone might have carried a grudge and waited for Headington-Lightfoot till he got out of prison . . ."

"But he's been out of jail for years and years, hasn't he? Why would someone from his past wait so long to hunt him up?"

"Maybe they couldn't find him right away. He did change his name, change his appearance—though not enough, and I'll mention that in a moment—and move to the opposite coast."

"But if somebody wanted revenge on him, it wouldn't be a casual witness, surely. And I can't imagine the insurance company sending out a hit man," Angela protested. "I'd say the only one likely to bear him a grudge was his poor ex-wife. After all, he lied to her. And burned down their house."

"No possibilities there. Lightfoot's ex-wife is dead."

"Then that's one thing he was truthful about at least," Angela said. "He told Edna that his wife was dead."

"Well, what about Felicia? Right now, I'm more concerned about Sam than about theoretical characters from Lightfoot's shadowy past," Caledonia said. "For instance, how did you find out Felicia Taggart and Felicia Dunlop were the same person, Lieutenant?"

"We've asked about every single person associated with that trial and traced them, insofar as we could, till we were sure they weren't in or near Camden at the time Lightfoot went under that train. We got interested in Felicia Taggart when we heard that she left town after telling all her friends that she was going to California to get into the movies."

"Of course!" Caledonia exploded. "Just like that silly little chippy!"

"I had Shorty looking through casting directories and old phone books and public records up in the Hollywood–L.A. area."

"And that's where you found her?"

"Right. She applied for a driver's license as Felicia Taggart with a Hollywood address. A few months later she changed her address with the DMV to Camden. A few more months and she changed the name to Felicia Dunlop and listed Sam's address as hers. Then it was no great trick to find their marriage license with her maiden name on it."

Angela was clearly excited. "Oh, what a wonderful piece of detective work! And now you think maybe Sam knew, through his wife, who this Alexander Lightfoot really was and killed him! But why? Why would he do that? Lightfoot didn't do anything to Felicia!"

"Well, damage is hard to assess in cases like this. Some of the dirt involved rubs off on everyone. Felicia became somewhat notorious, back in Connecticut. People who knew her always remembered that she was the defense witness who nearly got Lightfoot off. Maybe that's part of the reason she left for California—that and wanting to be in the movies, of course."

Caledonia shook her head. "Lieutenant, I think you're barking up the wrong lumberyard here. Just to begin with, Sam Dunlop is a gentle, honest man who wouldn't hurt a fly!"

"Mrs. Wingate, I've heard the same thing about every

second murderer I've arrested. There's always somebody to protest, 'He'd never do a thing like that!' "

"Maybe so. But in this case, it's the truth. But it's more than his gentle nature—it's that he was so sour about Felicia's deserting him, he wouldn't have lifted a finger to avenge her honor—or whatever you think he'd have been protecting by pushing Lightfoot under that train. Why, he took her belongings and dumped them into the street the week after she left, and the city collected them for the municipal landfill."

Martinez smiled but said nothing. Caledonia persisted, "Lieutenant, trust me, he wouldn't lift a finger to fish the woman out if she was drowning right in front of him, let alone committing a murder for the sake of her past reputation! You're wasting your time!"

"That's about half my job, wasting time. Like the fisherman who trolls up and down, up and down. Most of what he does is wasted, but if just one fish bites . . ."

"Lieutenant, you were going to tell us about the Graingers, weren't you?" Angela said. "For my part, I'll take Cal's word that Sam Dunlop isn't involved. But Fred Grainger now . . ."

Martinez smiled. "Oh, I'll tell you the gist of it. The substance is this: the Graingers recognized Lightfoot from pictures at the time of his trial. They paid special attention back then—even saved some newspaper clippings—because, they said, they lived in Westport, practically next door to where it all happened, and there'd been several suspicious fires in their own town. They wondered if there was a connection . . ."

"And was there?"

"No. At least, not that we know of. But they followed the trial because of that—and because of Dr. Grainger's profession."

"His profession?" Angela sounded skeptical. "But he was a pediatrician. What has that to do with insurance fraud and arson?"

"Nothing much. But remember that Dr. Grainger is getting terribly confused, and while he was talking to me, Lightfoot and the fire and his little patients got all tangled up in his mind . . . I did understand him to say that he used to worry about 'his children,' as he called them. And especially the ones whose parents couldn't afford health insurance. Well, he kept telling me that was Lightfoot's fault."

"But that's impossible! I mean, how could that be?"

"Well, insurance fraud is not really a victimless crime, although every insurance cheat we've run up against will tell you they've hurt nobody, since they only took money from a big company that had plenty of money to spare. The truth is, the insurance companies charge those losses off against all the rest of their customers; you and me—we pay. In higher premiums."

"Yes, yes—" Caledonia said, impatiently. "But what on earth has the increased cost of home insurance because of fraud got to do with children who can't afford medical insurance?"

Martinez shook his head. "Not much. But as I said, it all got tangled up in the old man's head. To him, Lightfoot was some kind of symbol of the degenerate state of morals of the world that, in his view, had meant pain and suffering for innocent children."

Angela bit her lip. "Well, Dr. Grainger sounds obsessive to me!"

"Oh, surely you're exaggerating," Caledonia said.

"You didn't see him, Cal, with the wind blowing his hair around, and the storm clouds behind him. Definitely menacing."

"All the same," Martinez went on, "however menacing you thought him yesterday, I don't believe he's a true obsessive. Mrs. Wingate vouches for Sam Dunlop on what she knows of his personality and behavior—and my feeling about Grainger is like that. It's little things. For instance, Mrs. Grainger told me that her husband threw away all those clippings about the trial when they were discarding things for the move west. An obsessive would have kept the clippings. Mrs. Grainger told me they hadn't even spoken about the case in years, nor thought about it so far as she knew—not till Dr. Grainger recognized Lightfoot. And I believe her."

"How did they recognize Lightfoot, by the way? I know it doesn't matter," Angela said. "But all the same—"

"It was the time they all went to the zoo. Lightfoot got to spinning yarns for some children. The adults stood aside and waited for him . . . but as they watched him talking and gesturing, a little distance away, something clicked for Fred Grainger. The Graingers had seen a lot of Lightfoot on television, after all, when he was Thomas Headington. And somehow . . . well, Grainger told me he'd been nagged all along by something familiar-looking about Lightfoot. In spite of the beard."

"Yes, Edna says the beard really didn't change Lightfoot all that much," Angela said. "Of course, she put it down to her artistic vision that, so far as she was concerned, he'd have looked about the same with or without the beard. But apparently even Grainger could see through the curtain of hair. Lieutenant, do you suppose he's homicidal? Unbalanced?" Angela felt more depressed than she had been when the fog was blanketing the garden earlier. "Oh, I hate this whole business. I don't really know Dr. Grainger well, and he did rather frighten me, but Mrs. Grainger seems so nice, and . . ."

"He doesn't seem in the least dangerous, to me," Martinez said soothingly. "Though I will surely have him checked out by the psychiatrist we sometimes work with. She ought to be able to tell me whether or not he's a 'possible' for my list of suspects. But right now, it looks highly unlikely. He'd be more likely to break down and weep than to commit a murder. He's that kind of person now . . . and he probably always was."

"Well, it was a theory, anyhow," Angela said. "But I'm glad if you think it's a silly theory."

"No theory is silly, and nothing's completely ruled out," Martinez said. "But I think you can put that one on the shelf."

"How are the Graingers doing?" Caledonia asked. "It must have been upsetting for both of them, having you question them. And especially if Dr. Grainger started raving . . ."

"Well, I think they're calm enough now. There were a lot of tears, as I told you, and a lot of harsh words—mostly about Lightfoot. Incidentally, they stayed so far away from Lightfoot and Edna, after Dr. Grainger recognized him, that they hadn't even realized she intended to marry the man. They might have roused themselves to tell her about him, if they had learned of the engagement, but I don't think they'd have killed him to prevent the wedding, any more than they'd have killed him for abstract vengeance."

"Perhaps we should call on them again," Angela suggested reluctantly. "He makes me nervous, but she's so sweet . . . and they weren't at breakfast, which might mean they're still quite . . ."

"Angela," Caledonia said, "leave them alone with each other for a while. We'll stay out of it, Lieutenant. I promise."

"Oh, speaking of breakfast," Angela jumped nimbly to a subject related only in her private thoughts, "unmitigated Wallace was there. I meant to tell you, Lieutenant. Wallace was as delighted to hear about Lightfoot's background as the Graingers were horrified at the discovery!"

"He was?" Martinez seemed mildly surprised. "I wonder why?"

"We think he's sweet on Edna," Caledonia snorted. "He was sorry she was upset by what Lightfoot was, but he thinks it's for the best that . . ."

"Upset? Does Mrs. Ferrier know about Lightfoot's background?" Martinez asked. "If she knew about him all along, of course, that would be . . ."

Angela had the grace to blush. "No-no-no . . . I told her.

Well, I thought she should know, you see. It didn't seem right, somehow, for us all to realize what a shabby kind of person he was, and for her to still see him as a knight in shining armor . . . So . . ."

"So Angela went right upstairs last evening and spilled the beans!"

"I should have known!" Martinez closed his eyes and took a deep breath. "Mrs. Benbow, I'd have preferred to tell her myself. So I could gauge her reaction firsthand, and . . ."

"Lieutenant, you should be glad I did it instead of you," Angela defended herself. "Her reaction was violent! Absolutely wild! She threw things at me—sofa cushions and an ornament from the desk and a box of his letters . . ."

"She threw them at you?"

"Well, not exactly. She threw sort of in my general direction and at the floor, really. I never thought she was trying to hit me. Though she did! I mean, those letters hit me as they fell . . ."

"Lieutenant," Caledonia said, "from what Angela tells me, Edna was just reacting the way a child might if it was told a beloved pet was dead—as though by saying 'No' and striking out at the truth you could make it not be true! You see what I mean?"

"I do indeed. I've been the bearer of bad tidings many times. It's a professional hazard. And sometimes the person getting the bad news lashes out at me! As though I had done something. I always thought it was wanting to hurt back, after you've been hurt—and when there's nobody or nothing you can really get at, you strike at the nearest available person . . ."

"Maybe so," Angela sniffed. "But I was pretty upset by it, I can tell you."

"I dare say you were, dear lady," Martinez soothed. "That's another reason I wish you'd let me tell her. I'm used to bearing the brunt of such violent reactions and it wouldn't have bothered me. Your instincts were good—but you had a bad experience I'd like to have spared you."

Angela beamed at him, mollified and forgiving of his having scolded her.

"I'd venture to say, if your report is accurate and if Mrs. Ferrier is not a superb actress, that Lightfoot's double identity was a complete surprise to her, then. At least, that is a reaction I associate with surprise."

"I'd say she was stunned, all right," Angela said.

"Then there goes another motive for murder," Martinez said. "It was always possible that Mrs. Ferrier had found out about Lightfoot's past and killed him herself—possibly in a rage because he deceived her, or because she feared being humiliated before her friends."

"Kill someone for embarrassment? Do people really do that, Lieutenant?" Angela asked.

"Oh, absolutely. Saving face is not a small matter, to some people. There are people in the world who simply cannot stand to be wrong. And to admit to one's friends that one had been about to marry a felon—a former convict—well, that would have been enough to turn love into rage and hatred, for some women. Especially women"—he hesitated, then went on tactfully—"women of her generation."

"Edna's not that kind," Angela said firmly. "Absolutely not. And anyhow, she didn't know before I told her. I'd swear to that."

Martinez sighed. "I hope you're right, Mrs. Benbow. I hope you're as shrewd a judge of character as I believe you to be. For the moment, I'll take your word for it. Well, I must be on my way ..."

"To question my friend Sam Dunlop?"

"Yes. Among others. We're talking to everybody who knew Lightfoot at all, and most of them we've talked to before. But we have nowhere else to look, right now, so we're talking to his garage mechanic, his druggist, his grocery clerk, and all his neighbors. We've spent a long time with the engineer of the train that struck him."

"The engineer? He's not a suspect, surely."

"Neither are Lightfoot's neighbors. Yet. We thought the engineer might have seen something and remembered— perhaps someone running beside the track, perhaps Lightfoot reeling and dizzy and falling toward the train, perhaps a fleeting glimpse of two people gesturing and threatening as though they were quarreling . . ."

"And?"

"Nothing. Of course those trains travel pretty fast. He didn't even know the train had hit anything till we told him, late on the day of the accident."

"Accident?"

Martinez shrugged. "Well, it was an accident so far as the engineer of the train was concerned. And it may turn out that Lightfoot simply fell under the wheels, after all."

"Oh, surely not!" Caledonia and Martinez grinned at each other, at the disappointed exclamation from Angela. "I mean . . . well, what about Miss Stoner's murder?" Angela went on. "You can't say she died from falling under that bookend by accident, now can you?"

Martinez smiled. "Of course not. But the death of Miss Stoner may be unrelated to the death of Lightfoot in any way."

"You don't believe that. You said you don't believe in coincidence . . ." Angela protested.

"But there is such a thing. And once in a while it does operate, whatever I like to believe. Look at the coincidence of Felicia Taggart Dunlop's ending up here in the same town as Lightfoot did. Now, ladies . . . I'll stop by again to-morrow or the next day. In the meantime, do keep your ears to the ground, but don't anticipate us. I mean, don't make announcements or ask questions that we'd rather do our-selves." The warning sounded stern, but he smiled fondly at them as he said it. And then he was gone.

"Whatever he says, I simply don't believe the two deaths

could possibly be coincidence," Angela protested. "But what link could there be between them?"

Caledonia shrugged. "Heaven knows—and we certainly don't. I mean, we don't know enough to even guess. We hardly know of any connection between Miss Stoner and Alexander Lightfoot, now do we? Except that she worked for Wallace Clayton, and Clayton is sweet on Lightfoot's fiancée!"

"Ah-ha! But we do know someone we can ask—someone who does know more about Stoner than we do." Angela crowed. "Unmitigated Wallace is probably still with Edna! Now, suppose we were to drop by to call on her, and . . ."

"No! Absolutely not! You've done enough damage to poor Edna, and she wouldn't be glad to see you today."

"Well, then, how about this? We go into the lobby and when Wallace leaves Edna, we ambush him for some more questions. What do you say to that?"

"Okay. It sounds harmless enough to me," Caledonia agreed, hoisting herself out of her chair. "Time I got a little exercise for today anyhow. The walk up to the main building will be about right, especially since I have to do that walk in an hour anyhow, when lunchtime comes . . . I might as well do it now. And then I can see you don't get into any trouble. Come along . . ."

Chapter 14

ORDINARILY, ANGELA and Caledonia—or anyone else entering the vast cavern of the nearly empty lobby with its marble floors, its classically gloomy decor, and its outsized furniture—would have plunked down onto the nearest couch to wait for whatever event or person or appointment had brought them to the echoing, heavily shadowed space. Newcomers might wish to gaze in awe at the fireplace, whose conical copper hood was large enough to serve as a teepee for a family of Cheyenne. Or at the mammoth oak cocktail table on which a Lippizaner stallion could have performed a capriole. Residents of Camden-sur-Mer noticed neither the fireplace nor the immense proportions of the furniture. They merely wished to sit down at their earliest opportunity. Old legs are not up to much strolling around for no good purpose.

In the case of Angela and Caledonia, since they had entered from the garden doors, the nearest seat would have been a couch that stood almost squarely in front of the desk and its switchboard, and that lay on the edge of the only patch of sunshine that oozed from the garden into the cool darkness of the shadowy lobby. But they walked resolutely past that couch, seeking a position more likely to afford them a view of the paths by which Wallace Clayton might leave the building's second floor.

They needed to be able to see both staircases—the main stairs, broad and carpeted with a curving banister, down which movie queens had once made leisurely entrances to the delight of fans waiting in the lobby—and the smaller utility stairs residents used when the elevator failed, also carpeted but narrow and laid out in straight, no-nonsense lines. And of course there was the elevator itself, next to the desk and about midway between the two stairways.

And that, as Angela pointed out to Caledonia, was about it. "Unless maybe Wallace is eccentric enough to take one of the service stairways in some other part of the building. Of course he'd have no reason on earth to use one of them unless he was trying to avoid us. And unless he's telepathic, he doesn't know we're waiting for him. So he'll come down one of the three ways we can see from . . . yes, I'd say we can see everything from just about here . . ." Caledonia stopped her forward progress abruptly in front of the fireplace, just about opposite the elevator entrance, and with a good line of sight to the foot of each of the stairways that entered the lobby—the grand staircase to their right, the utility stairs to their left.

"Perfect," Angela said. "You've picked a spot that will give us a reason for being here!"

"What do you mean, a reason for . . . Oh, peanut butter!" Caledonia realized that she was standing squarely in front of and almost touching the wrought-iron bird cage. At her outburst of annoyance, the little blue parakeet backed away from her to the far end of its perch, emitting its meaningless *chirrrk* . . .

"Listen to me, birdy," Caledonia said, bringing her face close to the bars and fixing the bird with a firm, unblinking eye. "If you and I are going to coexist for the next few minutes, you have to promise me to stay over there on the far side of your cage. I don't mind pretending to look at you, but I draw the line at actually fraternizing with you. So you keep your distance, do you hear?"

"Highly irregular," the bird said clearly.

"I don't know about that," Caledonia snapped. "It must

be apparent even to a birdbrain that I don't like you. And you don't seem to like me one bit better . . ."

"Same to your cat!" the bird remarked, eyeing her with what appeared to be simmering suspicion.

"And yours!" Caledonia said vigorously. "Just don't come close to me."

The bird uttered the deep, pained sigh it had borrowed from Tom Brighton and stared fixedly past her into the shadowy lobby beyond. It seemed to be ignoring her by an act of will.

"Good . . . good . . . we're beginning to understand each other, I see. I wonder when this little beast is going to be retrieved by its owners? It can't stay here forever . . . I hope."

"Oh, I meant to tell you, Cal," Angela said. "It is the property of Camden-sur-Mer. It belonged to Mrs. Roderick—"

"The lady who was moving in here a few months ago and had a stroke during the move? The one who was taken directly into the health facility across the street instead?"

"That's her. Clara told me the other day that Mrs. Roderick's family came and took most of her possessions away. They've decided she never will be able to live anywhere again but in hospital care, poor thing. Anyhow, the family decided they didn't want the bird, and Clara says Torgeson agreed to keep him. For the residents."

"For the residents' what? There isn't enough of him to fry for dinner."

"Oh, Cal! For our amusement, of course! Something to look at when we're in the lobby. A bright spot! Goodness knows this gloomy old place could stand something bright. And besides, lots of the people here used to own pets, and they miss having an animal around."

Caledonia groaned. "Animal! I don't call this little ball of feathers an animal!"

"Well, he's not a vegetable, for goodness' sake!" Angela's response was tart.

"That isn't what I meant and you know it. When I say 'animal,' I mean something soft and cuddly with fur on it ... something you can stroke and hold ... not a sharp-eyed, feather-covered pterodactyl with claws to slice you and a beak to tear you. You saw what this vicious beastie did when Grogan stuck a finger into the cage ..."

"Oh, Cal, he was just startled."

"He sure was. He yelled bloody murder!"

"I mean the bird was startled. Grogan probably poked that finger at him like a weapon. I don't think the bird would hurt anybody who came at him gently ... Look." And Angela moved next to the cage and very softly, very slowly, put her finger inside the bars, close to the far end of the bird's perch. The bird focused baleful eyes on the finger.

"You see?" Angela said triumphantly, turning to look at Caledonia. "He doesn't mind if you don't seem to menace him ... he's really—*OUCH!*"

The bird had sidled the length of the perch, leaned down, and taken the finger in his beak. Of course he couldn't truly bite—but he gave it the best nip he was capable of, pinching and twisting at the same time. Angela jerked her finger away, and her yelp sent the bird *chirrrk*ing and fluttering to the far end of the perch, where it huddled sourly, glaring out at them.

"That vicious little ... Did you see what he did to me? He—he bit me! He bit *me!*"

Caledonia was gleeful. "Oh, the poor little innocent is harmless, isn't hims! Hims wouldn't hurt anybody, would hims? Angela, maybe next time you'll take my word for it. That little fellow may be a canary, but he thinks he's a crocodile! You brought that on yourself. Don't go sticking your fingers in his cage anymore, if you don't want trouble. He's a feisty little devil, and—oh-oh!"

Swinging down the utility stairs came the jaunty little

linen-clad figure of Wallace Clayton, adjusting his bow tie, whistling softly and cheerfully as he came. Caledonia recognized the song: *"Let me call you sweetheart, I'm in love with you . . ."*

"He must be feeling good," she growled under her breath.

He saw them and altered his course to come near to them. "Ah, Mrs. Ah . . . Benbow and Mrs. Ah—Mrs. Ah—"

"Wingate," Caledonia supplied graciously, with her most autocratic manner firmly in place. "It's Wingate, Mr. Clayton. And I wonder if you could spare us a moment of your time?"

"Certainly. Delighted. I am, as you know, a retired man with time on my hands, and I . . ."

"I thought you ran an accounting business!" Angela blurted.

"Well, in name only. The office has been a convenient place to keep records and to separate business from personal matters, where my sister-in-law is concerned. I'll tell you the truth, ladies, I'm thinking of closing that office now." He sighed. "You see, it occurred to me, after I moved out here, that I might take on a few clients—perhaps keep working a while longer. I continued to do Edna's financial work for her, as you probably remember my telling you the other day. But somehow it just didn't work out."

"You didn't get any clients?" Angela asked innocently, as though she didn't really know.

"Alas, no. I didn't do any advertising, of course. But I'd have thought someone might take a chance and choose an accountant at random, perhaps some new arrival to the area might stroll past the office or pick my name from the phone book. Well, of course my office has a second-floor location, so I'm not very visible. And though I have a business phone listed in the directory, I didn't bother to advertise in the yellow pages. So I suppose my hope of getting more clients was foredoomed to failure. Miss Stoner often despaired that we would ever have a flourishing business and I know she fretted about it."

He smiled apologetically. "Actually, she fretted about practically everything. My health—my laundry—what I ate for lunch . . . Sometimes it got genuinely annoying. I've become quite self-sufficient since my wife passed away. I neither need nor welcome someone fussing over me."

"What I can't see," Caledonia said, "is why you kept the office open at all. Was it merely to make your work for your sister-in-law seem legitimate?"

"Legitimate?" His back stiffened in protest. "I assure you . . ."

"No, don't get me wrong. I'm sure it was perfectly honest." Caledonia did not, of course, choose to amplify the remark by saying how she knew he was honest. "What I meant was—well, Edna might have balked at forcing an otherwise retired accountant to continue to work just for her special benefit. She might have wanted to hire another expert instead of you. Just trying to be thoughtful. So you avoided that argument with her by appearing to have a business going in town."

Clayton's thin lips twisted into a rueful little smile. "My goodness, Mrs. Ah—Mrs. Ah—Wingate. You are perceptive indeed. That is exactly the way it was!"

"I see," Angela said. "I see. You really didn't care whether you had other customers or not."

He inclined his head. "Exactly. Oh, it's been a nuisance to have the office closed. But as I told you this morning, there's nothing there that can't wait till the police seal is off the door."

Caledonia walked a few steps away and settled her bulk onto the nearest overstuffed sofa, gesturing him to sit beside her. He moved rather reluctantly and sat gingerly on the edge of the cushion. Angela came and perched herself on the other side of him.

"What did your secretary think of all that?" Caledonia

said, as she waved him in to a landing beside her. "Your Miss Stoner."

"Miss Stoner?" He seemed a little surprised. "What would she have to say about it anyway? She is only—she *was* only my secretary! I wasn't accountable to her. It wasn't any of her business if I chose to run an office as . . . as . . ."

"As window dressing? As camouflage to help you do what you really wanted to do—work for Edna's welfare?"

"Well put, Mrs. Ah—Wingate. It was a form of camouflage, of course. But I would hardly confide that to Miss Stoner! Naturally!"

"So she thought the business was real? Just that it was unsuccessful?"

"Yes, Mrs. Ah—Wingate. I suppose it's fair to say that's true."

"You know, I don't understand why you hired Miss Stoner at all!"

"Well, an office needs a secretary to be a real office, now doesn't it?" he said smugly. "She was part of the . . . what you called window dressing. Keeping up the office certainly was expensive, but my fees for managing Edna's estate paid most of it, you know. And I'm not hard up myself. Frankly, it was worth it to set Edna's apprehensions at rest and prove to her that my caring for her concerns was not an imposition at all. Now, of course, without Miss Stoner . . ." He sighed. "Now I suppose I'll have to close the office entirely. It's going to be such an inconvenience!"

"You could hire another secretary, couldn't you?"

"Not for what I paid Miss Stoner. She was a very good office manager, an excellent typist, an efficient receptionist with what few inquiries we did get . . . and she was grateful to have the job. It isn't easy for a woman past middle age, they tell me! So she was willing to work for very little. No, she wouldn't be easy to replace. Younger people are too greedy nowadays, don't you agree?"

"Oh, certainly," Caledonia growled. "Why, some of them would demand enough to live on!"

"What about Miss Stoner personally?" Angela asked quickly. "Don't you think she might be hard to replace? As a person, I mean? For her talents and her ability?"

Clayton considered the question with a slight frown. "No. No, not really. She didn't do a lot, after all. I mean, the work was not very demanding. No, I think on that score I could find someone else."

Caledonia's determined smile had been slipping and now she looked positively stormy. "Can't you think of any other reason you might miss her? I mean, she obviously cared for you and she was a loyal employee, wasn't she?"

He thought about the question again. "I suppose so. But she should have been. After all, I was paying her salary, wasn't I? It goes without saying she should be supportive of her employer. And I think I made it clear to you that I didn't welcome it when she fussed at me about whether I'd eaten enough for breakfast, or whether I should carry an umbrella, or whether we were getting enough business to survive . . . Those things were simply none of her business, and she nearly drove me frantic. Indeed I shan't miss her constantly nagging at me!"

"I see," Caledonia said, her mouth set in a tight line. "She was worth what small salary you paid her—nothing more?"

Clayton looked surprised and slightly puzzled. "Essentially, that is correct."

"Tchap—Tch—P—P—!" Caledonia was spluttering with angry reaction, unable to get out a single word. Finally, she fairly spit out *"P—P—Peanut Butter!"* biting the consonants off viciously!

"Mr. Clayton," Angela intervened smoothly, "can you think of any reason anyone would want to kill your Miss Stoner?"

"Oh, dear, no! Of course not," Clayton said hastily. "But wasn't it—wasn't it an attempted robbery? I thought . . . of course they haven't said, but I thought all such things these days—with wild-eyed drug addicts searching for valuables to pawn, robbery seems the most logical—I mean, I took it for granted. That's the first thing I thought of, you know, when the police called my home in the middle of the night . . .

"What a shock to me! It was very late at night for an old widower like me, who generally goes to bed early. The phone startled me horribly! And when they told me she was dead—well, I tell you, it made me feel quite faint there for a moment. I thought I might have to call my doctor. My heart is strong, you understand, but a shock like that . . ."

Angela interrupted his fluttering reminiscence. "It could hardly be robbery. You didn't keep valuables at the office, did you?"

"No . . . nothing of any real value. The computer of course, but—"

"No records someone might want to steal?"

"I told you we didn't have clients, and nobody would want to look at Edna's records, would they?"

Angela bit her lip and took another tack. "Don't you think her death is connected with Lightfoot's in some way?"

"What? Connected with . . . ? Certainly not! How could it be? They had absolutely nothing in common. They didn't know each other. Did they? How could they have any connection! Unless, of course . . ." He paused.

"Yes?" Angela was pushing a little. "Go on. Unless what?"

"Well, I suppose it's possible that she was from his home area. From back East. It's all a little vague to me. I was never one to ask about my employees' personal lives. But she could have come from the East . . . Though why that would result in her being killed, I can't guess!"

Abruptly Caledonia stood, billowing up out of the couch so suddenly it seemed the couch set up sympathetic ripples that bounced Clayton to his feet as well. "Well, we mustn't keep you, Mr. Clayton. I'm sure you have all kinds of things to do . . ."

"Cal," Angela protested. "He just finished saying he didn't . . ."

"Well, I do have one more errand here in this building," he said, fussily smoothing the multiple creases that criss-crossed his linen trousers and the sleeves of his jacket. "I think I left my umbrella when I was in the dining room this morning."

"That's right," Angela said. "I remember. You had it over your arm, and you set it down on the floor under your chair! You ought to go in and look. If nobody found it . . . and it's pretty dark on the floor under the tables . . . it would still be there."

"Oh, dear . . . I do hate to interrupt your waitresses when they're setting the luncheon things . . . Perhaps if someone inquired whom they knew . . ." He looked hopefully at Angela.

"The girls won't mind," Angela said, ignoring his strong hint. "Just go right ahead."

He sighed and started toward the dining room door. "Well, I do believe I'll do that. I'm actually rather fond of that umbrella. I'd hate to lose it. It was a gift from Edna some years ago—my old college colors."

"Your college? What university did you attend?" Angela said politely.

"My father sent me to Chapel Hill . . . the University of North Carolina," Clayton said smugly. "It has a fine repu-tation, and of course he felt that nothing but the best would do." ("And you couldn't get into Harvard or Yale," Angela thought, but didn't say it aloud.)

"It was a career choice, you see. Prestige." He fussed with the buttons of his jacket. "Actually, I grew fairly at-tached to the school while I was there. Though I must say the climate in North Carolina was not really to my liking. It's not brisk and bracing like the air in Wichita. Nor quite as moderate as here. And that damp air . . ."

He shivered with distaste. "We used our umbrellas there, I can assure you! Here they're usually just a decoration. Well, ladies, it's been pleasant talking to you . . ." and he moved rapidly off, disappearing through the double doors leading to the dining room.

"*OOOOooooghgGG!* . . ." Caledonia exhaled forcefully and noisily, a sound of urgent protest. "That—that unpleasant little creep! That egocentric little twerp! That selfish, insensitive little clod! The only thing his alma mater meant to him was prestige! The only thing Miss Stoner meant to him was low-cost labor! The woman worried about him and his business, but he didn't even bother to confide in her it was just a kind of pastime—a front . . . He just let her worry. She worried over his health and tried to get him business and refused to talk about his affairs, even when you pumped her . . . But all he'll miss about her is that she worked cheap! And all he thought when the police called him about her murder was what the shock might do to him! That weasel! That insignificant, objectionable . . ."

"You know," Angela said, "it just struck me now, but during our breakfast this morning, he talked about himself and about Edna and about Lightfoot, but he never once mentioned Miss Stoner! I had to bring her up myself."

"And didn't you say she came from the Middle West?"

"That's right! She told me so."

"Well, he doesn't seem to know that. He hasn't bothered to find out anything about her personally—or if he did know once, he's forgotten. That poor woman cared about the Unmitigated Wallace but she was nothing to him—nothing at all." Caledonia took a deep breath. "I resent his attitude on her behalf!"

"I found it!" Half the dining room door had swung open and Wallace Clayton came through it, triumphantly brandishing the blue-striped umbrella. "It was indeed right there on the floor, where I'd left it. Thank you for the suggestion. Well, I wish you good day, ladies . . ." and he swung

sharply left and out the main lobby door, whistling "The
Daring Young Man on the Flying Trapeze" ... leaving
Angela and Caledonia glaring after him in silence.

Chapter 15

"I CAN'T settle down yet," Caledonia told Angela after lunch. "I've been thinking all morning about Sam Dunlop."

"When you weren't busy bristling at Unmitigated Wallace, you mean?"

"Oh, all right. Yes. But about Sam—you don't suppose he is involved in all this, do you? I can't believe it of him. But you know, he used to be crazy about Felicia. And if having that Lightfoot man around here represented a threat to Felicia—to her reputation or whatever—I wonder if he might try to protect her?"

"You said he was bitter after she left him, though," Angela said. "Don't you suppose he'd just feel rather pleased if she had to suffer a little discomfort over that old association? I would."

"I'm sure," Caledonia snorted. "And to be fair, so would I. I didn't even know Felicia very well, and I'd still have felt tickled to death to see her questioned by the police or pointed at and whispered about. I like Sam . . ."

"I know you do."

"And I'd think it was just a bit of what she deserved! Tell you what, Angela. I think I'll go talk to Sam."

"Right now? It's your nap time!"

"I know. But sometimes even that blessed moment has to be postponed. There's always time to take a nap; sometimes helping a friend can't wait."

"I don't really want to go down to—"

"I didn't ask you! Angela, Sam's my friend, not yours. So it's silly for you to put yourself out. Besides, this is a matter for some delicacy. I'll have to approach this in a roundabout way. And he wouldn't talk as freely if you were present. What I mean is, there's no reason you can't take your nap right now."

"You? Delicate? Roundabout?"

"Don't mock, Angela. I'll give the matter some thought on the way down to the lumberyard."

"You're going to walk?"

"Don't be silly. Not even for Sam's sake. I'm going in the little van. It's Tuesday afternoon and they make their regular run to the shopping mall Tuesday, Thursday, and Saturday."

"Is there room? You generally have to reserve a place . . ."

"They'll make room for me," Caledonia predicted, quite correctly, as it turned out. When she tried to ease her huge frame into the center seat beside Tootsie Armstrong, who was thinking of shopping for a birthday present for her niece, Tootsie decided it might be nice to wait another few days after all, and apologetically made space for Caledonia simply by leaving.

"Next week will be better for shopping," Tootsie fluttered. "Her birthday isn't till November, actually. I really don't need . . . Caledonia, you take my place." And Tootsie eased out of the van, balancing with difficulty on the tiny high heels she always wore.

Angela, waving goodbye from the lobby's front entrance, shook her head in grim disapproval of Tootsie's footwear, which Angela considered not only silly but dangerous. Then she turned her attention back to the van, which was just pulling away from the curb.

"Don't forget," Angela called out. "Delicacy! Tact!"

Caledonia nodded that she understood and agreed, but by the time the van dropped her at the lumberyard, she still had not thought of a roundabout approach to the subject.

"Sam," she began her conversation, "I have to talk to you. Privately." She glared at Contreras and at the pleasant-faced Carmella, working together over the Macintosh. (Contreras had found it easier to handle than he had imagined, and was spending his lunch hours being tutored by Carmella in some simple bookkeeping and word-processing techniques.)

"We'll go, Mr. Dunlop," Carmella said, starting to leave her chair.

"Nonsense. You two keep working. We can find another spot," Sam Dunlop said, limping forward to take Caledonia's arm, turn her around, and move her out of the office toward the storage bays. "You know, Caledonia, I think those two have something going on between them that will make them a lot closer than just teacher and pupil."

"Sam! You don't mean it! I thought your partner was a happily married man!"

"He is! A married man with a thirty-year-old unmarried son who's come by here three times in the past week to escort Carmella home after work! What I meant was, they might end up related—as a bride and her father-in-law! Oh. Here." He waved Caledonia into the first of the big storage spaces. "We can sit on some of the lumber stacked up in here and nobody will disturb us. Try this. There's a ready-made seat along these timbers here. Make yourself comfortable and fire away."

Caledonia eased herself gingerly onto a stack of lumber that had been shifted about so that it formed a kind of natural bench. Boards groaned slightly as they took her weight, but the seat seemed sturdy enough. For a moment she was quiet, taking in the clean, outdoorsy smell of the wood and sawdust, but inspiration still did not give her any ideas that could be called even faintly tactful. So she simply began.

"Sam, I wish Angela was here. She could do this a lot better than I can."

"Your little friend?"

"Yes. She's good at talking to people, I think. I'm not so good . . ."

"Well, just try. Just tell me what's on your mind. We've been friends long enough for me not to take offense, I think."

"It's Felicia . . ."

"Omigawd! What's that woman been up to now?"

"Nothing. I hope. Or rather, I hope *you* haven't been up to something because of her. Sam, did you know Felicia was a primary witness for the defense of Alexander Lightfoot?"

Sam sat down beside Caledonia and the lumber bench groaned again. "Witness for the defense? For what, for Pete's sake? I didn't know he'd been on trial for anything. I didn't read about it in the paper that I remember. No, wait! There's got to be something's wrong with that anyway. I mean, the paper said he'd only been here in Camden a couple of years. Felicia's been gone from here now for ten years—more, I guess—I can't keep track of the time."

"No-no-no . . . it was before she came back here. Back where she lived before she moved."

"In Connecticut?"

"Right. And his name wasn't Lightfoot then. It was . . ."

"Headington? The Headington case? Caledonia, are you going to tell me that Alexander Lightfoot was Thomas Headington?"

"The same. Nobody here knew it. Or rather, a few people had found out. And the police discovered it after he died. Fingerprints."

"Well, of course Felicia testified at the Headington trial. She told me all about that. But I didn't know the man was out of prison, let alone that he was here in town. And I certainly didn't know that Headington was one and the same with that Lightfoot fellow. And all I know about Lightfoot is that he was killed!"

"Sam, the police say that the trial was probably very hard on Felicia."

"Sure it was. It's one of the reasons she decided to move to California. People back East weren't very nice about it. They implied she had some private reason to try to cover up for him. Look, Caledonia, I don't love her anymore. In fact, I still resent her and what she did to me . . . walking out that way with no warning . . . taking our personal bank account with her and leaving me without enough to buy lunch for myself . . . but I've got to be fair about it. She was telling the truth as she saw it when she testified that Thomas Headington had never left the mall. She really believed that was so."

"I see. Well, that goes along with what I told Martinez— that you wouldn't kill Headington-Lightfoot in revenge for what he did, albeit inadvertently, to Felicia's reputation."

"Kill him? My Lord no! In a way, that whole business did me a favor. If she hadn't come West, I'd never have met her and fallen in love with her."

"And she'd never have deserted you and hurt you the way she did."

Dunlop got to his feet and limped back and forth in front of Caledonia, rubbing his hands together painfully. "Caledonia, I've got to tell you the truth. The reason I hate her so much now is because I loved her so much before. Hell, I probably *still* love her, in a funny sort of way. I mean, I wouldn't take her back . . ."

"I should hope not!"

"All the same, I miss her. I miss being in love with her—that was a good time in my life. A middle-aged bachelor like me falling for a pretty young thing like that—and she loving me back! It was . . . it was a miracle, to me."

"Did she, Sam? Did she really love you?"

"Oh, I think so. For a while. Till she got bored—and this other guy came along. Anyway, if she didn't love me, she gave a good enough imitation to make me happier than I've ever been before or since. I know I get violent with rage about her, but I also miss her. Can you understand that?"

Caledonia sighed. "Oh, yes. I think so. But Sam, when

the police come, if I were you, I'd concentrate on telling them how you resent her leaving, and not how much you miss her and how much you loved her ... and certainly don't tell them how you probably still love her, underneath all the anger. You know? Lie a little bit, Sam. Because they'll never believe you wouldn't kill for her, if you talk to them the way you talked to me."

"I'm not sure I can lie. I'm not good at it. Never have been."

"Except to yourself! You've been telling yourself you hate her all these years, even though it's only partly true. Poor Sam. I'm really sorry. But the police are going to come here, you know. They think you might—just might— have pushed Lightfoot in front of the train after you found out who he was."

Dunlop had been listening carefully. "You know, that doesn't make an awful lot of sense to me. What good would it have done to kill him? It wouldn't hide the past. And how would that help Felicia anyway?"

"Lieutenant Martinez says murderers don't necessarily kill for good reasons. Not what you and I would say were good reasons, anyhow. He says they're good reasons to the killers, all right, but they often don't make any sense at all to the rest of us. Because murder is a crazy solution to any problem! There's always a better way."

"He's right about that," Dunlop nodded. "I might have gone to Lightfoot and told him off, if I'd known who he really was. I might even have taken a punch at him. Just because I don't like liars and cheats. But I wouldn't have pushed him under a train!"

"Better not say that to the police either, Sam."

"Why not?"

"They'll think maybe you caught up with him by the railway line and took that punch at him just when the train came past. It would be manslaughter, rather than murder, but you'd still be the killer, in their books. Better just say you didn't even know who he was till I mentioned it."

"Well, I didn't."

"Good. I believe you." She eased herself up from her lumber-bench. "This wasn't really very comfortable! It started out all right, but the edge of the boards started cutting into my legs. Now . . ." she rubbed the backs of her thighs, "where was I? Oh, yes. The trick is to make the police believe you the way I do. Just be straightforward with them, Sam. But don't ever tell them you're still an old softie about Felicia. Tell 'em only what they need to know . . . that she's been gone a long time, and that you would never kill to avenge her honor, or whatever it is they think you did. Okay?"

"I'll try. And Caledonia . . . thank you for coming to warn me."

"I didn't come to warn you, Sam. I came to find out the truth. And I think I did."

"Well, then, thanks for believing me."

Later in the afternoon, Caledonia, who had returned to her quarters, phoned Angela and reported briefly the results of her interview.

"So, you do believe him? You don't think he's the killer?" Angela's voice had that lazy tone that means its owner has just roused from sleep.

"Absolutely not. Sam just can't tell an effective lie. So—that's how I spent my afternoon while you were slothfully asleep."

"Well, that's not quite true. I decided if you were out detecting, I could do a little myself. I went down to call on the Graingers!"

As soon as the van pulled away, Angela had turned back through the lobby and out into the garden, headed for the Grainger apartment. Thelma Grainger opened the screen to Angela's knock.

"Come in," she said softly. "But please, don't talk very loud. Fred's asleep, and he gets so tired these days—he needs to take a little nap after lunch."

"I'm not disturbing you?" Angela said in a whisper.

"No. I'm glad of the company."

"Perhaps if we stepped outside . . . walked in the garden . . ."

"Oh, I don't want to be too far away if he should wake and call out for me," Mrs. Grainger protested. "You've probably heard he's got a little hardening of the arteries, and it makes him confused now and then. Especially when he first wakes up . . ."

"Perhaps that bench there . . ." Angela pointed to one of the small wooden benches set here and there along the length of the garden walk. "If we sit there, you should be able to hear . . ."

When they were properly seated, Angela got right to the point. She might counsel Caledonia to tact, but she herself found diplomacy a waste of time. "I understand you weren't strictly truthful with us the other day," she began. "You really did spend a lot of time with Alexander Lightfoot—until you recognized him as a criminal."

Thelma Grainger nodded. "That's so. But when Fred recognized him—well, he really got violent on the subject. Didn't want to be anywhere near the man."

Angela nodded. "Did Fred get violent enough to do him some harm?"

Mrs. Grainger hesitated. "I told the police he didn't, but the thought has been nagging at me and nagging at me that maybe he might have got it into his head to do something— unusual. He gets these notions now, once in a while . . . It's especially when he first wakes up, when he's a little confused anyway. Just for a moment or two, he doesn't seem to know quite where he is. And after he recognized Headington, that day, it was terrible for a while. Every day when he woke up, he was back in Connecticut for a minute, and he was raging about justice and injustice . . . and about that man . . ."

"I see. So you're not really sure he didn't kill Lightfoot, then. Is that what you're saying?"

"Oh, goodness no! I'm positive he didn't. He's such a

gentle man. And failing, you know. I think that underneath, he knows that these notions of his aren't reality. At the same time that he's having this strong feeling he's back in Connecticut, I think he's aware that he's here in California. But all the same . . ."

"All the same you're afraid?"

"Yes. I'd do a lot to protect him. Life hasn't been kind to him, and now this mental problem . . . it doesn't seem fair. I haven't been much of a fighter myself. I'm more the type to let things happen, and just to find a way to live with them. But if I thought I could protect him . . ."

There was not a lot more for the two to talk about, so within a few minutes, they terminated their chat. Thelma Grainger was terribly anxious to get back into her own little apartment, where she could keep an eye on her husband— could be there if he needed her. And Angela wanted to think over what she'd learned.

A nap had intervened. Angela hadn't meant to fall asleep. But while she was thinking, she might just as well stretch out on the bed, she told herself.

"I should have known, of course," she told Caledonia. "So I was still asleep when you called just now. But do you know what I think about this afternoon? I think we've got yet another suspect that hadn't occurred to me before. Thelma Grainger. She might have killed Lightfoot herself with some notion of removing him as a threat to her husband. She's very protective of Dr. Grainger . . . she admits that. I wonder if she'd really include murder in her custodial chores?"

"Well, it's something to think about," Caledonia agreed. "Angela, are you coming down for a sherry tonight before dinner? Because if you are, I wonder if you have some peanuts or pretzels or something? Potato chips maybe?"

"Well, I might have some cocktail crackers . . . half a box from the last time I had a group in for bridge. Why?"

"Angela, I find detecting makes me hungry. Well, to be fair, everything makes me hungry. But detecting makes me absolutely ravenous! I just don't think I can wait for supper time. Come on as soon as you can splash some water on your face and wipe the sleep out of your eyes. And don't forget the crackers!" And she hung up.

Chapter 16

Over a small sherry at Caledonia's apartment before dinner, Caledonia and Angela talked about the murders. Over a main course of chicken kiev followed by a peach melba for dessert, they talked on, holding the volume down as low as possible to avoid being overheard. And finally, walking slowly out of the dining room and into the lobby, they continued talking, still in that urgent semiundertone. It wouldn't do to have this kind of speculation overheard.

"Let's stay here in the lobby, Cal," Angela suggested, moving over to the big sofa opposite the elevator doors. "It makes a change from the apartments . . . I feel a little restless. Like we're spinning our wheels somehow . . . something's there, but we're missing it."

"Well, why not?" Caledonia plumped down beside her expansively. "I don't feel like taking a walk, that's for sure. Not after that big meal. And I'm not going over there . . ." She gestured out the lobby's side door toward the large assembly room attached to the health facility across the street. The two separate buildings shared a single roof for economy's sake. There was the little hospital where residents went for anything more serious than a cold or a minor sprain—and there was a big, empty room where most activities were held that attracted large audiences: the community sings, the talent shows, the exercise classes, the bingo games, the concerts by visiting groups.

Angela and Caledonia enjoyed the bingo games as a rule,

and occasionally they even attended community singing and the talent shows, though both avoided the exercise classes. But after their first visit, neither would ever attend one of the "guest concerts," which ordinarily featured, not a hired entertainer, but the Magnolia Junior High School Choir in selections (quite beyond their range) from *Naughty Marietta* and *The Desert Song*—the Camden Girl Scout Troop # 43 wearing dishtowels for headgear and performing a nativity play—or the Foothills Elementary School students putting on a pageant that involved the entire fourth grade in imitation buckskins and paper warbonnets, portraying the guests at the first Thanksgiving dinner. Of course, not all programs were presented by juveniles. Once in a while a couple of old-timers who had gone down with the ship of vaudeville came out of retirement to play the spoons or to sing shaky love duets for their contemporaries.

"It's either 'The Little Rascals Put On a Play' or 'Ma and Pa Kettle Entertain the Old Folks,' " Caledonia had protested on the occasion of a magic show put on by a septuagenarian who, when he had his eyesight, used to play club dates in Vegas, but whose thick bifocals now made him fumble the cards so that he never once was able to pick out the one selected by his audience.

Later in the same show, as Caledonia reluctantly acknowledged, they had a fairly entertaining half-hour—but not as a result of the magic performance. The magician's rabbit, an enceinte doe, had felt nature's stirrings and escaped the tiny cage where she usually sat docilely awaiting her grand entrance from the silk hat. She had slipped through the half-open door to the hospital wing, left ajar so that patients might watch from their wheelchairs lined up in the infirmary lobby.

Frantic searching failed to come up with Mrs. Bunny, and the magician, with many apologies, had gone on to cutting off neckties and turning silk handkerchiefs into paper flowers until he was interrupted by a shriek from back in the hospital wing. Old Mrs. Dougherty, fatigued with waiting for the show to resume, had rolled herself back to her room, where she found the rabbit nesting in a pile of dirty clothes that were dumped beside the door to be collected for the laundry. Now, besides the cheerful mother rabbit, the pile also included three squirmy new babies, all apparently waiting, with Mrs. Dougherty's nightgown, for a trip to the washing machines.

But the visits of performers were usually on Wednesday or Friday nights. Tonight being Tuesday, almost all the other residents—at least those feeling up to an evening of togetherness—were across the street playing bingo. Carolyn Roberts, the energetic activities director for the center, arranged the bingo so that there were seldom any losers. She bought a multitude of little prizes (a sample jar of face cream, a four-pack of supersoft toilet paper, a deck of cards, travel-sized deodorant, a candy bar . . .) and had a stock of bicentennial fifty-cent pieces for those not lucky enough to snag what they called a "real prize." After a player had once won, he could not win again that evening. So as play progressed, more and more players dropped out until only a few remained. But everyone stayed on to watch and to talk. It wasn't a thrill to a real gambler, but it satisfied the residents as a social occasion. Gossip was exchanged, and there was companionship and laughter—it certainly beat another evening watching television alone in one's room. So even Grogan, Camden's part-time drunk and full-time cynic, showed up for bingo.

In fact, Caledonia and Angela had the lobby to themselves tonight except for Jimmy Stevens, the nighttime desk clerk. Jimmy was a student at Camelot Junior College, inland a few miles, and used his time on duty (when he wasn't answering an emergency or comforting a lonely insomniac) to study for exams. So his head was bent over a thick textbook. All the same, Caledonia and Angela moved away from the square of light that was the desk, and down toward the fireplace, where they could sit in comfort and be sure they weren't overheard.

"Now," Caledonia said, arranging the folds of her orchid satin caftan. "Where were we? Let's review from the top. First, we have two murders . . . and don't interrupt for a minute, Angela. Let me get my thoughts straight. We really know very little about Lightfoot, when you come down to it, except that he was a pretty shabby specimen of humanity at one time in his existence. And perhaps because of that, I suppose, any number of people might have wanted to kill him. About his present, or what was his present before he got himself killed, we don't know much. Not even what he was like. You probably knew him better than most. You said you talked to him in the lobby now and then . . ."

"I—I exaggerated. I think I said 'Hello' as I passed him and Edna a couple of times. That's all." Angela had the grace to look a bit embarrassed.

Caledonia smirked, but didn't take the chance to gloat. Instead, she went on, "We didn't really know Miss Stoner either. We'd only talked to her a couple of times. We know she was plain as a mud fence, slightly bossy, and apparently a gem of an office worker. But we haven't really found any reason at all why anyone would want to kill her, have we? One murder with no motives—the other murder with dozens!"

"Now Cal, if you're going to go speculating about motives, anybody could be the killer. In fact, that's what Martinez is doing now, isn't it? Investigating the possibility that some neighbor or business acquaintance had a grudge about something we haven't even discovered yet. Like—well, it's always possible Lightfoot owed the butcher and quarreled with him about the debt—or he quarreled with his paperboy because the kid always missed the porch in the mornings and Lightfoot had to search the shrubbery—or maybe there was an argument with a neighbor because somebody had a late party one night and Lightfoot sent for the police to stop the noise, and the neighbor resented it—or maybe he had a dog that dug up the neighbors' . . ."

"Enough!" Caledonia held her hand up. "Silence! Stop! Don't let your imagination run any further. I get the picture. We'd better stick to what we know and see if anything we've discovered so far makes sense."

"You know the trouble with our scenarios, Cal?" Angela sighed deeply.

Caledonia grinned hugely. "Sure I do! None of those ideas has anything at all to do with us! If the man was killed by his paperboy, we have no business being involved—and of course we're not likely to find out anything worthwhile, either. It has to be somebody we already know, if our contribution is going to be helpful to Martinez."

"Oh, Cal, I do wish it were Wallace Clayton! He's such an unpleasant man . . . besides, I have the uncomfortable feeling he's getting the inside track with Edna. He's been calling on her constantly . . . coming to see her, comforting her. Ever since Lightfoot's death Wallace has been underfoot."

"Bad pun!"

"Pun?"

"*Light*-foot, *under*-foot . . ."

"Oh, Cal, I didn't mean that. I was only trying to say that I've seen enough of Unmitigated Wallace in the past couple of weeks to last me a lifetime. I'd really hate it if he married Edna and moved in here and we had to talk to him every day!"

"I'd really hate it if he married Edna at all! He's such a tiresome person, and she's a pleasant woman . . . thoroughly nice from what I've seen of her," Caledonia said. "You probably know her better than I do, and you're certainly in a better position to judge her, because you've seen a highly emotional side of her, I never have, but I think you like her yourself . . ."

"Oh, I do. In spite of her throwing things at me!"

"Well, then. Wallace certainly isn't in the running for our 'Mr. Congeniality' award, is he? So let's take a long, hard look and see if we can't figure out a way to pin these murders on him!"

"Cal!"

"Oh, come on! You know I'm only kidding. Still, I'd like to go over again what we do know. It's possible there's something about him we've missed . . ." Caledonia hoisted herself to her feet and began to pace. She kept her tone low enough not to disturb Jimmy, still bent over his book and apparently oblivious to them. But walking allowed her to move her arms and emphasize her points, which she did vigorously.

"Okay. First, he's fond of Edna. We know that. And he thought Lightfoot was a bad influence on Edna, because she was spending so much money. Remember when he told us that?"

Angela nodded eagerly. "And he resented Lightfoot's presence, Cal, because it cut down the time Edna spent with him. He said so at breakfast today. He said he really minded not having her company . . ."

"Okay. He liked Edna and he resented Lightfoot. But of course, it's worse than just Lightfoot's taking up time Edna could have spent with Wallace. I mean, Edna wasn't merely dating Lightfoot! She'd decided to marry him!" She stopped in midstride. "Angela, do you suppose she announced her engagement to her brother-in-law rather recently? Say, just before Lightfoot was killed?"

"I don't know. But I bet we can find out." Angela started up, but Caledonia gestured her to stay where she was.

"Not yet. Let's think a little more about this. Let's suppose Edna tells Unmitigated Wallace that she's getting married to another man. Would that send the little egomaniac into a tailspin or wouldn't it?"

"I vote yes, it would!"

"Me too. He seems to think the world exists to serve

him. Why, girl, I bet he'd be wild with jealousy. So what would he do?"

"Well ... Cal, suppose he decided to talk to Lightfoot about it? Ask him ... warn him ... I don't know which ..."

"And suppose he finds out that Lightfoot is an early morning walker. Was he?"

"I think I heard he was very fit for his age. I assume he worked out, or jogged, or went for walks. Early morning would be a good time for a brisk walk, anyhow. So let's say he did. Went for morning walks, I mean."

Caledonia was warming to the subject. "Okay, and where do Camdenites go for their walks? Where's the best walking place in the world? Where you're bound not to get run over by some driver speeding through the fog, where there's plenty of space, where you don't get shin splints from jogging on concrete sidewalks ..."

"The beach!" Angela jumped up and began to walk back and forth beside Caledonia, her eyes shining. "And Lightfoot lived up the hill, on the far side of downtown. Anybody could figure out that he had to come through town and cross the railroad tracks to get to the beach. It wouldn't be hard to plan to intercept him on the way."

"So Lightfoot takes his walk this one morning and somebody catches up with him—somebody who's taken the trouble to find out exactly where he goes for his walks and when. That somebody catches him just about at the tracks ..."

"Wallace!" Angela breathed with delight.

"Yes, let's say Wallace. And Wallace starts out with something like, 'I understand you're going to marry my sister-in-law, Edna Ferrier ...' and of course Lightfoot says that's true. And Wallace says ... he says ..."

"He says," Angela said in wicked parody of Clayton's prissy voice, "he says, 'My good sir, she deserves a better man than you. I dare say you aren't fit to clean her shoes!' That's a good line ..."

"And exactly like something that little popinjay would say, too. Never guessing how true it really was!"

"And then," Angela went on, skipping a bit every third step to catch up with Caledonia's long strides, "and then Lightfoot would say, 'Get out of my way, little man' or something like that. I bet he could be arrogant."

"Well, Wallace always brings out the worst in me. I don't imagine Lightfoot would be any different in that respect. So then what happens? No, don't tell me . . ." Caledonia continued her march back and forth. "Our Wallace is furious. Lightfoot turns to go, and Wallace grabs hold of him . . ."

" 'Wait a minute,' " Angela squeaked, continuing her mimicry of Wallace, and plucking at Caledonia's sleeve as Wallace might have plucked at Lightfoot's. " 'Wait. Don't go yet, Lightfoot. We have to settle something. I don't want you hanging around her any longer. You aren't good for her . . .' " She snatched at Caledonia's sleeve. " 'Don't you turn your back on me, Mr. Lightfoot . . .' "

"But Lightfoot would shake him off . . . maybe give him a push . . ." Caledonia detached her arm from Angela's grip with a twist that made Angela stagger slightly.

"And that's when Wallace would lash out, I expect!"

"With what? With his fists? Or did he hit him with some weapon?"

"Maybe with his umbrella! If it was foggy the morning of Lightfoot's death, Wallace would have been carrying his favorite umbrella to ward off the mist . . . like he did today. He flourishes the thing a little bit . . . like a baton or a pointer . . . kind of like a fencer with a sword. Suppose he poked it at Lightfoot . . ."

"And Lightfoot pulled away . . ."

"And his arm flew out and just then the train was coming, and his arm was hit by the train, and it spun him around and down and under the wheels . . ." Angela was panting as she moved, demonstrating with sweeping hand gestures.

"Or he staggered and fell," Caledonia suggested. "Maybe he turned an ankle getting away from that umbrella . . . and he was down on the tracks. And he couldn't get up and out of the way in time . . ."

Angela saw him spinning and turning, a soft body meeting the tearing speed of flying metal . . . Caledonia saw him on hands and knees in the gravel, shaking his head in momentary shock, trying to rise, feeling the ankle give, and then suddenly the train was on him . . .

"Phew!" Caledonia threw herself down on the couch. "I can see it so vividly, I almost believe it's true!"

"Me too."

"I like the touch with the umbrella. You do this make-believe with more dash than I do, Angela. He takes that black, rolled-up . . ."

"Blue-and-white stripe."

"What?"

"Probably the umbrella he had with him today. You saw it after he picked it up in the dining room just before lunch. He waved it around . . ."

"No, I didn't. My back was to the door. I heard him call that he'd found it, and by the time I'd turned around, he was gone out the front door."

"Well, you should know it's blue-striped anyway. He said it was his college colors and that he was a Chapel Hill graduate . . . that's their colors. Sky blue and white. They have all sorts of slogans like 'Carolina Blue Heaven' and things like that . . ."

"Wallace had that umbrella this morning?" Caledonia said.

"Uh-huh. He said he'd had to carry it to ward off morning fog, or something . . . Even if he hadn't commented, I'd have noticed. Nobody else in all of Southern California ever carries an umbrella!"

"Angela, I'm going to call the lieutenant. You stay right here. Don't go away. I'll be right back." Caledonia heaved herself out of the couch and glided rapidly over to the desk.

"Jimmy, let me come in there and use your phone. It's kind of an emergency . . ." and she disappeared around the corner, out of Angela's sight, heading for the door that would take her into the office.

Chapter 17

LEFT ALONE so abruptly, Angela seated herself for a moment or two, still breathing heavily from the exertion of acting out the make-believe argument. But sitting still, even to recover her composure, was not easy for her. When she was breathing regularly again, she got to her feet and walked to the bird cage, hanging in the darkest shadows near the fireplace.

"Good evening, little fellow," she said, putting her fingers up at the bars to attract the bird's attention, but prudently leaving them well outside the cage, beyond his reach. "Have you got over your fit of bad temper? You were in such a rage . . . I don't ordinarily forgive someone who bites me, but in your case, I'll make an exception."

The bird simply stood and eyed her with speculation. It made no sound.

"Well, you're a bit dull tonight. No deep sighs? No comments on my cat?"

The parakeet merely stared at her, apparently lost in deep bird-thought. As Angela shrugged and turned her back on the cage, she caught sight of a small, linen-clad figure emerging from the base of the utility stairs. She was more than just surprised—she was startled (she had "jumped inside her skin," as she described it to Caledonia later) and taken aback to see that it was Wallace Clayton. He moved jauntily out of the shadows, adjusting his bow tie, smoothing his creased jacket, and whistling softly—this time it seemed to be "Let Me Call You Sweetheart."

"Ah, Mrs. Ah—Benbow! I declare, you really gave me a start! I didn't expect anyone to be in the lobby! Well, other than the desk attendant, of course. I expected everyone would be across the street. Edna said absolutely everybody plays bingo . . ."

"Oh! You were visiting Edna again?" She bit her lip. What a stupid thing to say! ("But you try thinking of something sensible," she told Caledonia later, "when the man you've just called a killer appears right in front of you like the genie out of the lamp!")

"Yes, indeed," he said smugly. "She relies heavily on me, now. I seem to be able to cheer her up."

"Well, you were here earlier, of course . . . I didn't expect you to come twice in one day."

"Well, not under ordinary circumstances. But she says she finds my presence soothing," he wagged a roguish finger at her, "and you did upset her very much the other evening . . . Tch-tch-tch, Mrs. Ah—Benbow, that was very naughty. But I can't be cross, for it's brought us even closer together, Edna and me."

"She asked you to come tonight?"

"Oh, no," he said, squaring his narrow shoulders self-consciously. "That was my own idea. She hasn't been eating properly . . ."

"I noticed. At least, she came to the dining room only once—and then not again!"

"Well, you upset her, as I say. She went back to having trays in her room. So I brought her a treat tonight . . . a container of chocolate chip mint ice cream—absolutely her favorite. And I coaxed her into eating a whole dish full. We talked a while and generally spent a companionable, pleasant evening together, till she got too sleepy, after eating so heartily—I—" He looked around. "Isn't your friend here? Mrs. Ah—Mrs. Ah—"

"Mrs. Wingate," Angela prompted. "She's gone to . . ."

"No, she's right here," Caledonia rumbled, as she came steaming across the lobby, her orchid satin caftan flapping behind her like a sail luffing after the wind changes. "Good evening, Mr. Clayton."

"Ah, Mrs. Ah— Wingate. Good to see you, too."

"You haven't got your umbrella, I see," Caledonia went on. "Do you only carry it when it rains?"

"Or when there's a fog," he said. "Fog droplets do as much to rumple a suit as rain does, you know."

"Where did you leave it?" Caledonia pursued.

"My umbrella? Why, at home, I suppose." He frowned for a moment, and then his brow cleared. "Ah, I see! You're thinking I might have forgotten it somewhere again, just as I did earlier today! Well, I'm not ordinarily so absentminded, Mrs. Wingate. But isn't that just like women? ... You're actually watching out for me the way Edna does. The way Miss Stoner used to . . ." He worked in a tremendous sigh. "Poor Miss Stoner. But she was rather a nag. It was always 'Have you had a proper breakfast?' or 'Why don't you pay the light bill on your way so we can save the price of the stamp?' or ... Well, at any rate, one got very tired of it." He sighed again. "I don't really enjoy my lonely life, but I confess that there are times when independence holds charms."

"Do you have more than that one umbrella?" Caledonia pursued.

"More than ... Well, I also have a black umbrella I keep at the office, of course. Just that one other, I think."

"You don't by chance have more than one blue-striped model, do you?" Caledonia insisted.

Clearly puzzled, Clayton stopped his forward progress. They had moved slowly as they chatted, and now they stood across the room from and nearly opposite the elevator. Clayton put his hands on his hips and swung to face them squarely, forcing the women to brake sharply, shoulder to shoulder, their backs toward the elevator and the desk.

"Why all this curiosity about my umbrella, Mrs. Ah—What does it matter whether I have two blue-striped umbrellas or not? Can't you be more direct? What exactly is it you want to know?"

"Yes, Cal. What do you want to know?" Angela might stand beside her friend in physical proximity, but with regard to Caledonia's line of questioning she was far out at sea.

Caledonia glared at Angela and made a shushing gesture with her hand. "Well, Mr. Clayton, I really want to know if you ever carry that blue-striped umbrella to the office. That's what I want to know."

Clayton shrugged. "Now and then, I suppose."

"Do you ever leave it there?"

"If it isn't misty or raining when I go home again, I suppose I could do. I suppose I *have* done."

"Was it there yesterday? The day Miss Stoner was killed?"

"How on earth should I know, Mrs. Ah—I can hardly be expected to remember . . ."

"Well, it happens I already know the answer to that question; it was there. When it was that you brought it in, I don't know, but it was there in the office yesterday afternoon."

He shrugged again. "I can't see how that possibly matters. Miss Stoner wasn't killed with an umbrella."

"No, but somebody removed that blue-striped umbrella from the stand in your office. You, I suppose, since you had it in your possession this morning. So I believe that you killed Miss Stoner, Mr. Clayton. And then took your umbrella with you as you left the office!"

Clayton was staring at her, momentarily stricken dumb. At last he croaked out, "I can't believe you're saying this. You're accusing me of having killed Miss Stoner just because I retrieved my umbrella from my own office?"

"No, because it was there before she was killed and it was gone afterwards. And because you have it now."

"B-but," he spluttered, "it's my umbrella! I have every right to carry it! Besides, how do you know it was there before she was killed?"

"Because we dropped by to see you that very day." Caledonia didn't elaborate on their motives. "You weren't in, but we got to look inside the inner office . . ."

"*You* did, Cal," Angela objected. "*I* didn't see a thing!"

"And the blue umbrella was right there in the umbrella stand, along with a cane and a black silk umbrella. I noticed it because it was one of the few spots of color in the whole room. But later that same night, it was gone. It wasn't in the stand at all."

Clayton, his brows thunderously knit and his lips pursed, glared at her. "And how do you know that! Don't tell me you dropped by to see me yet again in the evening!"

"No, Lieutenant Martinez had us come down to your office after Miss Stoner's body was discovered."

Clayton gulped and a tiny squeak came out of his tight lips. "The police brought you to my office? Why, for goodness' sake!?!"

"Because we were the last people to see her alive. And because Martinez wanted us to kind of look around—see if anything had been taken or changed since we were there earlier—"

"B-h-but why?" Clayton spluttered. "Why would they ask you to do that? I mean, they got me out of bed in the middle of the night and hauled me down there. They might have spared me the trip, if you'd already told them what they needed to know."

"Perhaps they didn't really trust your testimony," Caledonia said. "Most murders, we're told, are done by someone close to the victim. It would be a good idea to have details filled in by people who aren't really connected to the victim . . ."

"Or to the suspect," Angela filled in.

"Suspect! That's—that's outrageous! *Me* a suspect? I'm a

respectable businessman ..." He staggered back a step. "They *can't* suspect *me!*"

"Maybe *they* don't, but I do!" Caledonia insisted, moving closer to him. "Nobody else but you would grab up that umbrella. We don't carry 'em in Southern California, you know ... we don't even think to go get 'em when it's pouring rain! People here just make a run for their cars!"

"Furthermore, I bet not many people who'd just committed a murder would grab a blue-striped umbrella, even if they wanted one!" Angela added, moving closer as well. "If I'd just killed somebody, I'd want to be inconspicuous. I'd take the black umbrella, for sure!"

"But not you, right, Wallace?" Caledonia said. "Umbrellas feel perfectly normal to you, and that blue-striped one is your favorite. I didn't see it at first. I thought somebody had moved the umbrella stand a little, because it looked ... oh, I don't know—different somehow. But I've finally realized what was different about it. Your blue umbrella was gone!"

"But this is crazy!" He staggered back another step, as though his knees were weak, as though moving away from the two women might protect him from their accusing words. "I don't deny I stopped in my office for a moment early yesterday afternoon—almost immediately after lunch. I'd dined in a little cafe downtown, and it was convenient to come by ... just for a moment, mind you. Just to see if there was any mail or anything ... but that's all."

"You took the umbrella away with you then?" Caledonia said.

"Yes. I must have. I don't really remember, but you say it was missing after you were there much later ..."

"But why?"

"Why what?" He shook his head as though to clear it. "Why what, Mrs. Ah—Benbow?"

"Why take the umbrella at all unless it was raining? And the rain didn't begin till a lot later—just about the time

Miss Stoner was killed, the police think. So, whenever you were there, it wasn't right after lunch."

"Preposterous!" His voice had risen to a squeak so near to Angela's imitation of him that Caledonia very nearly smiled. "Preposterous! You have not a shred of evidence I was even there . . ."

"You just said you were."

"I'll deny it. Since it's going to be troublesome to me, I'll simply deny . . ."

"But you can't!" Angela said, triumphantly. "You can't deny it, because there's something else. You're probably the only person in the world who'd put the bookend back on the table after you'd used it to kill someone! You're the only person I know who's that much of a . . . a neatnik!"

"That's right!" Caledonia clapped her hands in sudden recognition of the truth. "With Miss Stoner—the only other person who gave a rap about a tidy office—lying there dead, who on earth would care if the books spilled all over the table anyhow? Only you. It had to be you!"

"Why ever did you kill her?" Angela asked mournfully. "That poor, homely woman hardly deserved to be knocked over the head with a statue of Venus!"

"*Aaaagch . . . !*" Wallace Clayton made one agonized, groaning cry, and then—faster than either Angela or Caledonia could think—he snaked out a bony arm and grabbed Angela around the neck, holding her head bent back against his shoulder, his skinny forearm pressed against her throat. "*All RIGHT!* You can push me just so far . . ."

"Now, see here, Clayton," Caledonia began, surging forward.

"You stay away or I'll break your little friend's neck!" Clayton snarled. "Stay away from me." His voice rose to a painful creak of protest. "You two and your meddling . . . It isn't enough you upset my dear Edna . . . made her cry! You have to come at me now and spoil everything!"

"Spoil everything?" With Angela held rigidly, and speechless, Caledonia seemed to ask questions for both of them.

"Of course! I had it so beautifully arranged! I had finally got rid of that dreadful Lightfoot man . . ."

"You did?"

"Of course! Somebody had to—for Edna's sake. Oh, I wanted to do it differently. I wanted to be civilized. So I offered him money to leave Edna alone, and he—he laughed at me. I sought him out that morning as he walked along and I walked with him a ways. I put my offer to him—I told him that I could make it worth his while to just leave town. And he laughed. He laughed at me!

"After that, I don't know—I must have hit him. I'm not really quite clear—I don't really even remember how it happened—and the train was there, practically on top of us. You see, he made me so angry, I . . . don't struggle, Mrs. Benbow . . ." He increased his grip on his arm, squeezing the do-it-yourself-garrote tighter under her chin. "I don't want to hurt you, but . . . if I must . . ."

"Let her go, Clayton," Caledonia pleaded.

"No. I have to think . . . I need time. Everything happens so fast . . . it's like that day with Lightfoot. I don't think I meant to push him—but he laughed at me! I didn't have time to work out what to do about it. Now you're rushing me . . . hurrying me . . . I can't think! I can't—"

"No, no," Caledonia soothed. "Nobody's going to hurry you."

"Aaaahghk . . ." Angela let out a strangled breath, but the sound was cut off quickly as Clayton tightened his grip again, and stepped backward, dragging her a little farther from Caledonia.

"Stay still, Angela. Don't make him any more nervous," Caledonia said softly. "Look, Clayton, I can see that killing Lightfoot was kind of an accident. That's what you're saying, isn't it?"

"Yes. Yes, it was. I was angry. I only wanted to get even with him for laughing at me. That's all."

"Well, if it was an accident, surely even the police will understand if you tell them about—"

"No! They'd never believe me. Not after Miss Stoner . . ."

"Why did you kill Miss Stoner?"

Caledonia kept her face directly toward Clayton, but shot a glance left toward the main door, then right toward the side door, unlocked tonight so the returning bingo players could get back into the building. Neither door moved. Nobody appeared to help them. She shot her eyes in the other direction, toward the front desk just hidden from their view, but Jimmy was apparently glued to his books; their voices simply hadn't carried sufficiently to break his concentration. And Caledonia hesitated to upset Clayton by shouting for help. No rescue likely from that quarter, either.

"It was the same as with Lightfoot," Clayton was saying. "It was so easy! Both times! And it really puzzles me, you know? One minute she was after me and after me— nagging about our never having any customers, nagging me about eating properly, nagging me about taking my umbrella because of the rain . . . and the next minute I hit her. Just grabbed the nearest thing and hit her! Of course, I didn't have time to think, you see? I really function better," he was almost pleading for Caledonia to understand, "I really am more effective when I can work things out to the last detail, you know."

"I'm sure . . . I'm sure . . . but now, your arm must be tired, and I tell you what. It isn't helping anything for you to hang on to Angela. So why don't you—"

"No! She stays right here," he insisted, renewing his grip around Angela's neck.

"Look, Clayton, I don't think she can breathe properly. She can't even make a sound, let alone talk. You may have killed two people by accident, but if you kill her, it won't be accidental . . . and you'd be better off . . ."

"SHUT UP!" It was the loudest Wallace Clayton ever spoke, through the whole conversation, and it was merely a high-pitched rasping squeak! "Shut up and let me think!"

"Oh, peanut butter, man! Think all you want, but let Angela go!"

"I said to shut up!" He tightened his arm once more.

Caledonia spread her huge hands helplessly and stood absolutely still. "All right—all right—don't get excited, now ..." Clayton glared at her, apparently trying to marshal his thoughts, but it wasn't easy while he kept having to renew his grip on Angela, whose awkward position made her a dead weight on his one arm, and whose distorted expression made it obvious that she was suffering even more discomfort than fear.

"I won't say anything more," Caledonia began in a soothing voice, when out of the darkness, almost exactly beside Wallace Clayton's ear, Caledonia's own voice rasped forth, *"Peanut butter! Peanut butter!"*

Clayton gasped and half turned. As he did, he relaxed his grip just a little on Angela's neck, and Caledonia lunged. One huge hand went around her little friend's arm, pulling Angela away ... the other hand landed outspread in the middle of Clayton's bony chest, sending him reeling backward into the shadows.

There was the clang of something hard meeting metal, a sigh, and Clayton collapsed downward, his eyes rolling upward in his head, and he lay motionless. *"Chirrrk ... Peanut butter!"* the parakeet protested, as its cage rocked back and forth dangerously.

Almost in the same moment, the lobby door opened and Lieutenant Martinez, followed by Shorty Swanson, entered with a rush. Both men saw a pair of legs, swathed in linen, protruding from the shadows near the fireplace and twitching in a way that could only mean their owner was severely damaged. They took in Angela, collapsed and gasping on the couch, and Caledonia, huge and menacing, towering above the fallen Clayton. It was enough to make them gallop the length of the room to take charge, waving Caledonia aside, checking on Angela, hoisting Clayton's limp form onto another couch, and sending for reinforcements.

"I'll get the details later, Mrs. Wingate," the lieutenant promised. "For now, I take it you've had some kind of confrontation?"

She nodded, still appalled at all that had happened.

"And you still believe what you told me on the phone? That Clayton's our man?"

"He told us right out that he was, Lieutenant. He says both killings were accidental—what he described as being murders committed in a flash of rage. But he was strangling the breath out of Angela here . . ."

"I'm all right," Angela said, recovering rapidly and surprised to find her voice was husky. "But I want to be at his trial, that repulsive little man, and I want to see them make sausage of him! He was choking me! Because he wanted time to think! That's what he said . . . time to think!!"

"Well, that's not quite all, my dear," Caledonia soothed. "He was using her to keep me away from him. He may not have had time to work it all out, but he certainly knew I'd have had the upper hand, if I ever got hold of him!"

"I can see his point, wanting to keep you away," Martinez said. "He's still unconscious! You must have delivered a real roundhouse, when you finally got to him."

"Oh, I didn't hit him," Caledonia protested.

"Yes, you did, Cal! You shoved him," Angela croaked.

"Well, yes, I pushed him. That's different. As soon as he let go of Angela for a second, I pushed him away from her. But what knocked him out was the bird cage! He hit his head on the wrought iron."

"You always said," Angela rasped, "that someone would hurt themselves on that thing!"

"When that bird came out of the darkness behind him and said . . . say, Angela, did you hear what the bird said?" Caledonia asked, sudden memory bringing a huge grin to her face. "Grandmother Parkhurst's favorite word . . ."

"Peanut butter," the bird pronounced solemnly out of the darkness. *"Peanut butter! Same to your cat!"*

Chapter 18

"SHERRY TIME!"

Caledonia hoisted the bottle of amontillado so it caught the late afternoon sunshine and threw warm amber lights against the wall behind it. "I presume we all want a nice little sherry to celebrate the close of another day, right?"

It was the Saturday following Wallace Clayton's violent confrontation with Angela and Caledonia. In the intervening time, Angela had been confined to her bed for two days, simply champing at the bit to get up and about, to find out all that had happened to Clayton when he was taken away under police guard, and to catch up on her friends.

"Nobody would come and tell me anything, Cal! There I was for forty-eight long hours . . ."

"Rot!" Caledonia snorted. "It was only forty hours total till you staggered up and came out amongst us again. You slept half the time from that stuff Doc Carter gave you anyhow. And I came to see you every day myself, both Wednesday and Thursday, morning and afternoon . . . and what's more, you had a steady stream of well-wishers. Even, I might add, including Edna Ferrier!"

"Oh," Angela breathed. "I was *so* relieved. I didn't know how she'd react to all this . . ."

Edna had showed up on Wednesday afternoon, apparently in good control of herself, and very apologetic about the last time they'd met.

"I'm very sorry," Angela had begun as soon as she saw Edna, and then realized that Edna was talking at the same time, and had said exactly the same thing.

"Oh, Angela, I'm so very sorry . . ."

After they started over, Edna said, "I feel as though this" —she gestured at the compresses on Angela's throat—"is all my fault. I could have told that wretched little fellow I didn't want him hanging around me, but I've always felt sorry for him. When my sister was alive, I tolerated him for her sake. But now—well, he's such a fussy old maid! He wanted to know everything I did, he wanted to regulate my budget, to choose my friends for me . . . he even tried to advise me on what clothes to buy!"

"He thought he was taking good care of you. That's what he said—that he wanted to take care of you."

Edna shook her head. "Maybe, but it came out as bossing me around. And I got so tired of his dropping in every five minutes! That's what it seemed like. I started faking headaches and bad colds, to get him to stay away. I'm not sure I'd have stayed in my room so long after Alexander died, except that I was afraid Wallace would show up and try to tell me how to recover from mourning."

"And he did anyhow, didn't he?"

"Yes, he certainly did. But, oh, Angela, I feel as though I could have spared you that awful business at the end when he was choking you, if only I'd been firm with him!"

"I don't really think so, Edna. He wasn't . . . he just wasn't normal! I think he was truly blind to what anyone thought of him. I mean, he thought the two of you were growing close!"

"Poor Wallace! And all the while I was only trying to think of ways to get rid of him!"

So Angela and Edna parted friends.

On the first afternoon she was out of her rooms— Thursday just before dinnertime—Angela felt a little weak, but in each hallway there were railings to hang onto, so she turned her steps toward Tom Brighton's apartment, not far from her own. It was high time, she thought, to fill him in on the outcome of their adventures. But when she arrived, she was dismayed to find a shiny new hasp affixed to his door with a large combination padlock swinging from it.

"What is the problem with Tom?" she asked Clara, as soon as she could make her way to the lobby. "His room has a lock on it. He's not . . . Oh, Clara! He's not dead, is he? While I was lying there in bed—he didn't—"

Whenever a Camden resident died, it was customary to padlock the apartment till relatives could arrive to remove personal possessions. A new hasp and padlock on a Camden apartment often meant the same as a funeral wreath on a door in the world outside.

But Clara was smiling. "Oh, gracious, no. Mrs. Benbow, he's not dead. Far from it!"

"But the lock . . ."

"We do lock apartments for other reasons, you know. Like if the resident's going to be gone for a week or more. Mr. Brighton decided to have that hip-joint replacement he's been talking about. He said it just got too painful, and he said that since he might not have much time left on this earth, he'd decided he wanted to spend it in comfort. So he went into the hospital on Tuesday morning, without telling a soul except the office here, because we have to deal with his mail and his calls."

"Why wouldn't he tell us, Cal? We're good friends, or so I thought!" Angela protested, when she finally found Caledonia, sailing up the garden walk on her way to supper. "Did you know about it?"

"Well, yes, but only by accident. I was in the lobby here when they delivered his computer . . ."

"His computer!"

"That's right. He's decided to get himself a new hip and a new toy at the same time. Apparently, he's going to do a lot of sitting and lying around, while he's recovering, and he figured he might as well spend the time learning something valuable. They unlocked his place briefly to have the deliverymen set it up for him so it'd be waiting when he gets back. Better than aspirin, I'd say, to take his mind off discomfort."

"But it'll be weeks before he gets home . . ." Angela began.

"Nope. He went into physical therapy today, they tell me, and he may even be home for next weekend! That's the biggest complaint I have about hospitals these days. They make you walk the moment you wake up from the anesthetic. They make you exercise as soon as your head clears. And they throw you out at the end of a week. You used to be able to count on at least having a rest when you went to the hospital. But no more!"

"Have you sent flowers in our name, Cal?"

"Absolutely not!" Caledonia grinned. "That's exactly the reason he didn't tell anybody—so nobody'd make a fuss. I tell you what I did do, though. I went to the store where he bought his Macintosh, and I bought him a chess game for it. It's waiting beside his computer right now, with a big red ribbon and a card from the two of us."

"Ah, that was very clever, Cal," Angela conceded. "I approve."

That was Thursday.

On Friday, Angela caught up with another bit of life that had gone on while she was out of commission. While she and Caledonia enjoyed their lunch—a crusty meat pie with tender vegetables and a deliciously rich gravy, followed by a hot, tart cherry cobbler with soft custard ice cream on top—Shorty Swanson came into the dining room.

He came straight to their table. "Afternoon, ladies . . ."

"Care to join us for lunch, Detective Swanson?" Caledonia invited.

He shook his head with genuine regret. "I'd love to. But the lieutenant would scalp me. He's out in the car. Sent me in with a message. He wanted to know if you could give him a little time about four or four-thirty tomorrow afternoon. He thought you'd like to hear how things came out with Mr. Clayton."

"Oh, wonderful!" Angela breathed. "I've been dying of curiosity!"

"At my place." Caledonia nodded. "Tell him to come straight through—not to bother having the desk announce him. We'll be waiting."

"Okay, I'll tell him." Swanson wasn't looking at them as he spoke. He was searching the dining room with his glance, wearing exactly the expression of mixed hope and despair, of bewilderment mixed with optimism, that a puppy might have as it hunted a crowded street for its lost master.

"She's in the kitchen, Detective Swanson," Caledonia said.

"What?"

"Chita. She just took an order and went to the kitchen. She'll be right out."

"Oh. I wasn't looking for—but since you mention it—Oh!" His face broke into a broad smile as Conchita came through the swinging door from the kitchen, carrying a tray of desserts (cobbler for most of the diners, plain ice cream for the few who couldn't tolerate the sour fruit). "Excuse me . . ." and Shorty made his gangling way between the tables headed for Chita.

Angela and Caledonia watched and listened with concentrated attention, but they couldn't make out a word that was exchanged. The couple was too far away for the sound to carry, and Swanson's head was tilted down so that his mouth was obscured from their line of sight as he spoke, while Chita's face was invisible because her back was toward them. So they couldn't even lip-read! But as the couple parted, Swanson was grinning from ear to ear, and his voice was perfectly audible to them as he called out, "Tonight at seven, then!" And when Chita turned back toward the kitchen, they could see that she, too, was beaming.

Furthermore, when Chita set their cobbler dishes on the

table, Angela caught the gleam of metal and stone, and reached out quickly to grasp the girl's left hand. There was a tiny solitaire on her fourth finger. "Chita! Is that an engagement ring?" Angela warbled.

Chita grinned. "I haven't got time to talk right now. Maybe Monday, when I'm back on duty. He finally said yes!"

"I thought it was you who didn't want to get married," Caledonia said.

Chita nodded. "Not till he agreed I could go on working. He got so mulish about it. He kept saying things like 'A woman's place is in the home'—and I just got tired of it. When he finally decided to let me be an adult, everything was fine. Got to rush now . . ." and she hurried off to finish serving the other diners.

The ladies finished their dessert in pleased silence.

Angela was prompt to arrive at Caledonia's Saturday afternoon, wearing her prettiest knit suit, the one in soft, periwinkle blue that she privately thought made her look ten years younger. She had hardly arranged herself on her favorite rose-velvet chair when the lieutenant arrived. Caledonia brought out the lovely cut-crystal stemware and the sherry.

"It wouldn't take me ten minutes, knowing all the background, to shake the dust off and say 'good riddance' to a man like Lightfoot, myself," Caledonia said. "But Edna is still feeling regret, apparently. I don't know whether he was truly reformed or not, but I'll take her word for it that they had a good thing going, and she truly misses the man."

"He was awfully good-looking, his manners were superb, and he had a kind of dashing air about him—"

"Angela!"

"Oh, don't misunderstand. I agree he was a thoroughly unworthy person. I was just thinking out loud that he must have looked pretty good to Edna. All she had to compare him to with was her husband Horace . . . nice, but not very colorful . . . and Wallace, the egomaniac, the fussbudget . . ."

"The pompous little jackass!" Martinez said. "Forgive me, ladies, but I've never come so close to—I really wanted to shake him and try to get him to talk sense. Do you know that, even now, he claims he's not really sure why he's under arrest? He acknowledges freely that he swung on Lightfoot and apparently knocked him off balance and into that train, but he thinks we should applaud him for getting rid of a blot on society. He claims to be quite puzzled about the fuss we're making over the killing."

"Well, he can't pretend Miss Stoner was a detriment to society!" Angela protested.

"Ah, but even in that case, he feels perfectly justified! He keeps saying, 'But she nagged me! She never let up on me! I really had to do something about it!' and things like that. It doesn't seem to dawn on him that he could have simply fired her."

"So you've reminded us often enough," Caledonia said, "and of course we agree."

"It's interesting," Angela mused. "That very overprotective attitude that drove him wild in Miss Stoner was the same attitude he adopted toward Edna! Of course he was so self-righteous, I'm sure he couldn't see it."

"To every man, his own fleas are gazelles," Martinez murmured.

"What?"

"An old Arab proverb, I'm told," he explained.

"Well, what's going to happen to Clayton?" Caledonia asked.

"Oh, he may be found incompetent to stand trial. The way he's smirking and bragging, the total lack of concern he shows about the killings—well, it isn't really a normal response. He'll certainly be removed to where he can't be a danger to society. But whether he's put into a mental hospital or into a prison is immaterial to me. My job is over when I gather enough evidence for a conviction, and when

I get him penned up so he can't be a danger to the public. Someone else has to take it from there."

"But, Lieutenant," Angela protested in her husky whisper, "he could get out again and be a danger to me! I mean, listen to my voice! He didn't care what happened to me at all, so long as I was an effective shield against Caledonia. And he—he hurt me!"

"He won't be free again any time soon, Mrs. Benbow. The evidence is too clear. And as I told you, he doesn't seem to mind admitting his guilt. He tells everybody who'll listen! So one way or another, he'll not be bothering you again. Ah, thank you, Mrs. Wingate." Caledonia had heaved herself up from the couch she occupied and brought the sherry around to refill the glasses. "This is really excellent . . ."

"You have good taste. Not like Angela," Caledonia said. "Angela likes that sticky sweet stuff."

"Cream sherry tastes good!" Angela rasped.

"To you, perhaps," Caledonia retorted. "To us civilized people, sherry ought to be drier. I don't know why she's so stubborn, Lieutenant. She likes this, but she insists on buying . . ."

"Caledonia, you're interrupting! She accuses me of doing that all the time, Lieutenant, but you'll notice who's getting in the way of what you have to tell us. Go ahead with your story. Don't pay any attention to her!"

Martinez smiled fondly at them. "There really isn't any more to tell. Wallace is certainly the person who killed Lightfoot and Miss Stoner."

"Isn't it remarkable?" Angela whispered in her husky little voice. "We looked so hard for a connection between the two killings. And there wasn't any!"

"Oh, yes, there was," Martinez corrected her. "Clayton. He was the connection. His incredible ego was the motivating force in both killings. Of course, according to him, both deaths were accidental. And I don't suppose we'll ever know whether he really tried to dispose of a rival under that train, or if—as he insists—he simply struck out in a flash of anger. But you could make a good case that he started out that morning determined to get rid of Lightfoot."

"What about poor Miss Stoner?" Caledonia asked.

"There again, I blame his ego. I believe he struck her down deliberately in an adolescent temper tantrum. And he said something very significant while we were questioning him—his lawyer couldn't get him to keep quiet, because he insisted on explaining himself, and he said, 'Everybody thinks it's hard to kill someone. But it isn't. Once you get over the feeling that it's going to be difficult, it's really very easy!' I believe that, in killing Lightfoot, Clayton discovered a lovely way to rid himself of inconvenience and annoyance. I think in time he'd have killed again. It was, as he said, quite easy. Well, at any rate, the case is closed."

"More sherry, Lieutenant?"

"Ah, thank you, no, Mrs. Wingate. Two of these are a gracious plenty before dinner." He rose gracefully to his feet. "Mrs. Benbow, I'm delighted you feel up to getting out of bed, and that your voice is on the mend. I should have known you wouldn't be defeated by a scuffle with a nasty little fellow like Clayton. And I'm so pleased . . . but as usual, I barely have time to pay my respects properly. I must be on my way."

"Not work on a Saturday night!" Angela protested.

"No, no . . . my nephew—my sister's boy—is performing in the school operetta. I promised to go with her. It's Friml's *The Firefly*, and he's playing the dashing hero."

"Singing the Allan Jones role." Angela sighed. "Oh, my, I wonder if your nephew is as handsome as Allan Jones was! When he sang to Jeanette MacDonald . . ."

Martinez rose. "He's only fourteen years old, Mrs. Benbow, and he's skinny and has acne. It's the Magnolia Junior High School chorus and drama group . . ."

"Oh, dear! We know them of old," Caledonia said. "They insist on doing every one of their shows for us. Sooner or later we see them all. All due respect to your nephew, but I imagine we'll be sleeping through his version of 'The Donkey Serenade' just any day now. Well, if you must . . ."

"I'm really sorry, but I promised." Martinez hesitated by the door. "Oh, one thing I meant to ask—I noticed that the bird and the cage are gone from the lobby. It was an attractive little parakeet, of course, but it occurred to me that black wrought-iron cage could be hazardous to navigation, in your dark lobby. It certainly laid Wallace Clayton low!"

"That was an accident! I told you . . ."

"So you did, Mrs. Wingate. But I shall treasure the memory of the first known use of a bird cage as an offensive weapon, all the same. You didn't say—did they remove the cage?"

"Yes," Caledonia said shortly. "They did. Now, Lieutenant . . ."

"Oh, dear, and I didn't even notice he was gone!" Angela chimed in. "I know you simply despised him, Caledonia, but he was cute. And I really owe that little bird something. If he hadn't learned to imitate you and hadn't spoken up, practically in Wallace's ear, that dreadful little man might still have me in a hammerlock." She chuckled. "The bird did sound exactly like you, Cal!"

"What did they decide to do with it?" Martinez said. "It seems a shame to dispose of it, even though I agree that the cage really had to be moved. For the safety of the residents. Do you know what was done with it?"

"Yes."

"Yes, you do know?"

"Yes. I do. Well, now, Lieutenant, you're going to be late—"

"She always gets like this, Lieutenant, when she's avoiding the subject. Caledonia, what is it about that bird? You didn't let them take it away to a pet store and sell it, did you? After it helped rescue me? After it learned your pet swearword and all? You didn't!"

"No, I didn't! Now will you get off the subject?"

"Mrs. Wingate," Martinez said, "now you've aroused my curiosity as well. I believe Mrs. Benbow is right. You are evading our questions. Mrs. Wingate, straight out, no evasions, where is that bird at this moment?"

Caledonia sighed. "You're not going to let me live this down, I know . . ." She strode across and flung open the door to her bedroom. "There."

In plain sight within the bedroom hung the wrought-iron cage on its heavy stand. The late afternoon sun streaked through the room and shone directly on the little blue parakeet, nibbling earnestly at a large piece of fresh lettuce. He looked up and squinted his eyes suspiciously at the interruption, then went back to work.

"Oh, Cal! How nice of you to give him a temporary home!"

But Martinez wasn't quite as easily satisfied as Angela was. Perhaps it was his police training. "You're still holding something back, Mrs. Wingate. Aren't you?"

"Me? Whatever would I—"

"Mrs. Wingate, something tells me you're going to keep that bird, aren't you? He's not with you temporarily. He's with you permanently!"

"Well, after all, he did us a service. And he had to be moved, you know. Trinita Stainsbury stumbled over the stand Wednesday—" Caledonia bristled, on the defensive. "Would you believe it, The Toad, Torgeson, was talking about sending for the Humane Society and having the little fellow put to sleep? Well, I said, 'Over my dead body!' I may not like birds, but this little chap is unique! After all, it's not many creatures who can bite Angela and live to tell about it!"

"He bit Mrs. Benbow?"

"Just a nip," Angela said quickly. "It was my own fault. I poked my finger into his cage . . ."

"Well, he doesn't bite me," Caledonia said, bending her hand so the Band-Aid on her forefinger was less visible. "Well, maybe just a sort of a love bite—while we're getting to know each other, you know. And he's already learning some new words!"

The bird looked up from his perch and cocked his head. *"Sherry time!"* he called, in a merry tone. *"Sherry time!"*

Martinez laughed aloud. "Well, that gives me yet another excuse to come back and visit you—perhaps next week—to see what else you've taught the new member of your household, Mrs. Wingate, as well as to check on you, Mrs. Benbow. Now . . ." He bent low and kissed Angela's hand, then Caledonia's. "Ladies, I'll take my leave." and he disappeared through the door.

"Cal, you fraud!" Angela chortled. "Saying you hate birds . . ."

"I do hate birds!"

". . . and then adopting this one!"

"Well, every rule has its exceptions. Tell you what, Angela. You don't tease me about the bird, and I won't make you feed him when you come here to the apartment."

"I wouldn't mind if you did! He surely wouldn't bite me a second time," Angela said. "He wouldn't dare!"

"Hell in a basket!" the bird called happily, mounting its perch and swinging vigorously to and fro. *"Peanut butter! Same to your cat!"*

Caledonia gently closed the bedroom door. "Well, Angela, what say we go on up for dinner?"

And the two of them walked together up the garden path toward the main building, content with the world and each other, warmed by the slowly setting sun, and basking in the double glow produced by good sherry and good friendship.